Marie froze as a shadow rose from the darkness.

Night Hawk.

Savior of women and children, and wild-horse tamer. How could he be real? He had to be a dream, a figment of her imagination, her idea of a perfect man.

Except she was wide awake, and this was no dream. She could smell the straw and horse scent of the stable. She could see the flicker of light on the man's hands as he inspected the gelding's fetlock, feel the wind rustling her skirts.

And hear the beat of her own heart.

He stood—all flesh and blood man—and his gaze pierced through the shadows and pinpointed her. "Miss Lafayette. What are you doing out of your father's house?"

"I didn't make a sound."

"Your skirts did." The light flickered over him, worshipping high, sharp cheekbones, a well-proportioned nose and a hard, carved jaw.

Something within Marie's heart clicked. Just like that. As a lock finding its key at the right moment.

Could he be the one? The man she'd been waiting for all her life?

Night Hawk's Bride
Harlequin Historical #558—April 2001

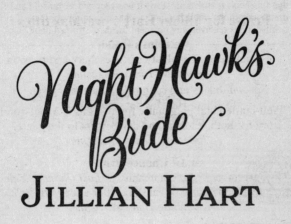

Night Hawk's Bride

JILLIAN HART

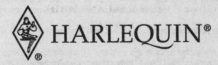

TORONTO • NEW YORK • LONDON
AMSTERDAM • PARIS • SYDNEY • HAMBURG
STOCKHOLM • ATHENS • TOKYO • MILAN • MADRID
PRAGUE • WARSAW • BUDAPEST • AUCKLAND

Special thanks and acknowledgment are given to Jillian Hart for her contribution to the Return to Tyler series.

ISBN 0-373-29158-2

NIGHT HAWK'S BRIDE

Please address questions and book requests to:
Harlequin Reader Service
U.S.: 3010 Walden Ave., P.O. Box 1325, Buffalo, NY 14269
Canadian: P.O. Box 609, Fort Erie, Ont. L2A 5X3

Chapter One

Fort Tye, Wisconsin
1840

The fort loomed like a fairy tale against the sparkling river and wild Wisconsin forest. Marie couldn't believe her eyes. Was this real? Was this truly where she was going to live?

She leaned out the open window of the stagecoach. Amid the rich green backdrop of the forest, the fort shone like newly polished wood in the hot summer sun. It was an impenetrable fortress like the castles of old. And it was her future.

"Welcome to Fort Tye, Miss Lafayette," Mrs. Webster said over the noise of the rattling stagecoach. "And stop leaning out of that window. Who would teach the children if something happened to you? Your father would have my head. Come in, now."

"I don't want to miss one single thing."

She felt as if a whole new world had been spread before her, and she was near to bursting with the wonder of it all. The beauty alone fascinated her. It was so different from back home with its tidy streets and tended houses all in a row.

This was a wild land untamed and filled with the possibility of adventure around every turn.

"Calm yourself, dear." Mrs. Webster, seated across from her, chuckled. "It's just a fort, nothing special at all and, believe me, after one Wisconsin winter, you'll be desperate to head back to your aunt's pretty little home."

Mrs. Webster didn't understand, and Marie knew she couldn't tell her why. She didn't want to speak of the pain of her childhood and of the father's love she'd always ached for. A love that seemed just out of her reach.

How did she say that here in this beautiful, wild land, she would live with her father again. Maybe this time she could make things right between them. Marie crossed her fingers and held the wish close to her heart.

"My Jeb works for your father, the colonel," Mrs. Webster continued from inside the stage. "Dear, you'll hurt yourself. Please, come inside. You're giving me a fright."

A sharp cry carried on the wind, and Marie tilted her head up. A hawk soared across a powder blue sky, wings spread as if to touch the brilliant sun.

"Have you ever seen anything like it?" Marie asked.

"Why, I must have seen a thousand of them."

The graceful bird glided on broad wings and out of sight.

The stage rolled around a corner, and a broad river sparkled with the sun's touch. A few houses and buildings huddled together near its grassy banks.

This is the settlement? It was smaller than she'd imagined. And beyond the huddle of buildings stretched a maze of thick woodland and danger. She felt a strange thrill looking into the shadows of the forest....

The stage bounced hard. Marie rapped the top of her head against the window frame. She rubbed her hand over the sore spot and didn't look away from that shadowed place in the forest. She felt as if there was something—*someone*—looking back at her.

The shadow moved, and darkness became a mounted man. Black hair, black eyes and bronze skin. He was as dark as the shadows. Dressed in trousers and a deerskin shirt, he looked as wild and proud as the horse he rode.

The stage jolted to a stop outside the fort's gates, and Marie almost slipped off her seat. She righted herself and turned toward the window.

He was gone. Only shadows carpeted the forest floor where no sunlight touched the thick ferns and bracken.

Had he been real or a dream?

Marie kept searching for him as she smoothed the wrinkles from her skirt.

"You take care now, dear, and give my regards to your father." Mrs. Webster hesitated at the door. "I hope Fort Tye is everything you've hoped it to be."

"I hope so." All her life she'd imagined accompanying her father to one of his posts, and now it was truly happening. Marie grabbed her reticule from the seat and took one last look out the window. The man—image, shadow or dream—was gone.

There goes your romantic fancy again. Marie sighed. She was always daydreaming, something her father frowned on.

Please, let him be glad to see me. She knew he'd be here to greet her—he'd promised her in his last, brief letter. Nerves gathered in her stomach and made her hands clammy beneath her gloves as she grabbed the edge of the door frame and climbed onto the narrow step.

Where was he? She searched the strange faces of the people bustling around the entrance to the fort. Where was Papa? This time he'd promised to meet her. And she wanted to believe this time was different than all the other times he'd forgotten or been too busy.

The sinking sensation in her heart felt as heavy as lead. Careful to keep her chin up, she hopped off the last step and touched solid ground.

Maybe he was late. Or she hadn't seen him yet in the small crowd. The stage *was* a few minutes early....

She stood alone, feeling like the stranger she was. Everywhere she looked people greeted one another, stopping outside the wooden steps to the mercantile to exchange news. Everything looked so different from home and she felt lost. Surely Papa hadn't forgotten her this time.

"Miss Lafayette?" A uniformed soldier broke apart from the crowd. "Your father, the colonel, sends his apologies. A situation arose—"

"I understand." Marie tried to steel her heart against the disappointment. It wasn't this man's fault Henry was the way he was. "Will he be along shortly?"

"I'm afraid he'll be engaged for most of the afternoon. I'm Sergeant James. I'm your father's assistant." The officer avoided her gaze, as if he didn't know what to say. "Are these your trunks?"

"Yes." She hated the look of sympathy in his eyes. Sympathy for her. "He forgot, didn't he?"

"No, miss, he's simply busy—"

"He didn't realize that I arrived today." Marie refused to let the hurt show in her voice. "Don't worry, Sergeant, I'm used to it. I know my father."

"Just wanted to spare your feelings, miss." The sergeant tugged on his cap. "I'll see to your trunks."

Marie began to thank him when a horse's high, shrill neigh trumpeted above the sounds on the busy lane.

Suddenly a pair of iron-strong hands banded around her arms and yanked her back, away from the dirt road.

She stumbled against an unyielding, male-hot chest. Even through the layers of her traveling clothes, his heat scorched her and tingled along her skin.

For one brief second she felt the strangest thrill. She couldn't describe it. Her heart was racing, her chest tightened and an odd ringing filled her ears.

She knew she ought to be terrified, but she wasn't. Time slowed down, and there seemed to be nothing in the world but the protective shelter of his arms. She didn't even know who held her, whether he was friend or foe, young or old.

Then he released her.

Time snapped back, the noise from the street and the crowd filled the air, and Marie nearly stumbled. Breathing again, she felt him brush past her arm. He was running toward the street, and she saw the danger.

A runaway horse clipped past her so close she could feel the heat of his breath. His lethal hooves slammed into the ground, obliterating her shoe prints in the thick dust. The renegade flew past her, then swerved to avoid the stagecoach.

A little girl stood directly in his path. Marie leaped into the road, but she was too late. A man wearing a deerskin shirt scooped the child to his chest and rolled out of the renegade's path.

Not soon enough. The gelding was on top of him, skidding to a stop, bugling his fury. Wild, out of control, it reared up, hooves slashing the air, and then landed again. Marie heard a man's grunt of pain, and a bullwhip cracked in the air behind her. The wild horse leaped over the man in the road and flew toward the river.

"Are you all right?" The sergeant appeared at her side. "You could have been killed."

"I'm fine."

"Cassie!" A woman darted out of the mercantile and raced down the stairs. "Cassie!"

The man holding the child rolled one final time and climbed to his feet. Marie saw his face, the dark eyes and long black hair, the chiseled bronze face that could have been made of stone.

The man from the forest.

Just seeing him made her heart beat painfully fast. He was like no man Marie had ever seen before. She could only stare as he brushed the dirt from the child's locks and handed the girl over to the housekeeper responsible.

A tender gesture. Marie couldn't believe her eyes. How could such a tough man have such gentle hands? She remembered the strength in them as he'd pulled her safely out of the gelding's path. The same strength that kept a frightened child safe now.

Instead of crying, the little girl stuck her thumb in her mouth and gazed up at the man holding her. The child went wordlessly into the worried housekeeper's arms. The woman couldn't stop thanking the man enough for saving the child.

He's bleeding. Marie saw the stain on the man's shirtsleeve, spreading with each passing moment. He'd risked his life for a child, and she couldn't look away.

The housekeeper crossed the street, muttering about how fast children could move. The men mounted up to join the army officer to bring in the dangerous horse.

Marie stood on the side of the street as the men rode off, the dark hero among them. He guided his black stallion bareback without aid of bridle and raced out of sight.

Admiration burned like a new flame in Marie's heart.

"Looks like they'll need help bringing in that killer." The sergeant appeared at her side with a plump, elderly woman at his side. "This is Mrs. Kelsey. She'll look after you while I help with the roundup.''

"Thank you, Sergeant." But he was already swinging up onto his horse.

"Dear me, what a sweet little thing you are." Mrs. Kelsey took Marie by the hand and tugged her toward the brightly painted mercantile. "I hope you weren't frightened at all. If it hadn't been for Night Hawk, I'd hate to think what would have happened to both you and that little girl. I was standing at the window, and what I saw nearly scared me to death."

Night Hawk. His name must be Night Hawk. Marie hesitated on the top step and gazed toward the bend in the road.

She could no longer see him, but the image of him lingered. Dark, brave, proud. His long black hair brushed by the wind. A man who would have traded his life for a child's without hesitation.

"Come right in here, dear, and let me get you some cold water." Mrs. Kelsey held open the stout wooden door. "You need to sit down after a scare like that."

"Really, I'm fine." Marie could still feel the heated imprint of Night Hawk's hands on her arms. "Is the child all right?"

"There's not a scratch on her." Mrs. Kelsey's voice lowered as she led the way down the aisles and through the noisy store. "Now, sit right down here on this stool and I'll fetch you a drink."

"Please, don't go to any trouble—" Marie started but couldn't finish the protest.

Mrs. Kelsey had already bustled away, her skirts

rustling. She returned with a dipperful of sparkling
cold water. "Drink it all, dear, you'll feel better."

An elderly woman stepped close to the counter,
clucking sympathetically. "Poor dear, a near miss like
that. Why, you must be the colonel's daughter come
to teach our children."

"That's right." Marie took the dipper with trem-
bling hands. A few drops landed on her dusty skirts.
She could still feel the heat on her skin from Night
Hawk's touch.

She drank the entire dipperful because Mrs. Kelsey
kept fussing. When she was done, she looked over her
shoulder through the small front window that offered
a view of the dirt road and the river beyond.

Where was Night Hawk now? Was he safe? How
badly had he been injured? Questions buzzed inside
her like the conversations in the crowded little store.
Most of the customers were discussing the renegade
horse and how close the little Ingalls girl had come to
being killed.

But no one mentioned Night Hawk.

Marie returned the empty dipper and thanked Mrs.
Kelsey. The minute she slipped off the stool, the older
woman was there, shaking her head.

"You're still trembling, dear, and flushed as can be.
Stay right here and when Sergeant James comes back,
I'll have him take you home straightaway."

"I came to no harm, thanks to Night Hawk."

As if saying his name had brought him to her, the
door opened and he filled the threshold. Noble and
mysterious, wild and civilized. The conversations si-

lenced and a tension filled the room. Night Hawk headed toward the front of the store.

Directly toward her.

Marie slid off the stool, her knees suddenly like water.

But he wasn't looking at her with his dark, fathomless gaze. "Mrs. Flanders, how is Cassie?"

The housekeeper grabbed hold of another rambunctious child, a boy, ready to dart down an aisle and out of reach. Then she shifted Cassie on her hip. "First thing she did was try to run off. As you can see, it put no fear into her at all."

"I'm glad." Night Hawk's stone face relaxed into a slow grin and he brushed one bronzed knuckle against the girl's pale cheek. "Did you like me grabbing you like that?"

"Night Hawk! Let's do it again." Cassie smiled adoringly up at him.

"Not today, cowgirl." Night Hawk withdrew his hand and stepped away.

He *was* part dream, Marie decided.

Then the man named Night Hawk focused his eagle-sharp gaze on her. She felt it like a touch to her soul.

"Are you all right, miss?" He strode toward her with the grace of a wolf stalking prey. "I must have startled you, but I didn't want you harmed."

"I owe you a great debt, sir." Marie eased around the corner of the wooden counter, and there was nothing between them. "I cannot thank you enough. You saved two lives."

"I did only what any man would do."

"No other man took the risks you did today." Marie heard the breathlessness of her own voice.

"Miss Lafayette." Sergeant James appeared in front of her, separating her from Night Hawk with his presence. "Your father wants you delivered to his quarters immediately."

Marie blushed at the officer's rudeness. "I'll be ready in a moment. I—"

"Now, miss."

Marie could feel half the customers watching her.

"Good day to you." Night Hawk nodded formally and backed away.

It was too late to call him back, not with the sergeant watching her with narrowed eyes and the attention of so many strangers. Strangers whose children she would be teaching at summer's end.

Disappointed, Marie watched Night Hawk stride toward the door. A thousand questions itched inside her, and she desperately wanted to talk with him. Did it show on her face? Was that why the sergeant took her by the elbow and led her, stumbling, to the door.

When she tripped down the steps, Night Hawk was nowhere in sight. She looked through the shadows created by the immense log walls. She scanned the crowds of busy soldiers inside the fort once she'd followed the sergeant inside.

No sign of him. Had he vanished back into the shadowed wilderness?

"Why wouldn't you let me speak with him?" she demanded, frustrated.

"I'm under strict orders to bring you straight to the colonel's quarters," Sergeant James said in a clipped

manner as he saluted the guards at the fort's wide
gates and wouldn't look at her.

No, there was more to that. Was it Henry's orders?
"It's because Night Hawk's an Indian, isn't it? I saw
how everyone acted in the mercantile."

"You're wrong. His being an Indian has got nothing
to do with it." The sergeant flushed. "He is a different
sort of fellow."

Marie heard what the officer wasn't saying, and it
made her angry. "It *is* because he's a native."

"Your father is more progressive than that!" The
sergeant's commanding tone vibrated with anger, as if
he didn't like being questioned by a mere woman, and
it drew looks from uniformed privates mounting up in
the nearby stable yard.

"Night Hawk keeps to himself. Doesn't seem to
have much need for us. He's a real lone wolf type,
and you'd be wise to keep your distance from men
like that. Your father won't permit it."

So, that was the way it was. Did Henry still think
of her as a little girl to be commanded and supervised,
like any new enlistee? If that was true, then he was in
for a surprise.

She was a grown woman, and she could make up
her own mind about a man's character. Remembering
how Night Hawk had brushed his knuckles down little
Cassie's cheek with a father's tenderness eased the hot
anger inside her.

A thousand questions buzzed on her tongue, so
many she didn't know where to start. She was nearly
out of breath trying to keep up with the fast-paced

sergeant, who looked more unpleasant after their exchange.

"Tell me, please." She lifted her skirt and hopped over a rivulet of water from a garden's irrigation. "Does Night Hawk live here in the settlement?"

The sergeant's mouth narrowed, and he walked even faster.

Marie practically ran to keep up. "Night Hawk was injured. Does he have family to look after him?"

The sergeant scowled at her. The intent was clear to her. He wasn't going to tell her a thing.

She wasn't discouraged. Somehow, some way, she'd find the answers to her questions. Meeting Night Hawk today had left her feeling as if she'd been interrupted in the middle of a sonata, the harmony of notes fading in the air, unfinished and without end.

As she hurried past huge log buildings and the smaller log homes of officers, she remembered the low rumble of his voice, like summer thunder, and the protective shelter of his arms.

Maybe—just maybe—she'd see him again.

Chapter Two

What a wondrous night. Marie let the screen door slap shut behind her and padded across the porch. Like enchantment, the night sky glittered with the light of a billion stars. Big, white beautiful twinkles that made the heavens seem close enough to touch.

If only Papa were here to see it with her. He hadn't come home at all, and she'd eaten supper fixed by an unfriendly housekeeper alone in the echoing dining room.

A series of sweet mellow bongs spilled through the open parlor window. Eleven o'clock. Late for Papa to be out on her first day here.

She fought the harsh sting of disappointment. Her father was a busy man, that was all. She understood that. Surely a crisis had come up and detained him. That's what it was.

But she didn't think so. He'd promised he'd greet her at the stage. He'd promised he would have a new horse at the stables for her. Had he broken that vow, too?

There was only one way to find out. She took the

steps two at a time and hit the dirt path with both feet, stirring up a cloud of dust.

Overhead a hawk cried, and she tilted her head all the way back to watch it spin across the handle of the Big Dipper. Exhilaration thundered through her.

Was it the same one she'd seen earlier today? Or its mate? The bird glided gracefully on wide wings, wild and free, commanding the night.

This wilderness was truly an amazing place to live. What other wonders would she see? *Maybe Night Hawk.* The thought came unbidden like a whisper in the wind.

It was easy to recall how he'd looked framed by the mercantile's doorway. As dark as forest shadows, he was striking with his shoulder-length jet-black hair, bright sparkling eyes and mysterious good looks. Just imagining him made her heart leap. A strange, shivery feeling gathered in her stomach.

Light from the stables tumbled through an open half door onto the path, as if beckoning her closer. At this late hour, no one should be inside the stables. Maybe it was her father, a part of her hoped. Was it possible he hadn't forgotten about her mare? Eagerly she pushed open the door.

A single flame burned in a lantern hung from one of the overhead rafters to light her way. She took two steps and froze at the sight of a huge dark horse cross-tied in the aisle, half-masked in shadows. His eyes rolled, and he tossed his head sharply. The ropes holding him snapped taut, keeping him trapped.

"Whoa, fella," a man's forest-dark voice soothed. It wasn't her father's voice. "Easy, now. There is no danger."

Marie watched in amazement as a shadow rose from the darkness at the horse's side, taking shape and substance as the light touched him.

Night Hawk.

He didn't appear to see her lurking in the doorway.

"Easy, boy." Night Hawk stepped into the light, circling around the nervous animal that watched him defiantly. Almost viciously.

How powerful and wild the gelding looked up close. He stomped one huge front hoof and tossed his enormous head in the air as high as the ropes would allow. His ears flattened against his head. She recognized the horse now. It was the same one that had almost hurt her and little Cassie Ingalls.

"That's no way to behave, boy." Night Hawk's words held no trace of fear.

The warmth in his voice made the sensitive skin at Marie's nape tingle.

"You can be a gentleman, I know you can." Night Hawk spoke with the hush of a lullaby and the power of a summer storm.

The horse responded with uneasy trust. She couldn't believe her eyes. The untamable runaway that had nearly turned killer today stood quietly for Night Hawk.

The big man knelt and ran his hand along the gelding's front leg, never losing touch with him. Night Hawk's words became too low to hear, but the gelding's head drifted down to eat from a small tin bucket on the floor.

The scent of corn and molasses tickled Marie's nose.

What kind of man was Night Hawk? Saver of

women and children and wild-horse tamer. How could he be real? He had to be a dream, a figment of her imagination, the fantasy of a perfect man. Yes, that was it.

Except she was wide-awake and this was no dream. She could smell the straw and horse scent of the stable, see the flicker of light on the man's hands as he inspected the gelding's fetlock. And hear the beat of her own heart.

He stood—all flesh-and-blood man—and his gaze pierced the shadows and pinpointed her. His eyes were dark like the night. "Miss Lafayette. What are you doing out of your father's house?"

How long had he known she was there? "I didn't make a sound."

"Your skirts did." The light flickered over him, worshiping high, sharp cheekbones, a well-proportioned nose and a hard, carved jaw.

Marie felt a lightning bolt strike her, but there was no storm, no thunder. Her feet left the ground, she was sure of it. When she looked down, she saw the straw-strewn earth directly beneath her shoes.

The wind gusted, snapping her skirts. The gelding trumpeted, loud and shrill and sidestepped violently, fighting his restraints.

Night Hawk spoke, gentle soothing sounds of his native tongue while holding tight to the gelding's halter with one hand. He stroked the horse's gleaming coat with the other. The animal fought, and the man's muscles corded beneath the deerskin shirt, holding him steady.

Night Hawk's touch was magic, and the dangerous horse calmed.

Unbelievable.

"He cannot harm you. I have him cross-tied and hobbled." Night Hawk caressed one bronzed hand down the gelding's neck with the ease of a natural-born horseman. "Devil is not used to a woman's skirts."

"Should I leave?"

"No. I can control him. You have nothing to fear."

Something within Marie's heart clicked. Just like that. As a lock finding its key at the right moment.

Could he be the one, she wondered. The one she'd been waiting for all her life?

Excitement flickered through her in hot, bright flames. She dared to step forward, wanting, no—*needing*—to be closer to him. "I saw you save the little girl's life. How badly were you injured?"

He didn't meet her eyes. "I will heal."

"I saw the blood on your shirt. In the mercantile. When you spoke to me." She felt breathless, as if there wasn't enough air in the building.

"Cassie Ingalls is my friend's daughter. I would trade my life for my friend."

"Or for any child." She could *feel* it, the kind of man he was at heart—brave, noble and humble. A dream man who couldn't possibly be real.

But the real flesh-and-blood man stepped out of the shadows and into the light. "Does your father know you're here?"

What did she look like, a girl and not a woman grown? Heat flamed her face and it took all her self-control to modulate her words. "I'm my own woman, Mr. Night Hawk."

"Just Night Hawk." He spoke deep like rolling thunder and as gentle as twilight.

Another jolt spiraled through her.

He cupped the stallion's front hoof in one hand, leaned his solid shoulder against the horse's side and lifted.

Marie saw the rivulet of blood streaking the animal's delicate fetlock. "He's injured."

"That's why I'm here. No one under your father's command could get close enough to treat him."

"Then you work for my father?"

"No. I came as a favor." Night Hawk reached up to reposition the lantern and didn't look at her.

Bright light illuminated the angry gashes on the gelding's neck and the man's big, healing hands. Such gentle, masculine hands.

Marie shivered deep inside. She couldn't move away. "It looks to me as if you need some help."

"Does it?" He lifted one dark brow, measuring her. "You're not afraid of Devil?"

"Not with you here."

He nodded toward the shadows. "You can fetch that basin for me."

She lifted the hot enamel container from the shadowed dirt floor. Mossy-smelling steam brushed her face as she knelt in the crackling straw beside the horse.

"Closer to me," Night Hawk urged.

Closer? She was already near enough to see the bold, high cut of his cheekbones and the wide, lean cut of his shoulders. He smelled pleasantly of night and wind. She managed to crawl a few more inches on her knees.

He dipped a cloth into the steaming basin and wrung it well. He was big but his ministrations were gentle as he cleaned the blood from the horse's wounded fetlock.

She had never seen tenderness like this in so strong a man.

"Now that the wound is cleaned, come closer," he said. "Help me with the bandaging."

Unable to speak, Marie obeyed. Kneeling together in the shadows, she could feel his body's radiant heat.

Night Hawk held a roll of muslin to the gelding's fetlock. "Hold this in place for me. Right here." He caught her hand and pressed it to the bandage just above the gelding's hoof.

His touch was like sunlight, his nearness like dawn. New sensations burst to life within her.

Then Night Hawk released her hand, but the sensations remained. He bent over his work, wrapping the horse's wound. His rock-hard biceps brushed Marie's shoulder. His jaw grazed the crown of her head. Bright, hot yearning ripped through her, leaving her trembling but not weak.

He knotted the muslin strip and eased the hoof back to the ground. The gelding nickered, as if in thanks.

"You have a gift." She breathed the words, and embarrassment warmed her face. Couldn't she hide this admiration for him better than that?

"A gift? No, nothing special. Not like my father had." Night Hawk straightened, towering over her, tall and proud, and then extended his hand to her. "I merely have a love for horses."

"So do I." She placed her palm against his and

climbed to her feet. Touching him this way felt unreal. As if it were part of an amazing dream.

If only he would look at her. If only some of what she was feeling reflected in his dark, mysterious gaze. But she could tell he wasn't interested in her. Not one bit.

He thinks I'm too young. She bit back the urge to ask his age. To ask a thousand burning questions about him.

Night Hawk spun in the direction of the door. "Here comes your father."

She didn't hear anything. A few seconds later footsteps tapped on the path outside and a tall, imposing man marched into the dark stable.

"Papa!" She launched herself past Night Hawk and Devil, skirts rustling, heart lifting. "I'm so glad to see you. I've been waiting all day. I knew you were busy—"

"Now, daughter, contain yourself." Colonel Henry Lafayette held up both hands as if the sight of her running at him, arms wide, was no way to behave.

Marie stopped short and folded her arms around her middle.

"I had an unavoidable crisis. Only just got it resolved. A bear is threatening the settlers, hardly surprising on the frontier, but there you have it. Sergeant James tells me you've settled in. What are you doing here?"

Why had she expected, after years apart, he would be different? She hugged herself, feeling alone. "I came down to look for the mare you promised me. You did remember, didn't you?"

"I'm a busy man, Marie. Horses are dangerous. Not

only that, but I can't think it would be the best for your reputation. Ladies ride in buggies, not on the backs of animals." Henry's face changed and Marie saw a brief apology.

Then it vanished, leaving only the commander's stern manner. "And what about your behavior tonight? This is the frontier. You can't walk around on your own, especially at this time of night."

Disappointment tasted bitter. She should have known. It's just that his letter asking her to come had been so surprising. Now she could see she'd misinterpreted his meaning. He hadn't wanted her as much as she'd hoped.

Night Hawk's moccasins made no sound on the straw-strewn floor as he approached. "Colonel, sir, I have been watching over your daughter. As you see, no harm has come to her."

"I owe you a debt of thanks, Night Hawk." Henry shifted his attention on the silent man in the shadows and, again, his stern demeanor faded. "How is the gelding?"

"Devil needs a few days' rest. I'll leave instructions with the stable master." As if she wasn't there, Night Hawk turned and looked past her. "Good night, Colonel."

Night Hawk stepped into the shadows and disappeared. Marie stared into the darkness, wishing, just wishing.

"Honestly, Marie," Henry boomed loud enough for every last soldier in the nearby barracks to hear. "I expected you to remain home until I arrived."

"Oh, Papa. I couldn't wait forever in an empty house."

"How am I to maintain discipline in my ranks when I cannot command my own daughter? This is no way to start out your tenure here."

"My tenure?" She'd been a fool to think anything had changed between them. She'd traveled all the way from Ohio for this? "I'm not one of your privates ready to jump at your every command. I am a grown woman—"

"That is quite enough, girl." Henry pushed open the door. "Come, before I lose my temper."

Marie steeled her heart and headed into the night. A pleasant breeze caressed her face and tangled through her long wavy locks, scattering them every which way. She heard her father's gait behind her, tapping brisk and even.

"Good thing you came across Night Hawk. I run a tight fort and I command good men, but that doesn't mean you should wander the grounds without an escort. The stables aren't a proper place for a young lady."

"I can take care of myself. I'm not the girl you remember."

"No, but you are my daughter, and if anything should happen to you, I could never stand it." A touch of warmth softened his stern manner. "I want you safe, Marie. A gently raised young lady such as yourself is not used to the dangers of the frontier."

"I'm not afraid—"

"You could have been trampled today," Henry interrupted. "You would have been had it not been for Night Hawk. That's twice I'm indebted to him now. Twice. Do not put yourself in danger a third time."

Marie followed her father up the steps and onto the

porch. Not knowing what to do, she leaned against the railing and gazed out on the night. Her father sat down in the shadows, and the wooden chair creaked. A match flared to life, a brief flame against the darkness. The first burst of smoke lifted on the wind.

From Ohio, with his letter in hand inviting her to join him, it had seemed like an opportunity to make things better. Was it even possible to change things between them?

He might be her father, but he was a colonel first. Always a colonel. Never a parent to remember birthdays and gifts. Never someone to turn to when the loneliness became too much to bear.

"Go on up to your room and get some sleep, Marie." He sounded gruff, just short of harsh, but he sounded strangely affectionate, too.

"I'll choose my own bedtime, thank you. The night is beautiful and there are so many things I want to say to you."

"Not tonight, daughter." Embers glowed at the tip of his cigar as he inhaled. "I've had a tough day."

"I see." So, he would dismiss her. His daughter. She pushed away from the porch.

"Mrs. Olstad will have breakfast on the table at six hundred sharp. I'll see you then."

"Yes, Papa. Good night." She fled before he could answer, turning her back on the lonely night and the canyon of distance between them.

She hurried up the staircase and down the dark hallway, trying not to turn their first not-so-warm encounter into a disaster. He was tired. She was disappointed. Maybe tomorrow would be better.

Her room was dark, just as she had left it. The white

curtains lashed at the open window as if beckoning her. It was still early and she wasn't a bit tired, so she knelt on the soft cushions of the window seat and let the wind breeze across her face.

It was a night made for dreaming, with stars so bright and the wide horizon brimming with possibilities. A hawk's cry snared her attention and she watched the noble hunter cut the sky with silent wings.

Marie breathed in the fresh air and listened to the call of a coyote. The swirling emotions inside her began to ease.

A movement in the shadows caught her eye—a broad-shouldered man, lithe and powerful. Night Hawk. Mounted, he rode tall and proud, his long brave's hair dancing with the wind.

Her heart soared just like the hawk overhead. The strange floating, shivering sensation she'd experienced in his presence returned.

She'd never felt so alive and the feeling remained long after he'd ridden from her sight.

Night Hawk saw the young hawk circling overhead in an ever-widening spiral away from the fort. Other creatures filled the night sky—the hoot owls, the mosquito-eating bats and a mature male eagle hunting the fields for food for his young.

It was likely that only the young hawk had no mate to fly with and no young to hunt for. A solitary life was no comfort for a bird.

Or a man.

The wind gusted, stirring a woman's scent clinging to his shirt where he and Marie Lafayette had briefly touched.

The colonel's daughter.

A cold weight settled in his gut, and Night Hawk urged Shadow into an easy lope. Even to notice the smallest detail about the colonel's daughter was trouble.

In truth, he hadn't noticed her. He'd memorized her wavy, dark brown hair and how she smelled fresh as morning sun on a spring meadow. The oval cut of her face was soft and so beautiful it hurt to look at her.

You've been without a woman too long, he told himself. But even as he thought the words, they rang false. It wasn't lust he felt. It was something greater, like the sky without horizon, like time without end.

Who did he think he was? Marie was too young, too pretty and too white. She was the colonel's daughter. She was out of his reach like the stars above.

He halted his stallion in the shadow of his home where there were no windows lit and no woman waiting.

If loneliness battered him, he refused to feel it.

He dropped the pack he carried on the front steps and made a vow never to think about the colonel's daughter again.

Chapter Three

"You're late."

Marie pulled out the wooden chair and eased onto the tapestried cushion. "I had trouble finding all my clothes. Only one of my trunks arrived."

"Then I'll have Sergeant James see to it." Henry's stern demeanor softened. "Did you sleep well?"

"I tried." Marie couldn't contain her excitement. "I've never heard so many strange sounds in one place. Coyotes howling, owls hooting and creatures moving in the forest outside the fort walls."

"We'll see if you're of the same opinion next week." The colonel sounded harsh, but his dark eyes twinkled.

There was hope, Marie decided as she grabbed a slice of crispy bacon. For the first time in her life, she was alone with her father over a meal. It was a time to talk, to bond and share opinions and experiences like other families.

Where did she start? "Papa, I'd love to see the new schoolhouse. I—"

But Henry wasn't listening. He'd turned toward the

opened front door, just visible through the parlor, where footsteps pounded across the porch.

"Excellent!" he boomed. "Come right on in, Major. Do you have the report?"

"I do, sir." The screen door whispered on its hinges as a man entered. He marched across the parlor with a painfully straight posture and wearing a spotless blue uniform. "This is the latest report from the field."

"Give it here, Major. I have decisions to make." The colonel snatched pages of parchment from the lesser officer's fist. Paper snapped as he flipped through the pages, skimming. "Yes, it looks complete. Major, you must meet my daughter. Ned Gerard, this is my only daughter, Marie. Marie, say hello."

"I know how to speak without your instructions, Papa," she reminded him gently. Really. Hadn't he looked at her enough to notice she was no longer a child needing instructions? He was embarrassing her.

But the newcomer, Major Gerard, struggled not to chuckle as if he knew Henry all too well. He was a pleasant-looking man.

"I'm pleased to finally make your acquaintance, Miss Lafayette. Your father has spoken often of your teaching achievements."

"Achievements?" Leave it to her father to make teaching English sound like she'd negotiated the Louisiana Purchase. "I'm not the best teacher there is, but I am lucky to be here."

"I'm sure you'll be a wonderful aid to your father's work." The major bowed slightly.

Marie noticed her father's face was hidden mostly

by the papers he was studying. But his brows knit together as if he were smiling.

Smiling! Marie grabbed her plate and stood, working hard to contain her anger. "You gentlemen appear to have business to attend to, so if you'll excuse me, I'll leave you to it."

"Marie," Henry warned. "You'll stay and finish your meal at the table. This is the frontier, but that doesn't mean we can give up any—"

"Goodbye, Papa." Marie tapped across the room, refusing to give in. "Pleasant meeting you, Major."

"And you, ma'am."

She could feel Henry's fury all the way into the kitchen. Too bad. He wasn't going to do this to her. She absolutely refused to allow it.

Introducing her to the major. Next it would be an invitation to supper. Then her father would be pressuring her to marry the major. She hadn't come here to let her father run her life, that was for sure.

She marched down the kitchen steps and into the backyard.

A three-foot-high split-rail fence walled in a well-tended vegetable garden and a cool patch of mowed grass. Ancient sugar maples cast long morning shadows across the yard. She spotted a log bench beneath them. It was the perfect place to enjoy her meal.

She ate in solitude, if not exactly silence. Outside the small haven, she could hear the sounds of the soldiers beginning their busy day. Voices rang. Doors slammed. Someone—perhaps a new recruit—raced past, hidden by a row of bushes, muttering to himself that he was late again.

A rabbit darted out from behind a clump of beets to nibble on delicate carrot greens. He lifted his chocolate-brown head, wrinkled his nose while he studied her and then returned to his breakfast.

Marie finished hers. This strange new land wasn't home yet. Last night she had missed her comfortable bed—the familiar feel of it, the sound of Aunt Gertrude rising to prepare breakfast, and the regular routine of their days together.

Here in Fort Tye, there were no lending libraries, no ladies clubs and no supper theater. But Marie watched a finch light on a limb of the sweet-leafed sugar maple, and a sense of rightness filled her like heaven's touch.

Happiness was awaiting her. She could *feel* it.

Night Hawk's entire body screamed with exhaustion as he hauled fresh water from the well. The two huge buckets felt like boulders as he emptied first one and then the other into the trough.

The bay mare in the corral with him nickered softly to her newborn foal and gratefully dipped her nose into the water. It had been a long night and a tough morning, but Joy had brought forth a strong foal. The tiny filly walked at her dam's flank, her knobby knees threatening to buckle. Her bristle-brush mane ruffled in the wind as she nursed.

The big black dog napping in the shade of the house let out a single woof and climbed to his feet. Tilting his big head, he listened to the faint clip-clop of a newly shod horse.

Night Hawk dropped the buckets. It wasn't his

friend, Josh Ingalls, riding over the crest of the hill. Judging by the faint jingling of a harness and the rattle of wheels, it was a buggy from the settlement. The dog wasn't used to many visitors. Night Hawk ordered Meka to stay.

He wasn't surprised when one of the fort horses crested the rise, pulling the colonel's buggy. He tried not to curse the Fates tempting him when he saw a spray of blue fabric ruffling in the wind—the hem of a woman's fine dress. Sunlight gleamed on a lock of wavy dark hair, and his blood fired.

The colonel's daughter.

He gritted his teeth, but the images of the night returned in a fiery rush—her porcelain face in the lantern light, the summer-breeze scent of her skin and the feel of her next to him like something lost finally found.

She was the colonel's daughter, he reminded himself and forced the images from his mind.

The sergeant at Miss Lafayette's side reined in the thick-legged army horse a good distance from where Meka sat on his haunches warily watching the newcomers.

"Night Hawk." Humphrey James climbed down from the buggy and offered his hand to the woman. "We've come to look at your horses. Miss Lafayette would like to purchase a mount. Something gentle and easy to handle. An older mare, I should think."

"Sergeant, I'm capable of speaking for myself." In a graceful sweep of blue silk, Marie Lafayette stepped out of the shadowed buggy and into the dappled sunlight. "Night Hawk. I asked around the settlement this morning and everyone agreed that you had the best horses.''

She spun in a half circle, her full skirts and dark locks swirling as she quickly scanned the pastures and corrals of grazing horses. ''Looks to me that they were right.''

''They were wrong. I have no mares to sell you.''

''What? You have plenty of horses.'' She flipped one silken lock behind her ear, and a look of wonder flashed across her gentle features as she noticed the corral. ''You have a new baby.''

''She was born this morning.'' He couldn't keep the pride out of his voice, or the way his gaze kept straying to the colonel's daughter.

''She's beautiful.'' Marie knelt outside the wooden corral where dam and foal were alone. ''How old is she?''

''Four hours.''

''Look how well she walks. And her legs are so long.''

She curled her delicate hands around the wooden rails. ''I've never seen such knobby knees.''

''That only means she'll grow up to run fast and far.'' He itched to step closer. Just close enough to smell the sweet scent of Marie's skin and the wild-flowers in her hair.

The foal wobbled away from her dam's side and stretched her skinny neck toward the fence and Marie's fingers.

A part of him ached to be the foal, stretching toward the beautiful lady dressed in a rich blue dress like a tropical bird on this plain and simple land. Night

Hawk's chest felt as if it had filled with sand. Too many longings filled him. Yearnings for home and family, for a woman to love.

The foal lipped Marie's fingers, then leaned a sun-warmed cheek against her palm.

His heart simply stopped beating.

"What's her name?"

"I haven't gotten around to that yet. What do you think?"

Marie's spine tingled at his question. She couldn't imagine having the right to name this fragile and amazing creature. The adorable filly's lips were velvet soft against Marie's skin.

Then the wind caught the hem of her crinolines and ruffled a lace edge. The foal hopped backward a few steps and braced herself on her knobby knees. Those long legs were at off angles, but still she managed to hold her balance.

"It's all right, little one." Marie tucked the offending lace edge beneath her blue skirts. "See?"

She felt Night Hawk's gaze on her like a touch to her cheek. Felt his scrutiny as the filly ambled closer, braver now that the lace had vanished. The wind picked up Marie's skirts again and the foal leaped so fast she was a blur as she flew to her mother's side. Her long wobbly legs promised a lifetime of speed.

"Wind." Marie decided. "I would name her Wind."

"Good choice."

He towered over her, silhouetted by the sun's golden light. Marie gazed up at him and a jolt of pure sensation traveled from her heart to her soul, leaving her trembling.

What was it about this man that made her feel so much? And so strangely? As if she were alive for the first time? Before she could think about it, Night Hawk tore away and kept his back to her, striding on his moccasins to where the sergeant stood in the shade of the buggy.

"Sergeant," he said in a cool, even tone. "Please see Miss Lafayette safely to the fort."

He was sending her away? She climbed to her feet. "I came to purchase a mare and that's what I intend to do."

"Either Josh Ingalls or Lars Holmberg may have an older mare for sale. Sergeant, take Miss Lafayette to see one of them." Night Hawk didn't look at her. It was as if he saw not a woman but a child too young to be bothered with.

He whistled to his dog, which leaped to his side, and strode off toward the fields.

"Come, let's try Mr. Ingalls." Sergeant James held out his gloved hand, waiting to help her into the buggy. "No doubt he will be more cooperative. Night Hawk is a loner. He doesn't take to people butting into his business."

"But I want to buy a horse from him." Only him.

"Ingalls is a good man. He'll give you a fair price for an old, gentle mount. Something for a young lady to learn on."

She was getting tired of being a young lady. She was a woman, capable and intelligent, and she wasn't going to let a man who handled horses the way he did refuse to negotiate with her.

Determined, she set off across the stable yard. The sunlight was warm on her face and the tall seed-heavy grass snapped against her skirts. Grazing horses lifted their muzzles to study her.

Where had he gone? She scanned the lush green acreage of grazing pastures and growing crops, all neatly fenced.

There he was—near the tree line. He was nothing more than a shadow against the dark woods, but she'd recognize his proud profile and the set of his wide shoulders anywhere.

She watched his spine stiffen as she drew nearer. He deliberately kept his back to her as he lifted an ax from a thick stump.

Let him try to ignore her. She would show him. She wasn't a feeble-minded female who could be pushed around.

The dog let out a friendly *woof* and wagged his tail in greeting until a low word from Night Hawk commanded him to sit. A few dozen horses grazing in the field lifted their sculpted heads in unison and trotted eagerly toward the split-rail fence. Their coats gleamed in the sunshine—an array of rich browns, vibrant reds, pure whites and deep blacks.

A few of those horses were mares. Wait—every single one of them was. Anger kindled, and she could barely contain it. To think that he'd lied to her!

"You said you had no mares," she challenged. "But here's a pasture full of them."

"They are not for sale."

"That's right. Because you won't sell to a woman."

He lifted the ax high and sank it deep into a tree already on the ground. Steel drove into wood, and the log split its entire length. "I never do business with women."

"Then let's pretend I'm not a woman just for the few minutes it takes for me to pick out a mare and pay for her."

He lowered his ax. Instead of answering, he narrowed his eyes to study her. "Are you sure that you're the *colonel's* daughter? I expected someone obedient and well behaved."

"I am well behaved. But don't make the mistake of thinking any woman ought to be obedient. I suppose that's how men think, a woman would be easier to manage if she wore a bridle and had a bit in her mouth. Just like these horses."

"What if I agreed?" One brow crooked.

"Then you, sir, are not what I had hoped." She fisted her hands, not sure now if he was serious or if he was teasing her. "No wonder you're alone. No woman in her right mind would have you."

"Maybe I have three wives who obey my every command."

"Yes, but there's no one else here. If you have three wives, they obviously came to their senses and left you."

Now he laughed, rich and deep like summer thunder rolling in from the horizon. "I *do* think women and horses should be treated the same."

And he could say that with sincerity in his voice and integrity warming his eyes? She said, "You've finally convinced me. I don't want to do business with *you.*"

How could she have been so wrong about him? Marie marched through the grasses, disappointment whipping through her.

"I've changed my mind, too," he called out. "I will sell you one of my mares."

"One of your old, obedient, submissive mares?"

"If that's what you wish."

"You have no notion of what I wish for." Now she was really mad. He mocked her? Or was he amused by her? And what of the man with the gentle hands and iron strength she'd seen last night? Who tended wounded horses with care and made her feel alive? "I know what I don't want, and that's a horse from you."

"Too late. One has already chosen you." Night Hawk gestured toward the field.

A mare walked on the other side of the fence, her ears pricked and her mane and tail dancing in the wind. Her big brown eyes held a shining question.

"I told you, I'm no longer interested."

"She's interested in you."

"The sergeant will take me somewhere else. Somewhere I won't have to be insulted."

Night Hawk's gait whispered behind her, and the mare's hooves clomped on the hard-packed ground alongside her.

Don't look at either of them, Marie commanded herself.

"It's said it's best when the horse chooses her master." Night Hawk caught up with Marie, adjusting his long-legged stride to match hers. "When one heart searches for another and finds its match. Look at her."

Marie tingled at his words and at the depth of them. "I'm not looking for a submissive horse. I'm looking for spirit."

"You misunderstood me." His hand curled around her elbow, branding-iron hot and iron solid. "I meant what I said. A woman and a horse should be treated the same—with respect. I will only sell a horse to a rider who understands that."

"Is that why you wouldn't sell me a mare earlier?"

"No." He released her and stepped away. "Look at the mare."

She was beautiful. The mare's red coat gleamed like fire beneath the sun's touch, and a narrow stripe of white delicately marked her well-shaped nose.

A spark of affection flickered to life in Marie's heart, just like that.

The sorrel reached above the rail. Marie laid her fingers on the mare's nose. She would never want any other horse.

"I can't believe it." The sorrel caught a bit of lace on Marie's sleeve with her teeth. "She's mine. My very own horse!"

"She's not broken to ride."

"She seems gentle. Could you train her for me?" Laughing, the sweetest trill of music and delight, Marie extricated her sleeve from the mare's teeth. "I'm in love with her already."

No, his conscience warned him.

Yes, his heart answered. "I could train her to a buggy in no time."

"No, I don't want to drive her. I want to *ride* on her back and race the winds."

Night Hawk was enchanted. The colonel's daughter burned with the light of a thousand suns, this quiet softly shaped woman with a will as strong as oak. A longing burst inside him so fierce it left him weak. Far too weak.

"Please, don't tell my father. He has very rigid ideas of how women should behave, but I'm not his little girl anymore. I make my own choices."

No. That should be his answer. "It will be our secret."

Her smile made her too beautiful to gaze upon.

Night Hawk broke away from this woman he could never have and stared hard at the mare. "I will contact you when she's fully trained. We'll agree on a price then, with your father's approval."

"Papa had his chance. He could have chosen an old plodding mare for me to learn to ride on, but he didn't. So I figure he doesn't have the right to complain about whatever horse I purchase with my own savings."

"I don't want to anger the colonel. He's been good to me and my people."

"Don't worry." An ember of mischief glimmered within her. "I can manage my father."

Longing speared him. It's loneliness, he told himself. He'd been without a woman's company for more years than he could count. All he had to do was say goodbye. Then Marie Lafayette would climb back into the buggy and drive out of his life.

"I will leave word with Sergeant James when your mare is ready," he promised. "Good day."

He spun on his heel. Every step he took put welcome distance between him and the colonel's daughter.

Dainty feet padded against the dusty earth behind him. "Night Hawk."

He should have kept walking, but he turned.

She looked like a dream with her long brown hair waving in the wind as she ran. The sky-blue fabric hugged her soft woman's curves.

Marie smiled with the innocence of a woman who didn't know the power she possessed over a man. "Does the mare have a name?"

He watched her slim, long-fingered hand caress over the sorrel's white blaze with a woman's tenderness.

The heat in his veins burned.

"I call her Kammeo." His words sounded strangled to his own ears, yet it was the best he could do. Want swept over him like a wildfire, and he couldn't control it.

"It's a beautiful name. What does it mean in your language?"

There was no trace of prejudice. Only a bright curiosity and a quiet interest that left him speechless.

He couldn't deny his attraction to her. To a woman too fine and genteel for the likes of him. He'd bet his land and every last horse he owned that Colonel Henry Lafayette wouldn't want his precious daughter alone with a man like him.

Night Hawk hardened his heart, turned his back on her and walked away without answering her.

If she had shown abhorrence for his culture or disdain at his people's ways, it would have been easier.

So much easier to keep his back turned. To put distance between them.

But she'd been respectful. *It's a beautiful name. What does it mean?* He could still hear the music of her voice and feel the bright light of her presence as he returned to the far pasture.

Trees shaded him as he lifted his ax and swung, taking his frustration out on trees that had fallen last winter.

Over the thud of the ax, he heard the squeak of the buggy's wheels as it bounced along his rutted road. Dust lifted like fog in the air and larks playing in the grasses startled skyward.

Meka lifted his big head and howled a melancholy goodbye.

Night Hawk could feel Marie Lafayette's gaze like a hot burning flame to his back. He worked until she'd driven past and then he stared into the cloud of dust in her wake.

Loneliness settled around him like the dust to the earth—a loneliness that ached and thrashed within the deepest places of his heart.

He had no family. No wife. No children. That was how he'd always feared his life would remain.

Maybe that was why he felt such an attraction to Marie Lafayette. That was all. Loneliness. A man's natural yearning for a wife.

He felt warm velvet of a horse's muzzle graze his knuckles. He hadn't realized that he'd stopped splitting rails and was leaning against the wood fence. Kammeo, with her coat of red flame and spirit, lipped him quizzically as if asking where Marie had gone.

Kammeo. It meant *one and only.* It also meant *soul mate.* A man's one and only love for all time.

Fate would not be so cruel, Night Hawk was certain, as to make his *kammeo* a white woman he was forbidden to love.

Chapter Four

The wonder of Marie's day remained even when the front door slammed open with the force of a bullet and rattled the windowpanes in the house.

"Marie Janelle, front and center this minute!" Henry's voice filled the house like a cannon blast.

"No need to shout, Papa." She laid the last sweater into place in the bureau draw and pushed it closed. "I'll be down in a minute."

"Now."

"When I'm finished emptying this last trunk."

She winced at the angry drum of his boots on the floor. Not even the thick wood ceiling between them could muffle it. There was no time like the present to start standing up to him and to change their relationship.

His footsteps punched up the stairs and knelled down the hallway. Marie took a deep breath and lifted the last of her sweaters from the bottom of her trunk.

"Good evening, Papa." She crossed to the bevel-mirrored bureau. "It doesn't sound as if you had a pleasant day."

"Not when I discovered you coerced my sergeant into taking you from the settlement."

"Coerced?" Marie saw her father's reflection in the mirror behind her. Angry tension stiffened him like a well-seasoned board, and his face was ruddy. "I merely pointed out that I would find the way on foot if I had to. The stable master refused to allow me the use of a horse and buggy. Your instructions, he said."

"I don't want you running off, Marie. It's unsafe." Soldier-fierce, he clomped into the room, and yet when she looked again in the mirror, gray gathered at his temples and marked his beard. The fall of once jet-black hair over his brow had turned completely gray.

They'd lost so much time, she and Papa. So much time to be a family.

"Papa, I didn't mean to be difficult." She pushed in the drawer and faced him. "I know there's a bear threatening settlers, but I had Sergeant James with me. He was armed—"

"A musket won't always stop a raging bear. Everyone knows that." Henry's anger flared but beneath it lurked something else, something harder to discern.

Marie closed her trunk lid. "As you can see, nothing happened. You don't need to be worried after the fact."

"Worried?" Henry sounded surprised. "I'm furious that you'd disobeyed a direct order, Marie."

"It wasn't direct to me. I was furious because you broke another promise."

"I'm a busy man."

"You're my father, not my commanding officer." She yanked the empty trunk from her bed and set it with an angry thunk on the floor. "I bought my own horse today, so there's no point in you rushing to find me the mare you promised."

"My secretary was supposed to—"

She slid the trunk with force into place beneath the second window. Papa always had his excuses and she wouldn't listen to them. She wanted more than excuses. She wanted more than his attempts to be her father—attempts lacking heart.

She settled the trunk into place with a final thud and straightened.

Henry merely looked angrier. "I brought you out here to help me with my work. There are children who need to learn. Both the settlers' children and the Indian children have to be prepared for the changing world awaiting them. That is what I fight for every day. Bettering the lives of the civilians I defend."

"That's good and fine, and I admire your principles, Papa. I always have. But I came here because my father asked me to. My *father*." She marched past him, losing her temper. "I'll be downstairs."

He followed her out into the hall. "Marie, Mrs. Olstad is putting supper on the table. You straighten up. I want you presentable in five minutes. Major Gerard is coming—"

Not wanting to hear more, Marie flew down the stairs and through the kitchen. Ignoring Mrs. Olstad's disapproving frown, Marie dashed outside and shut the door behind her with enough force to echo up the stairwell. It wasn't a slam, just a statement. She wasn't going to settle for a colonel. Not when she wanted a father.

The evening was hot and humid when she stepped out onto the porch. Sunlight played through the tips of trees, casting long shadows. The wilderness outside the tall, stout fort walls beckoned her.

This was her adventure. She'd come to Fort Tye for several reasons. Being with her father was only one of them. There were children to teach, a new world to explore. And maybe—just maybe—a love to discover.

Night Hawk. The thought of him made her bones melt. A thrilling, shivery feeling rippled through her. How angry he'd made her when she'd thought he was like so many men she'd met—all looking for a wife they could command around like her father did his soldiers.

But she'd been wrong. *A woman and a horse should be treated with respect,* he'd said in that voice as deep as winter. Oh, he'd been playing with her, all right, and her heart warmed with the memory.

"Miss Lafayette." A polite baritone broke into her thoughts. Major Gerard, hat in hand, strolled down the stone path, watching her with a curious gaze. "You look lovely this evening."

"Thank you, Major." Marie tucked her thoughts of Night Hawk aside for later, when she was alone. Right now she had Major Gerard to deal with. "I know my father is expecting you."

"He was good enough to invite me." The major climbed up the steps and stopped awkwardly, holding his hat, looking uncertain. "My name is Ned. Please, may I call you Marie?"

"Of course." There was a lot to like about the kind

officer who seemed boyishly shy as he attempted a nervous smile.

"Please, come in. My father would want you to be comfortable." Marie led the way into the parlor. "What do you drink?"

"Your housekeeper is known to have cold tea on hand for a few of us who don't partake." He hung his hat on the coat tree before she could offer. "I'm sorry, ma'am. I'm here so often. I report directly to your father. I oversee the training of the enlisted men."

He was proud of his work and proud to work for her father. It was hard not to like him, but she didn't want to give him the wrong impression. Likely as not, her father had already done enough of that. She offered Ned a seat before leaving him alone for the kitchen.

He thanked her and sat awkwardly in the uphol-stered wing chair near the front window.

Her temper was back, and she fought to stay calm. In the hot kitchen, she grabbed a glass from the hutch shelves. She'd come to change things between her and her father, not to have the same old battle over mar-rying her off.

"Marie! Leave that to Mrs. Olstad. Honestly." Henry thundered into the kitchen. "I want you to make a good impression tonight. Ned Gerard is just the sort of man I want for you."

"What sort is that?"

"A West Point graduate. Impeccable family name. You know I want only the best for my daughter." Henry snatched a tomato wedge from Mrs. Olstad's drain board. "I don't want you to let this opportunity pass by. Living with your aunt has given you the idea that you can be happy as a spinster for the rest of your life.''

"I don't want to be a spinster, Papa. Really.'' She could be as stubborn as he could be. After all, she was his daughter.

Marie spotted a covered pitcher on the drain board and reached for it.

"Leave that to Mrs. Olstad, Marie. We can't leave our guest waiting.''

"You go in alone, you old schemer.'' Marie couldn't summon up enough resentment to be truly angry. "I'm not going to marry him.''

"You don't know that for certain. No one knows where love will take root. Or how it will grow.'' Henry stole another tomato wedge from the worktable. "Don't be long, Marie. For me.''

She began to protest but stopped at the sudden look of sadness in his eyes. It was a kind of sadness that she knew well. They hadn't been close since she was a little girl. Could it be possible that he shared this same loneliness? This hurting ache for the bonds of family?

There was a limp to his step as he marched from the room. The sunlight slanting through the window burnished the gray in his hair.

Yes, it *was* time for a change between them. As long as he stopped trying to marry her to every West Point graduate he met.

A movement through the window caught her attention. A huge black dog slipped out of her sight on the other side of the picket fence. Night Hawk's dog.

Night Hawk couldn't be far. Her pulse soared. Her sadness drained away. Thinking of him and knowing he could be near sent a thrill through her that was brighter than the sun.

No one knows where love will take root. Or how it will grow, Henry had said. And he was right.

She dashed out the back door. The wind tangled her hair, and she wrestled it out of her eyes so she could see. Breathless with anticipation, she tripped down the steps and raced along the path to the gate.

But the lane was empty. There were no shadows, no dog and no dream man.

He *had* passed this way. She could feel it in a way she couldn't explain. Seeing him again was only a matter of time.

Where was his will of steel? Night Hawk cursed himself as he drove the sickle through the waist-high grass. For the better part of two weeks, he'd thought of her. Every time he visited the fort to check on Devil's injury. Each time Kammeo caught his gaze in the field. He hadn't started working with the animal yet.

He was afraid that would make him dream of the woman more.

Fragrant stalks dropped to the mowed ground, and he swung again, taking down more grass. Sweat flew off his brow as he cut his way to the edge of the field. Winded, he leaned the blade against the fence and reached for the jug he'd left in the shade.

Cool water poured down his throat and he swallowed until it was gone. More sweat ran down his face and chest. He'd been up since three this morning making hay while the good weather held.

Meka's low bark cut through the afternoon's serenity. Night Hawk squinted into the sun and saw a figure crowning a low rise where earth and sun made illusion. There was a suggestion of a woman's dark wavy hair and soft curves—Marie Lafayette.

Night Hawk cursed. Not even twelve straight hours of hard work could drive the colonel's daughter from his mind. He grabbed his shirt off the fence's top rail and slung it over his shoulder.

When he looked up, the illusion remained, with her long hair rippling, her green skirts swirling around her soft woman's body—a body made for a man's pleasure.

Want drummed in his blood.

Then Marie moved, dream became reality. She was breezing closer, bringing the sunlight with her. Meka barked again, and only a sharp command kept the dog from bounding over to greet their unwelcome guest.

Night Hawk hardened his heart. He *had* to send her back to the fort. It was the right thing to do—no, it was the only thing to do.

"I came to see Kammeo." She stepped out of the sunbeams and offered him a shy smile. "Would you let me watch while you train her sometime?"

Night Hawk pulled on his shirt and drew it down over his sun-bronzed chest. "What are you doing out here on your own? It's dangerous."

"The bear was caught this morning. I'm perfectly safe." She held out her hand to let the dog scent her. "I didn't mean to interrupt your work."

"You didn't." He snared the empty jug and then whistled to his dog, ordering Meka to heel. "Come, we'll take you home."

"I came to visit my mare. I didn't see her in the pasture." She lifted her skirts and breezed after him, her dainty feet hardly touching the ground. "I came through the woods along the lakeshore. I've never taken such a beautiful walk."

Every step she took beat through him. Why? Why was his physical reaction to this woman so turbulent?

"The sunlight sparkled on the lake," she continued, "and the woods were enchanting, like something out of a fairy tale. I've never been in such a wild place."

She was beauty, the finest he'd ever seen and far more enchanting than this tiny piece of the world. "You're not afraid of the wilderness?"

"Afraid? It's amazing. Except for the meadows and the lake, and the farmers' fields of course, the trees go on forever. I've never been serenaded to sleep by wolves."

"Wait until you hear the cougars."

"They're musical, too?"

"Let's just say the sound might make you miss the quiet back home." Merriment twinkled a little in his dark eyes.

"Between the birds that hunt at night, the bugs that chirp and sound like they're the size of bears in the dark and the wolves braying, I'm sleeping blissfully."

"I bet you are." Night Hawk unlatched the wooden gate and stood there, laugh lines crinkling around his eyes. "It's quieter in the city."

"Astonishingly."

He held the gate open for her. Her skin tingled as she swept past him. Maybe it was because she remembered seeing his bronzed chest, bare and glistening at the sun's touch. Or maybe it was the man.

While he latched the gate, the big black dog bounded toward her, tongue lolling and sharp teeth bared in a doggy smile.

"Meka! Sit," Night Hawk ordered.

The dog launched into the air and placed his front paws on Marie's shoulders. His tongue swiped across her chin in a friendly greeting, and delight filled her. She couldn't resist hugging him. "I never had a dog when I was growing up."

"Down, Meka." Night Hawk snapped his fingers and strode close enough to cast her in his shadow.

The dog swiped his tongue across her knuckles and then obeyed. "He's a ferocious one, I can tell."

"And he doesn't like strangers." Night Hawk quirked one dark brow and his mouth narrowed as if he were trying not to laugh. "Especially women."

"I can tell. He's also the smallest dog I've ever seen."

"If you compare him to a bear. Meka, *sit.*" Night Hawk snapped his fingers and the huge dog sank to his haunches, tongue hanging out, a sparkle in his eye, imploring to be stroked.

Marie couldn't resist running her fingers across his broad head. His fur was warm from the sun and bristly soft. A bronzed hand much bigger than her own settled on the dog's head and stroked only a hairbreadth from her fingers.

Marie burned as if she'd touched the sun.

Night Hawk moved away, as if he were upset. "Come, Kammeo will be glad to see you."

As though his words had brought her, a whinny carried across the windswept meadow where a horse skidded to a stop at the split-rail fence, her red mane flying in the wind.

But what drew Marie's attention, and kept it, was the way Night Hawk's blue cotton shirt was unbuttoned, showing a wide strip of golden skin and hard, delineated muscle.

"I've been getting her used to a bridle. She doesn't like it." Night Hawk stroked one big hand down the horse's cheek. "I'm having a small problem training her. I don't know anything about a lady's sidesaddle."

"Neither do I."

"That must be how you ride in Ohio."

"I've never ridden a horse before."

"Now I understand why your father 'forgot' to buy you a mare." Night Hawk climbed over the rails and then held out his hand.

Marie looked at his wide palm, callused from hard work, and laid her hand on his. Heat seared through her like lightning across a dark sky. Light burst within her so bright it hurt.

Night Hawk's eyes went black. His strong fingers curled around the side of her hand. Had he experienced this, too?

She concentrated on fitting her shoe on the lower rung and climbing. Her skirts caught the wind and twisted tight around her ankles, but Night Hawk held her steady.

Her feet touched the ground, but she couldn't feel it.

A warm velvet horse's nose bumped against her shoulder in greeting. Dazed, Marie stroked the mare's neck and tried to marvel at the heated coat that stretched tautly over the steely muscles beneath. Night Hawk moved close, tying a rope he'd lifted from one of the fence posts, and slipped the makeshift halter over Kammeo's nose.

"She is your first horse, and you will be her first rider." Night Hawk shouldered close to slip the pliant hemp over the mare's ears. "You'll learn together."

Excitement thrilled through her. He nodded once in understanding, as if he could read her secret wishes and dreams.

"Hold the rope tight, right here." He placed her hand firmly in front of his.

At once she felt the quivering life force of the mare and the steady steel of the man. Like a dream, he led the way deeper into the field, walking beside Marie as if he belonged there. As if he were a part of her.

He spoke low, and Kammeo moved. The rope pulled taut, and Marie felt a connection to the man that she couldn't explain. Night Hawk halted behind her, with only the wind between them. Her body tingled and burned as if they were touching, chest to back, thigh to thigh.

"Don't be afraid," he murmured.

She blushed. He'd noticed she was trembling, but she wasn't afraid.

"Keep her going in a circle."

His words breezed against the back of her neck, sending arrows of pure sensation down her spine.

"Hold on tight."

She needed to hold on to her senses, that's what she needed. But Night Hawk stepped away, leaving her alone with the rope. Kammeo didn't miss a beat and when Night Hawk spoke, the mare broke into a disciplined trot, leaving Marie to rotate in a smaller circle of her own, faster against the wind and the sun.

He leaned against the fence. "Are you getting dizzy?"

"Not yet, but if she goes any faster..."

"Turn and walk backward. I can come help."

"No." Simply looking at him, with his hair bound at his nape and his shirt snapping open to let the sun worship his bronze chest, pleased her immensely. She wanted to feel his touch more than anything in the world.

Embarrassed by her thoughts, she turned, leading with her back shoulder, and the world stopped spinning so fast. Kammeo broke into a blinding gallop. The land became a swirl of green grass and golden sun.

Then Night Hawk's hand covered hers and brought the mare to a stop. Disappointed, Marie swayed into a steely chest. Lean, muscled arms enfolded her and kept her steady. How wonderful it was when wishes came true. He smelled like summer wind and mowed grass, and he felt hotter than the sun.

"Are you all right?"

"I will be." If she could catch her breath and find the good sense that had obviously taken leave of her.

Marie stumbled away, not sure if she was dizzy from twirling or light-headed from being in his arms.

Kammeo stood obediently and waited while Marie approached, and the mare nickered in friendship. The horse offered her cheek to be rubbed.

Grateful for something to do, something that would keep her from thinking about the man two paces behind her, Marie stroked her fingers along the horse's sleek coat.

Kammeo leaned into the touch with an appreciative-sounding groan.

"You two are a good match." Night Hawk's shadow fell across Marie as he untied the makeshift halter. "I will have her saddle-trained by the end of the month."

Marie watched, captivated, as he rubbed his big, gentle hand down the mare's satin neck, talking low and kind to the animal. Full of spirit, Kammeo took off at a hard gallop, tail and mane streaming like fire in the wind.

"That's what I want to do. I want to race her with the wind." Longing filled her as she watched the red mare fly across the meadow.

He laughed loud and true, as if from the depths of his soul. "Your father is going to ban me from the fort for selling you that horse. I'll train her for you, but that's it. Ride her fast or not, I refuse to be responsible."

"Being banned from the fort wouldn't be *that* much of a hardship."

"Joke all you want. I am not angering the colonel." Night Hawk couldn't believe it. The sedate, upstand-

ing English teacher the colonel had been promising
the area settlers was nothing short of a lie. Or maybe
the colonel and his love of discipline and command
was too blind to see the spirited filly he'd sired.

Spirited fillies were hard to handle, that was for
sure.

"Teach me to ride like you do." Her skirts whispered behind him. "Please. I won't tell my father if
you don't."

"He'll know, believe me." Night Hawk tossed the
coiled rope over the fence post, fighting with himself.
No one had made him laugh in a long time. Maybe it
wouldn't hurt....

No, he shouldn't do it. He *wouldn't* do it. "Let me
grab my musket and I'll see you home."

"I can find my way back." Marie's chin lifted.

Her bonnet ties and long wavy curls framed her
face, and he couldn't look away.

It was as if he'd seen her face a thousand times in
his thoughts since he'd saved her from the runaway
horse. Turning his back and walking away from her
hurt as if a knife were slicing him.

Maybe walking with her wasn't such a good idea.

"I'll wait on the path near the lake, then," he said
without looking at her again. "I can keep an eye on
you for most of the way to the settlement. Meka will
stay with you. He'll scare off any wild animals."

"Thank you." She placed her woman-soft hand in
his as she climbed over the fence.

Fire seared through his veins for the brief moment
it took her to reach the ground.

"Can I come back and watch you train her?" An

innocent longing gleamed in her eyes. Her face was flushed from the excitement and pleasure of working with Kammeo.

"Can I stop you?"

"No." She was passion and beauty, and far out of his reach.

He couldn't keep from noticing the sway of her body beneath that dress. He couldn't halt the pounding desire for her in his blood.

She'll never be yours. He knew it. But that truth didn't stop him from wanting her long after she'd disappeared from his sight or deep into the night where he lay alone in his bed.

Always alone.

Chapter Five

A dog's welcoming bark shattered the serene lake-side meadow. Loons and warblers rose from the tall grasses with squawks of protest. Butterflies feeding on the fragrant wildflowers scattered on the wind. On the sun-bright water, a pair of ducks and their half-grown chicks glided farther into the lake.

The huge black dog bounded down the grassy path, his tongue lolling. He leaped at her, his face friendly. Not knowing how to stop him, Marie accepted his big paws on her shoulders and rubbed his ears until Night Hawk's voice thundered across the shoreline.

"Meka. *Down.*"

Marie laughed when the dog lunged at her basket. "You'll have to wait like a gentleman," she told him.

"If you're looking for gentlemen, you're in the wrong territory." Night Hawk halted on the path in front of her, winded from running. His chest rose and fell, attracting her gaze. He wore dark trousers and a white shirt with the sleeves rolled to his elbows. She noticed his shirt was unbuttoned again and showed a wedge of bronze chest.

He'd been working in his fields, shirtless, and she'd missed it. Longing swept through her. "You said I could come back. I brought baked goods so you'd let me stay longer this time."

"Baked goods?" The stony look on his face softened. "Give me that basket."

"You must have a sweet tooth."

"A great big one." When he took the basket from her, he was careful to keep his fingers well away from hers. As they walked, he kept a respectful distance between them.

"Were you cutting more hay?" she asked.

"Oats this time. The cut grass is still drying." He didn't look at her but strode with leashed power that made her think of a wolf stalking prey.

She'd thought of him many times in the passing days, but she realized her remembered images of him paled when compared to the reality. He seemed taller, imposing, and so essentially masculine that she felt small next to him.

"My niece Morning Star said she met you." Night Hawk held aside a low fir branch that hung over the path so Marie could easily pass. "She said you came in your buggy with the sergeant."

"Morning Star is your niece?" Marie hadn't considered that the native family she'd visited yesterday morning could be related to Night Hawk. "I bet she'll be one of my best students."

"She was first in her class last year when the school was first opened." Pride expanded his shoulders even wider. "She rode over this morning on her pony and told me all about you."

"Is she excited for school to start?"

"She can't wait. I'm told she likes reading best."

"I'll remember that." Marie thought of all the children she'd met so far. "Some parents are hesitant to send their children to learn from the fort teacher. I'm hoping my visits will make a difference."

As they crested the small rise and Night Hawk's land spread out around them in gentle rolling hills of green and gold, of grazing horses and thriving crops, Marie couldn't imagine being lucky enough to live in a cozy log cabin like he did. Or gaze through the window to see foals romping in the pastures while their mothers watched.

He held out his hand to help her over the fence.

Fire consumed her in hot, bright sparkles that made it impossible to ignore. She was thoroughly attracted to the man.

Kammeo broke over the crest of the hill, mane and tail flying, strong legs churning the ground as she galloped. The sight of her stole Marie's breath.

She's mine, all mine. Happiness wrapped her up like a thick down quilt, and with Night Hawk at her side, Marie imagined just for a moment what it would be like to stay like this forever.

Another foolish daydream, but even as she tried to force the wish from her mind, it remained.

Kammeo charged down the hill like a warhorse and skidded to a stop dangerously near. But Night Hawk didn't move a muscle, so Marie wasn't afraid. She reached into her skirt pocket.

Kammeo nickered in approval and, as if she'd read

Marie's mind, had her teeth around the treat in Marie's hand the instant she'd taken it from her pocket.

"Spoiling her already?"

"I'm trying my best." Marie laughed as the sugar cookie disappeared in one quick bite. "Lucky I have more. Have you worked with her already today?"

"No, I train the horses in the afternoon." He said nothing more as he turned, leaving her alone with Kammeo.

The horse nudged Marie's pocket, wise to its contents, and made an affectionate nickering sound. How could Marie resist? She withdrew another cookie and loved the feel of Kammeo's soft lips on her palm.

Was she really here and not dreaming? Marie marveled at this exceptional moment in time. The warm sun kissed her with a welcome heat, and the shivering grasses and wildflowers sent dazzling fragrances into the clean air. Birds chirped and butterflies glided. Kammeo leaned her nose against Marie, pressing from her breastbone to her stomach, and contentment filled her, warm and sweet.

She knew the instant Night Hawk returned. The sun felt brighter and the wind sweeter. Harmony flooded her, like a melody finding harmony. All the pieces of her life fell into place. A beautiful sense of rightness filled her as Night Hawk shouldered past her, the bridle in hand.

She resisted the urge to lay her hand against the high plane of his cheek. But she *knew*.

Everything in her life had happened for a reason— and it was to bring her here—to this meadow, to this man.

* * *

"She's still afraid of my weight." The colonel's daughter spun toward him in the shaded circle of the corral. "I'm doing this wrong."

"No, she needs time to learn to trust you." Night Hawk fought to keep his feelings for the woman neutral. "She's getting tired, aren't you, girl? Don't worry, Marie. She'll let you know when she's ready."

"I'll trust you on that."

"You seem to like working with her."

"Sure, but I remember you saying that *you* would train her."

He laughed because he saw the teasing sparkles in her eyes. "You said you wanted to ride like I do. That is something only you and Kammeo can do together."

"I knew you were going to say that." Marie laid one slender hand against the fence. Exhaustion marked her delicate skin, but her face was flushed with pleasure.

He ought to send her home. Every instinct he had roared at him to keep his distance. But his heart overruled. He told himself he had a fondness for a fellow horse lover, that was all. But he was only lying to himself and he knew it.

"I'm out of cookies." The gentle trill of her laughter drew him. Kammeo was nosing at Marie's skirt pocket again, determined to find the treat she deserved for putting up with that scary experience of having a little weight on her back. "Night Hawk, what do I do?"

"I'll get some grain." He liked rescuing Marie, if only from her overly affectionate mare.

When he returned with a small pail of grain and a currycomb, he found Kammeo chewing contentedly and Marie rubbing her nose. The picnic basket was in the grass just outside the fence, evidence that Marie hadn't waited for the grain.

"Gave in, did you?" He set the pail on the ground in front of the mare as she stole another cookie from Marie's hand.

"I couldn't resist."

"How do you keep discipline in a classroom with that soft heart of yours?"

"I use the same method I do with Kammeo. I win them over with cookies."

"The children in this settlement are lucky that you came to teach them. Is that what you brought me in your basket? Cookies?"

"Yes. You should have seen the outrage on Mrs. Olstad's face when she came in from shopping to find me making a mess in her kitchen. She must think I'm some sort of pampered, spoiled little girl. She didn't believe me when I promised I wouldn't set the kitchen afire and I'd clean up afterward."

"I bet she wasn't happy when you proved her wrong."

"She forbade me to step foot in her kitchen again, but I'm planning on winning her over. I'm not sure cookies will work."

How Marie charmed him. Like stars drawing the moon across the sky, Night Hawk felt a potent, undeniable attraction. Intense desire turned his blood to liquid fire. Never had he wanted anything as much as the right to draw Marie into his arms and claim her as his.

A dangerous need. One he refused to give in to.

Hands trembling, he pulled a currycomb out of the second pail and concentrated on grooming the horse. Long, gliding strokes along the mare's flank that kept him from thinking about Marie.

But he heard the tap of her shoe on the earth and a clatter of steel against the small bucket. Marie wasn't so easy to ignore. She gently assured Kammeo there were no more cookies in her pocket.

He should send Marie home now, while he still could. He'd finish training the horse himself and there would be no more visits. No more temptation.

That's what he should do.

"I brought something besides the cookies," Marie said as she watched him across the span of the mare's withers. "It's not for you, I'm afraid. I brought some books Morning Star might like to read. You said she rides her pony over to visit you. I don't think I'll get a chance to see her before school starts."

"What kind of books?"

"A few children's stories about horses. I hope that will keep her excited about going to school."

As the wind caressed her hair and the sun graced her with fire, Marie wasn't just beauty, but spirit too.

One that touched his.

Night Hawk felt his steel will melt like a candle beneath a hot flame.

How was he going to resist her now?

The excitement of preparing the schoolhouse was a shadow when compared to the brightness Marie felt from being with Night Hawk. She loved teaching but it wasn't the reason she hummed as she tottered on the low stool to hang the curtains she'd made.

"Miss Lafayette?" a woman's modest voice broke the silence.

The curtain rod fell from Marie's fingers. "Goodness, you surprised me. I didn't hear you on the steps. Please, come in."

Spring Rain, Morning Star's mother, studied the desks lined in neat rows. "The children will learn well here."

"I sure hope so." Marie hopped off the stool and rescued the fallen curtains. "I hope all your children will be attending?"

"We shall see. My husband is not sure. He doesn't see the use in his sons knowing letters and numbers." Spring Rain hesitated in the center of the room. "Morning Star is my first husband's daughter, Night Hawk's brother, and so Running Deer will allow her to attend school. Night Hawk brought your books this morning. I came to thank you."

"I hope she enjoys them." Marie fit the wood rod over the wooden pins, and the green gingham curtains cascaded into place. "Would you like some tea? I have cookies, too."

"My sweet tooth is my weakness." She accepted with warm laughter. "Your father has done great things in this settlement. It has been hard with my people leaving. Only a few of us remain."

This was about Night Hawk, Marie realized as she poured two cups of tea.

"I know that Night Hawk is training a horse for you." Spring Rain accepted the cup and cradled it in her hands.

"Yes. She's a beautiful mare." Marie set the plate of cookies on the desk between them.

"Night Hawk is an attractive man," Spring Rain said quietly. "He has magic with horses. His father was a great horseman."

Marie heard what Spring Rain was afraid to say. All of it. How Father had made things better for her people and the settlers, bringing teachers and trying to make a community where everyone belonged—whether they spoke German, Swedish, English or Sauk.

"I won't hurt him, I promise." Marie spoke the words sincerely, meaning them with her entire heart. "I'm only buying a horse from him."

"But there is more." Spring Rain set down her cup, the cookies forgotten. "He has known many heartaches and losses. He is alone and that is not good for a man capable of great tenderness. You may not see what I do, but you can hurt him. I came to ask that you think on what I've said."

Genuine concern filled the woman's eyes. She nodded once and left with the whisper of deerskin and the pad of moccasins.

Marie stood and pulled the edge of the curtain back. Four boys and a girl stood quietly in the shade of a sugar maple just outside the schoolyard. Spring Rain hurried to them, head down as if she still struggled with her emotion. The little girl with twin black braids looked up at the schoolhouse and waved.

Marie waved back, her heart heavy. She hadn't realized all that was at stake in this settlement where so many different people had come to make a better life.

This surely was a place where a woman like her could fall in love with a man like Night Hawk. Without consequences. Without prejudices. Without causing harm.

Still, the memory of Spring Rain's concern remained in Marie's thoughts the rest of the morning.

"That's right, Kammeo," Night Hawk praised as he tightened the cinch. "Marie, hold her tighter."

"She's starting to shy."

"Just speak calmly to her." Night Hawk remained at Kammeo's side, close enough to reach the leather reins in case Marie had any trouble.

She uttered soft, soothing words that reassured the mare, who wasn't sure about the leather thing resting on her back.

"Good Kammeo, good girl." Marie circled past him, tossing him a victorious smile. Her skirts swirled around her ankles, gracefully hugging her soft hips and lean thighs.

Fire ignited into a sharp physical want. The blood thickened in his veins.

What was wrong with him? He had better control than that. He fought it, but the drum of desire within him remained.

"I brought tarts today," Marie informed him as they finished currying Kammeo after her training session. "I picked the apples this morning."

"Mrs. Olstad let you in her kitchen?"

"Not yet. She baked for me and complained the

whole time." Marie ran her fingers across the mare's neck. Soft, supple fingers that stroked and caressed.

What would it be like to know her touch? To feel the satin heat of her skin to his? A groan rose in his throat and he turned away, hauling the saddle to the stable to hide his response. Every step away from her brought him only distance but no relief.

She wasn't meant to be his, but still his body yearned to know her touch on his skin.

This is crazy, he told himself. No good could come of these feelings. He wasn't the sort of man she was looking for. He knew without asking. Allowing these feelings of love and attraction to flourish would cause him grief and nothing more.

He'd be logical, not emotional. Sensible, and force out his physical attraction to her. That's what he'd do.

When he returned from the barn and saw Marie laying out her red checked blanket in his shaded front yard, all reason fled. Desire for her flared like a wind-swept firestorm, incinerating every good intention.

He wanted her. The way a man wanted a woman. Fierce and sweet, fiery and tender and all-consuming. He could no longer lie to himself. Denying his lust for her wouldn't extinguish it.

"Meka!" Marie's carefree scolding was accompanied by a chuckle. "Out of my basket, right now. You'll wait for your treat like everyone else."

The big black dog, who was more of a loner than Night Hawk, wagged his tail and dove into the basket. Unrepentant, grinning broadly, Meka chewed and swallowed.

"You're proud of yourself, are you?" Marie rubbed

the dog's head as she snatched the basket from the front step.

She knew the moment Night Hawk came into view. She could feel his presence. He was watching her, smiling, cradling something from his garden in the crook of his left arm.

"You have watermelon!"

"I have to contribute something to our picnic. I can't let you bring all the sweets." Night Hawk lowered the melon to the blanket and cut it.

His nearness sparkled like sunlight. It felt as if they were connected like dawn and twilight, earth and sky.

"For you." He held a bright piece of juicy melon and she ate from his fingers.

Marie lingered at the forest's edge. If only she could stretch this moment and the next, then maybe their time together wouldn't end.

As if Night Hawk felt it too, he halted one step from the main road to the fort. "We'll have you in the saddle tomorrow."

"You mean, I can ride her?"

"She's ready." Night Hawk handed Marie the empty basket he carried.

Excitement trilled through her, both at the thought of riding her mare and the man who towered next to her, dark like the shadows, proud like the ancient forest. Meka tore off into the underbrush chasing a gray jay, leaving them alone.

Marie watched Night Hawk's gaze focus on her mouth. In the space between one heartbeat and the next she felt her entire body blaze. *He's going to kiss me.* The knowledge pummeled through her. *Yes, kiss me.*

His eyes darkened as if he was tempted, and then he took an abrupt step backward. Disappointment didn't douse the fire sparkling in her veins.

"Tomorrow," he said.

The fire within her only burned hotter. Tomorrow— it was a promise and a gift.

She pushed through the low boughs that guarded the private trail from the main road. Long shadows met her as she hurried toward the fort's busy gate. When she looked over her shoulder, she saw only shadows but felt the heat of his gaze.

Night Hawk feels this, too. She wouldn't wonder and wish any longer. There was no mistaking that he'd wanted to kiss her. She was inexperienced but woman enough to know Night Hawk liked her.

The ground felt like clouds against her feet as she rushed past the dark mercantile and noticed that it was closed for the day. Was it that late already? She lifted her skirts and ran.

There were only two soldiers standing guard at the gates. The fort grounds were empty as she dashed through them. Her spirits fell at the sight of her father rising out of his chair on the porch. He frowned at her as if she were a soldier dodging orders.

"I know I'm late, Papa," Marie began the instant she was close enough. "I lost track of the time. I hope you didn't wait supper on me."

"Of course we did." Henry rose slowly. "Major Gerard came to dine with us. He's waiting inside."

"Oh, Papa. Not Major—" Marie caught herself in

time as a movement blurred in the shaded doorway. "Good evening, Major. My father tells me I've kept you both waiting."

"No need to apologize." Ned Gerard smoothed a long shock of blond hair across his forehead with a hint of nervousness. "A gentleman never minds waiting for a beautiful lady. Let me take that basket for you. Were you picking berries?"

Marie kept hold of the wicker handle. "No, I was watching Night Hawk train my new mare. She's almost ready for me to start riding."

"What mare?" Henry's voice lowered to a chill. "I distinctly told you that if you wanted a horse, I would provide you with one."

"I told you I bought a horse." Marie skipped up the steps and wished just this once he would greet her with warmth and not reproach.

Ned opened the door for her.

"Major," Henry growled. "Would you be so kind as to inform Mrs. Olstad she may begin serving the meal? I need a moment alone with my daughter."

"Certainly, sir." The major caught Marie's gaze with a hopeful look, one that told her he was glad to be dining with them tonight. With her.

Henry snuffed out his cigar on the banister rail while he waited for the door to close. He didn't look at her, but she could feel his fury. "I did not give you permission to procure a horse on your own—"

"I don't need your permission, Papa—"

"But spending an afternoon alone with a man without a chaperon. I don't know what's become of you, Marie." Henry's disappointment showed in every deep line on his proud face. "I expressly told you Sergeant James will escort you—"

"I can take care of myself."

"I don't want my only daughter wandering the dangerous wilderness alone without an escort. I want you to marry well and you can't do that if your reputation is in tatters."

"Because I want to ride a horse? There's nothing wrong—"

"Because you spend time alone with a man. How many afternoons have you gone to him, Marie?"

"But you said Night Hawk—"

"Think of what it looks like, what a false rumor could do to your reputation." His commanding manner softened and he looked almost caring. "I could not bear it if you were wrongfully shamed, Marie."

If he'd been commanding, she would have argued with him. But seeing the rare and precious concern in his eyes—a father's concern—she felt the fight ebb out of her.

"I'm doing nothing wrong, Papa." She laid her hand over his. "Not one thing."

"You are a good girl, I know that. But other people—"

"Are other people." Marie couldn't withdraw her hand and end this rare moment of contact.

Maybe she was too soft, but she loved her father. She wanted his love in return. "Fine, I'll tolerate this meddling you're doing tonight—and only for tonight. But I'm never going to fall in love with Major Gerard."

"How can you know a thing like that? He's the right sort of man."

"It's something a woman knows deep in her heart. Now stop trying to matchmake and come inside. I don't want to keep supper waiting another moment. Mrs. Olstad is angry enough with me already."

To Marie's surprise, Henry *almost* smiled.

Chapter Six

The stars blazed in a velvet black sky so bright they hurt Night Hawk's eyes. But on a night like this, serene and unsettled, the brilliant sky comforted him. It was the same firmament his ancestors had looked to since people had come to this place of wooded hills and sweet meadows. Tonight the bear burned brightly, and the warrior stood close guard to the horizon.

Remembering the formations in the stars brought pain and gladness to Night Hawk's heart. His father had taught him about the heavens when he was a boy. About the turning wheel of stars and moon that guided a warrior through the forest, told a hunter when the geese would migrate, when the bear would hibernate and when trout would brim the river.

At a time like this when Night Hawk was troubled, he could sit on the rise that overlooked the woods and lake below, where the moon blazed a path of light across the dark waters. Memories ran like a river's current, fast and breathless and too difficult to hold on to.

Meka nudged Night Hawk's hand for a pat, and he stroked the dog, burying his fingers in short thick fur.

I wanted to kiss her. Night Hawk groaned with the memory of Marie's mouth as soft looking as a wild rose petal. Blood thickened in his veins. A need for her whipped through him until he shook with it.

He launched to his feet, pacing through the meadow where nighthawks hunted and owls glided by on soundless wings. Frustration pounded him like wind-driven hail.

Meka's bark echoed across the low-rising meadow, announcing a late-night visitor. Night Hawk turned toward the road, already recognizing the faint crisp clip of a powerful gelding's gait. The colonel.

Night Hawk felt his stomach clench, and he knew this was no business call. Henry Lafayette hadn't come to discuss business or request help for an injured horse. Not at this time of night. Not judging by the brisk, almost angry snap of his horse's gait.

Preparing for the worst, Night Hawk ordered Meka to heel and cut through the meadow. A last quarter moon cast scant light across the wildflowers waving in the breezes. A badger snarled at the edge of the clearing, where a small creek whispered a melody, and Night Hawk knew just how the badger felt.

"Henry," Night Hawk greeted the dark rider. "This must mean your daughter has told you about her mare."

The colonel drew his gelding up short, the man's tension causing the animal distress, as he dismounted heavily from his saddle. "Marie is young and impulsive, but I expected better of you, Night Hawk. You've always been a man I can trust whenever I've turned to you for help.''

"I had no intentions to harm your daughter, Henry, and you know it.'' Night Hawk understood a father's protective nature, yet he would not be intimidated by anyone. He was a warrior, a brave who'd fought his first bear at thirteen, who'd lost his father and many of his clan a year later. He'd been a man long before the colonel had set foot on this land they called Wisconsin.

"Your daughter is no child, Henry, and I am no weak-willed man. You know well I'd never harm your daughter or any woman, white or Indian.''

Henry drew himself up taller, his rounding middle tensing, his shoulders straightening as if ready to fight for his daughter's honor. Seconds ticked by, marked by his short, angry puffs of breath.

Then his shoulders relaxed. "I know the man you are, Night Hawk. I didn't come here to accuse you.''

"You came to vent your anger on me. A father's anger at a daughter no longer his child.''

"She's a woman all right and she needs a firm hand.'' Henry sighed, a long pent-up frustrated sound that made him less the imposing colonel and more a concerned father. "I shall have to lock her up in her room until the school term starts.''

"She'd merely climb out the window. She's a young bird spreading her wings.''

"And she'll ruin her reputation if she's not careful,'' Henry muttered, showing the true issue behind his anger and frustration. He marched up the dark road, dragging his gelding by the reins.

"Her reputation is in no danger with me. You believe that?"

"Yes."

To his credit, there was no hesitation in Henry's answer, and it stung Night Hawk's conscience. Hadn't he been dreaming of Marie's mouth the same instant her father had been riding down this road?

Shame filled him, as thick and cold as a winter's fog. Ashamed because he'd delighted in the warmth of Marie's presence, fed her watermelon from his fingers and wanted to see her again. Hell, he didn't want to *see* her. He wanted to taste her sweet lips and hold her the way a man embraced a woman.

Night Hawk stepped inside his back door and grabbed a bottle of scotch from the pantry shelf, kept for the colonel's visits. He faced a truth he'd known all along.

These forbidden afternoons with Marie had to end. *Now*. Her laughter would no longer grace the wind. Her brightness would no longer complement the sun in his meadows. Her woman's beauty would no longer make hunger sing in his veins.

He snatched two clean cups from the kitchen shelf and headed into the cool night, resolute. He was wise enough to let go of what he could never have.

"The problem I have is this." Henry thanked him for the scotch. "I've got a daughter who needs to settle down. She's twenty-one. Another few years and she'll be a spinster too old to marry. That's why I brought her out to teach at the settlement's school. She doesn't know it, but I intend to see her married before her term here is over."

Night Hawk set the bottle aside and leaned against the corral fence. He could see what was coming and he didn't think he could stand listening to the colonel discuss possible husbands for Marie—all white, all successful and with much to offer her. "You need to discuss this with your daughter, Henry."

"I just want to make you see what I'm up against. Why she can't be wandering about the countryside coming to your ranch to visit a damn horse. And why she can't have whatever horse you sold her in the first place."

"You want to protect her."

"I want her married. I want to stop waking up at night worrying about what is going to happen to her. Is she safe living on her own? Is she happy? Am I ever going to have a grandson?" Henry took a deep swig and emptied his cup.

Night Hawk handed him the bottle.

Henry poured a liberal dose. "I've busted my hind-quarters trying to work my way up in this world to provide a better life for my daughter. And now she thinks she's grown-up, when she's nothing more than a child. She needs an advantageous marriage."

To a high-ranking officer. Night Hawk swallowed his disappointment and stared hard into the scotch, smooth and dark in his cup. His stomach clenched, and he set the cup aside. "One of your majors?"

"Exactly. That's the way a man thinks. See the logical advantage and work toward the goal. But a woman—" Henry drained his cup. "They buy a horse they don't know how to ride."

Night Hawk stalked away. He wasn't going to discuss Marie with her father. Henry wanted a confidant, but Night Hawk had his pride. Heart aching, he strode through the familiar shadows of his backyard, past the garden to where the mare leaned over the top rail, nickering quietly.

"Good girl, Kammeo." He rubbed her cheek. The comforting feel of a horse's velvet warm and steeled power comforted the breaking of his heart.

No, he wasn't in love with Marie. Not yet.

"The mare is nearly saddle trained, Henry." Night Hawk battled to keep his business tone. "I just need a few more hours with her. She can be in your stables by the morning."

"No deal." Henry stood, hands empty, his anger spent. "I don't want to break an agreement, but Marie won't be needing a horse. She'll have Ned Gerard's ring on her finger by the time the leaves fall, mark my words. If you need the money, I can buy the mare for the fort—"

"No." Night Hawk let his answer boom through the darkness. Watched its effect on Henry.

"Ah, yes, well, I know where you stand. My captain of horses is one of the best I've seen." Henry scooped his reins from the post, sounding regretful, sounding contrite. "I know you disagree with his methods."

Disagree? They went against everything Night Hawk stood for, but he remained silent. His words wouldn't change how horses were treated at Henry's fort and would only bring discord between them.

"Good night." Henry mounted with a creak of leather and the impatient sidestep of his gelding. "If Marie comes this way again, I want your word that you will escort her home immediately. And notify me.''

''Keep watch on your own daughter, Henry.'' Night Hawk could make no promises.

Nor could he watch the man leave. Night Hawk climbed through the rails and laid his hand on Kammeo's back. He felt the animal's life force, strong and vibrant and as brilliant as Marie's.

The two belonged together.

He knew what he had to do, knew it meant he would never look up and see Marie appearing from the shaded wood or feel her laughter ripple across his skin. He eased onto the mare's back and waited while she twitched and sidestepped, first afraid, then uncertain, then accepting.

Night Hawk steeled his heart and told himself it didn't matter. He was like the hawk that hunted alone against the stars. And always would be.

''A note came for you.'' Mrs. Olstad tapped on Marie's open bedroom door. ''I hope you don't think I'm your personal messenger. See it doesn't happen again.''

''Yes, thank you.'' Marie took the folded parchment from the frowning housekeeper and unfolded the paper.

A bold, proud scrawl marked the page. ''Look in the stable,'' was all it said. She didn't recognize the handwriting.

Night Hawk? Was he at the fort to check on another horse? Was he hoping to see her?

Joy swept through her like morning sunshine. He'd

kept his parting promise to her—they would meet to-day. She tingled from head to toe as she selected her favorite bonnet from the top shelf of her wardrobe and then hurried a comb through her unruly locks.

He was going to teach her to ride! Oh, the thought of his hand on her elbow as he helped her into the saddle. The anticipation of his mellow voice as rich as the night. She hoped this time he would be brave enough to cover her lips with his....

She flew down the stairs and out the kitchen, Mrs. Olstad's rebuke to not run in the house followed her out the door. Slow down, she reminded herself. She didn't want to show up at the stable out of breath and covered with dust. But it wasn't easy as she walked down the path that wove to the back of the fort.

The stable doors were open. The interior felt oven-hot as she made her way inside. The stalls were empty. The scrape of a pitchfork against wood meant a stable boy was cleaning.

Where was Night Hawk?

She ambled down the main aisle, and her step echoed in the rafters overhead. She expected to see him kneeling down in a box stall, tending to a horse. Maybe they would walk back to his ranch together and they would spend all afternoon in the sunny meadow riding Kammeo. Marie could already feel the wind in her hair and the happiness from having Night Hawk at her side.

She started down the back aisle; the scrape of the pitchfork grew sharper as she approached.

"Are you Miss Lafayette?" A boy, who didn't look more than a day over fifteen, tramped into the aisle to her right, holding a dirty pitchfork by the worn wood handle. "Night Hawk come by with something for you. Told me to make sure you saw it."

"He's gone already?" Disappointment doused her joy like ice water. "What did he leave me? A saddle?" It was the only thing she could think he might bring to the stable.

"Well, partly." The lad pointed with the pitchfork's tongs. "Last stall to your right. He says it's yours."

A horrible feeling washed through her. If Night Hawk had sent a note but hadn't stayed to see her—

A familiar neigh split through her fears. Marie missed a step when a horse's red muzzle reached into the aisle. The horse nickered in welcome, shaking her head up and down with excitement.

"Kammeo." Marie curled her fingers through the mare's mane. Where was Night Hawk? Why had he left?

Footsteps shuffled in the row behind her, not Night Hawk's gait but the stable boy's. "He said she was ready to ride. Left a saddle and bridle in the tack room. I sent word to my captain, but I ain't heard if I'm supposed to saddle her for you."

"She's ready to ride? That can't be right."

"That's what he said."

Had Night Hawk finished Kammeo's training without her? No, he wouldn't have done that. He wanted her and Kammeo to learn together. That was the reason he agreed to sell the mare to her in the first place.

What was she to do now? She hadn't paid him. She didn't have any idea what a horse like this cost.

"He said there was somethin' else." The stable boy

stared hard at the floor. "I remember. He said the mare is a gift."

A gift? Marie pushed away from the mare, shaking as if she'd been caught in a blizzard's arctic wind, and rushed down the aisle.

Blood pounded in her ears as she ran. Why hadn't Night Hawk kept his promise to her? He'd nearly kissed her yesterday evening. His affection for her had burned like an unmistakable blaze—in his eyes, in his voice, in his touch.

Why had he done this without an explanation?

Papa. He must have spoken with Night Hawk. Anger drove her out of the stable and down the path toward the administration buildings. She jerked open the door just as her father was walking out.

"Marie Janelle!" Henry glared down at her. "Your hair is a mess, and your dress! What has gotten into you, young lady?"

For once she ignored his criticism. Too much anger raged in her heart—a woman's heart and not the girl he wanted her to be. "I want to know what you said to Night Hawk."

"What matters is you, Marie." Henry lowered his voice and closed the distance between them. "Look at your dress. It's covered with dust."

"You *did* speak to him. What did you tell him?"

"A young lady your age wears her hair up and not tangling down her back like an urchin."

"Papa, will you listen to me? You told Night Hawk about your dreams of a West Point graduate for a son-in-law, didn't you?"

Henry's face flushed. "I talked to him about the

horse, Marie. I don't want you getting hurt. You're to stay in the settlement where you're safe. School starts next week, and I want you to meet some more of the settlers' children this afternoon.''

This afternoon. When she was going to meet Night Hawk. White-hot anger lanced her like a newly sharpened blade. ''I'm not one of your soldiers, Papa. Maybe if I say it enough, you'll eventually notice it. I'll do what I want.''

''I'm restricting you to the grounds.''

''You can't do that—''

''I *am* the colonel of this fort and I already have.'' Anger flushed Henry's face.

He was right, and she hated it. She whirled away and kept going even when he called her name.

Tomorrow, she would make her way through the woods, along the lake and into the meadow to see Night Hawk. She had to make certain he understood that the colonel didn't control her.

She knew what was important in life, and she wasn't afraid. Not one bit.

Don't be nervous, Marie told herself as she hurried along the path by the lake. He was probably expecting her. He knew she'd come to thank him. He needed to know that whatever her father told him wasn't true.

Please, let him understand, she wished fervently as great blue herons startled into flight along the water's edge.

A shadow blurred across the trail ahead of her and barked a welcome. Meka! Her troubles lifted. Night Hawk was close, she was certain of it.

"Yes, I remembered a treat for you." Laughing as the dog nearly knocked over her basket, she reached inside and offered a sugar cookie.

It was going to be all right, she told herself as Meka escorted her along the path. Night Hawk was waiting for her, and he would understand. Surely he knew Papa well enough to see how the older man would get carried away with his matchmaking plans. Their precious time together would not need to end.

Soon she climbed the crest of the hill and Night Hawk's land spread out before her with breathtaking wonder. She saw no sign of him. He wasn't where the horses grazed in succulent green meadows. The house and the stables looked empty.

Maybe he had gone to town. Maybe he had taken the road and she, the path, and they had missed each other. But even as those thoughts formed, she knew they were excuses, excuses meant to protect her foolish heart.

Night Hawk would have taken Meka with him. When he went to town, the dog remained loyally outside the fort, waiting for his master's return.

There was only one reason Night Hawk would have left Meka behind.

To escort her safely back to the settlement.

No, there had to be another reason. Instinctively Marie fought to find another explanation—any explanation. He'd gone to help a neighbor, gone to tend a horse at the fort, run an errand, needed to check on his niece. Anything that would make his absence only an absence.

But it was a fact. Whatever Papa had told him had

had a definite impact. How could she repair the damage?

She set her basket on the ground and curled up on the bottom porch step. Meka nosed the lid, trying to get into the cookies, and she scolded him. The big dog lay down at her feet, a true companion, and they waited together.

The white thunderheads speeding in from the south crowded out the hazy sun. Their underbellies turned dark with the promise of rain. The wind turned gusty, almost cold, driving the scent of ripe apples and plums from the nearby orchard.

Marie jumped when the first distant lightning bolt speared through the threatening clouds. The horses in the fields took off at a gallop, racing the perimeter of the pasture.

A curtain of rain brushed the tops of the distant hills. A storm was coming. Suddenly the rain fell in hard cold bullets that bent the grasses double and rebounded on the earth. Marie climbed the steps and sought shelter beneath the porch roof. Lightning flashed in eye-searing streaks, thunder boomed and wind drove the rain hard.

Still Night Hawk didn't return.

Marie waited until the lightning had passed and the wind slowed before she let Meka escort her home.

He'd been racing the storm when Shadow broke through the trees. Rain fell in steady sheets, but even through the downpour, his gaze found her. Head down, bonnet drooping from the rain, her skirts soaked and clinging to her slim hips and thighs, Marie made her way through the wet meadow toward the lake and the trees. Toward the path that would see her safely home. Meka lifted his nose and scented the wind but remained by the woman's side.

Night Hawk eased Shadow into the trees and waited, protected from the rain by the sheltering maple but not from the pain in his heart.

She moved like morning when the sun was new, even in the rain, even when he'd disappointed her. She turned one last time to gaze at the house, to scan the meadows and hillsides.

He nudged Shadow farther back in the thicket.

She lingered, as if she sensed his presence. Even as the rain drenched her and the wind lashed at her skirts. Even as she shivered from so far away.

He felt the same cold move through him that appeared to quake through her. Like icy claws that scraped through flesh and bone all the way to his soul.

It's for the best, he told himself. But his heart didn't believe it.

He was no stranger to the difficulties of life. And no stranger to losing what could be.

In the space of a heartbeat, Marie hurried down the trail and vanished from his sight, just like that, like a dream fading at dawn's light.

Night Hawk didn't bother to lie to himself. To pretend she hadn't enchanted him. That she was like any woman and easily forgotten. He knew what she was—his guiding light.

Without her, his world would be dim and cold from this day forth.

Chapter Seven

The cozy, quiet sounds of children working out math problems on their slates filled the one-room schoolhouse. Marie paged through her primer, debating how big an assignment to give her next class.

The crisp autumn days were pleasant, and she knew many of the children still had chores to complete this time of year. The harvesting of the major crops was over, but hay still had to be cut and hauled, gardens harvested and fruits and vegetables stored and preserved.

A small lesson would be good. She closed the book and called the second math class to the front. Ginny Ingalls, Morning Star and Rose Holmberg clambered to the front, nervous over their lesson to come.

Ginny began solving the first subtraction problem given her. While Marie listened patiently, a movement through the window caught part of her attention.

Night Hawk rode his stallion down the street, back straight, shoulders set, hard jaw unflinching. The wind whipped his long black hair, and he and the horse moved as one. He was poetry and power, wind and fire, and Marie's entire being ached with longing and loss.

"Is that right, Miss Lafayette?" Ginny asked, bringing her attention back to the three small children standing before her.

"Perfect, Ginny. Morning Star, let's see if you can solve this one." Marie gave a second math problem, and Night Hawk's niece quickly answered.

If only there was a chance to get away, to steal the time to see Night Hawk.

A part of her feared he would remain in the shadows again.

He caressed his fingers down the line of her jaw, feeling a softness he'd never before known. A wisp of her dark, wavy hair brushed the side of his hand. Lust rolled through him as powerful as the leading edge of a tornado.

Like a tornado, he couldn't fight it. Couldn't outrun it. Couldn't defeat it. He ran the pad of his thumb over Marie's lower lip, petal pink and soft before he covered her mouth with his.

The brush of lips, the play of tongues, the mingling of breaths wasn't enough. He was rock hard and she was moaning, low in her throat like a plea.

She was softer than silk beneath her dress, where lace-edged drawers pulled away at the tug of his hands. He laid her down and they met like earth and sky, lightning and thunder, his hard shaft and her yielding flesh...

Night Hawk woke with a roar. Lust beat in his veins as he threw off the sheet.

A dream. It was only a dream and yet he could taste

the sweetness of Marie's kiss and feel her heat on his body. He was iron hard and aching for her, and he cursed the cruel fate that made her his dream and not his reality.

The night held the crisp hint of the autumn to come. The last of the apples and plums ripe on the tree scented the cool air as he stumbled out into the darkness. His erection strained against his drawers as he leaned his forearms on the coarse fence rail and breathed deep.

The solitary hawk circled high ahead, crying once, the sound of his loneliness shooting across the face of the full moon.

Why tonight? Why after all he'd given up and all his self-control did his mind betray him now?

He'd seen her today in town through the window of the little schoolhouse. That's what made him dream of her tonight.

He was a wise man, and so he did not think of her again. But he feared his body would remember this dream and his mind would never forget.

Marie bolted upright in bed. Her breath came in great gasps as if she'd been running for miles. She pushed off the muslin sheet and felt her way to the window, where the light of the moon tumbled between the billowing curtains.

The cool air smelled of the night, of mystery and promises made. What had she been dreaming of tonight? She could feel the image just beyond her reach, like a memory on the brink of being recalled.

A shadow flashed across the bright disk of the

moon, wings spread with majesty, and the bird's loneliness haunted her.

Would she be always alone? All her friends had married, finding men to provide them with security, homes and children. But there was more to life.

After she'd returned from his ranch the final time, her father had been outraged. A scout had spotted a twister north of Night Hawk's land. What if she'd been caught in it? Henry had roared.

Then school started, and she spent nearly every waking hour working. After classes ended, there was the schoolhouse to clean and lessons to plan. She had twenty children, nearly all of them at different levels and with different needs. Many could barely speak English.

She hadn't stopped thinking of Night Hawk. She wanted the chance to make things right between them.

Troubled, she watched the lone hawk glide across the golden moon.

The Saturday afternoon was hot, and she'd promised Henry she wouldn't go far. But before she knew it, she was at the lakeside where fragrant ruby berries were ripe and ready to pick. The trail that would take her to Night Hawk was not far away.

Maybe she'd finish filling her basket and then—

Something rattled the bush at her feet. She jumped back and the basket tumbled from her fingers.

It wasn't a snake or anything dangerous. The limb kept shaking. Curious, Marie knelt down and pushed the branch aside. She saw a huddled lump burrowed against an exposed root, shaking with fear. The breeze ruffled against it, lifting soft down, and her heart stopped. It was an injured hawk.

Blood stained the ground, and Marie tried to ease into the narrow space. The bird lifted one wing and tried to flee, but it cried out in pain and collapsed. Breathing heavily as if certain it was about to be killed, it ducked its head, no longer looking at her, trembling so hard every feather visibly quaked.

Poor helpless thing. Maybe she could get it into her basket. She reached out, and it struck with its beak. Pain tore through her fingertip.

It was terrified enough of her to fight. She couldn't save it, but she couldn't leave it here. What should she do?

The hawk trembled harder, daring to gaze at her over his bloody wing.

Night Hawk. She was on her feet and running along the lake until she found the familiar trail.

Meka's bark welcomed her the moment she crested the last rise that gave way to meadow. Seeing the big dog loping toward her and the man turning from stacking hay made her skid to a stop.

Was she welcome here after what Henry had told him?

Fallen leaves tumbled through the air between her and Night Hawk, and the sun held a hint of a chill. She squared her shoulders and faced the man who approached, pitchfork in one hand, his shirt in the other. His bare chest fascinated her. How strong he looked with every muscle delineated beneath bronzed skin.

"I didn't think I would see you again." He drove the tines of the fork deep into the ground with a powerful ripple of his biceps, then pulled on the shirt he carried. "You shouldn't be here."

How many weeks had she wanted to explain? Now there was no time. "I found an injured hawk in the meadow by the lake. I thought you might know how to help."

Night Hawk stared at her, his face a mask of stone, his gaze nothing but shadows. "Show me."

She led the way down the trail and along the lakeside to where the bushes edged the sparkling water. With every step she took, she could feel him only a pace behind her, feel his stoic reserve and his powerful masculinity.

"He's here." Marie knelt and pushed aside the low bough so that Night Hawk could see the hawk huddled beneath.

"Looks like he's taken a bullet." Night Hawk knelt close. The iron-hard length of his shoulder and arm, thigh and knee pressed against hers.

Heat engulfed her. A thrilling spiral of flame and desire consumed her. The feelings inside her raged hotter and brighter.

Night Hawk calmly reached for the bird. Didn't he feel the conflagration that blazed between them?

"You mean someone shot him?"

"Maybe on purpose. Maybe not." He crooned to the hawk in his native tongue, using low, soft sounds.

The creature tried to escape, but the moment Night Hawk held the bird in his hands, wings tucked down and legs held tight, there was no more struggle.

"More likely a duck hunter missed his target. Unfortunately for this fellow." Night Hawk cradled the bird to his chest and stood. "I'll take care of him. Meka will take you home."

"But I—"

"You belong at the fort and not alone with me." There was nothing polite in his steely stance. Nothing civil about the wind lashing his long black locks and molding his cotton shirt to his wide chest.

He looked like a warrior. She longed to deeply know the man. "Is that what my father told you?"

"He said many things." Was that sorrow in his voice? "I agree with him."

"Maybe I don't."

Night Hawk cocked one brow in surprise.

"He doesn't dictate my life, although he won't stop trying. Did he mention wanting a West Point graduate for a son-in-law?"

A hint of a grin touched Night Hawk's mouth. "He did mention how important it was for you to make an advantageous marriage."

"He wouldn't know one if it hit him square in the forehead." Marie watched Night Hawk's stony visage crack into a hesitant smile. "How will you take care of the bird?"

"Come. I'll show you."

Those words simply spoken made her spirits soar higher than any bird. Or ever would.

His body hadn't forgotten the forbidden dreams that had tortured him night after night. And as he tended the hawk with Marie at his side, he fought his hunger for her.

A desire tore at his steely control every time Marie's sleeve brushed him, every time a lock of her hair caressed her face. Every time his gaze clasped on the shape of her mouth or the soft, round fullness of her breasts.

"You know a lot about birds." Marie's fingertips brushed his as she handed him a strip of muslin soaked in herbs. "I've never known anyone who could handle a wild hawk before."

"All it takes is knowledge." Night Hawk swiped the bloody wounds along the bird's left wing. "I found a baby hawk when I was a young boy."

"You had a pet hawk?"

"I raised her. I taught her how to hunt. And released her when it was time."

"Did she ever return to you?"

"No, but I did see her now and then when I was on a hunt with my father." Memories ached with both pain and warmth. "She would call to me from the sky and when I woke in the morning, she had left some of her night's hunt on the doorstep to my lodge."

"So she did return."

"Not as my pet. That was a long time ago." He didn't want Marie to ask any more questions, for he knew where they would lead. Away from that treasured time of his boyhood to the turbulent years of the war when his people had won their battle for this land, but the cost had been high. Too high.

He could not think about those losses. Of the brothers who did not return, and his father, who paid with his blood for this land. This land Night Hawk would never leave.

"I've done the best I can." He pressed the last of the soaked cloths to the wound and bandaged them.

"There's nothing more to do but wait. We'll see if he lives."

"I'm glad I came for you." Her fingers lighted on his wrist.

Her touch felt *right*. His heart thundered with the knowledge. His blood beat with it. He gritted his teeth to keep the moan of want trapped inside his chest. She was young and innocent. She had no idea how he felt, how a man felt when he thirsted for the woman who would make him whole.

"It's late." Dusk was falling and so it was the excuse he used. "Your father will be displeased."

"My father doesn't run my life."

"I cannot afford to anger him." Night Hawk untied the makeshift tethers. "You can't risk your reputation. What about an advantageous marriage?"

"Night Hawk." Her hand found his. This time her touch was not a brief caress but a lingering claim. "I don't want what my father wants for me. The only man I will ever marry is the one I love with all my heart."

She didn't want him. He was sure of it. She would never want him.

And yet her slim fingers slid between his and clasped tightly. Locking them together. Making him wish...

No. It was not to be. She was young and impressionable, that was all. He didn't have the strength for more heartbreak.

He pulled away from her touch, denying her claim and telling himself it was the right thing to do. "It's too dark to send you home with only Meka. Wait here while I call my horse."

"You don't want me to stay?"

He fisted his hands, helpless against the hurt glinting in her eyes. Hurt that he'd put there by pulling away. By doing the right thing.

"It isn't what I want. It can never be what I want." The competing forces of desire and integrity, of loss and yearning threatened to tear him apart. He wanted to hold her. He wanted to love her. He wanted to slake this carnal need for her once and for all.

She was too innocent to know about the desire tormenting him.

He escaped to the blue-gray shadows of twilight and let the cool wind drum against him. Even though he fought to control it, the fire within him raged.

Her skirts whispered behind him. "Will the hawk need care through the night? I could stay."

"No. I will tend him."

"But I wouldn't mind." She stepped into the shadows at his side. "I found him. I feel responsible for him."

"He is warm and fed because of you. You've done more than most. You're bleeding."

She stared down at her fingers. He had to have noticed her wound earlier, when she held the basin while he cleaned the bird. It was too dark to see her wound now. "It's better."

"I can bandage it."

He led her to the house on the small rise, dark and lonely. She waited as he lit a candle and then another. Flame tossed gentle light across handwoven rugs and a polished wood floor, honeyed walls and carved furniture.

Home. Every piece of her being cried out with the certainty. This man. This land. This house.

"Come." He held out a chair in the kitchen and she settled into it.

Tingling with the excitement of being near him, she watched while he lit a lantern and gathered a basin and supplies from a drawer. Everywhere she looked she saw beauty—grape leaves carved into the chair backs, the scrollwork on the cabinetry, carvings and Indian blankets hung on the walls.

He cradled her hand with his, lifting it toward the light. "This may sting."

"I'm brave." That made him smile. His touch was firm but gentle. Her heart raced as he swabbed a scrap of clean cloth across her injured knuckle.

This is how it would feel to be loved by him. To know his touch on her skin.

He rolled a strip of muslin around her finger, leaning close to tug it tight. The pulse beat in the hollow of his throat fast and frantic. His chest rose quick and light.

Just like hers.

"Done. Now we can take you home." Gone was the mask of stone and the distance. Night Hawk smiled, his entire heart showing.

The greatest joy filled her, buoyant and sweet. When he pressed his lips to her palm, she knew.

This was the man she would love for the rest of her life.

It was wrong. He knew it. But that didn't stop him from holding out his hand and helping Marie onto Shadow's back. He meant to settle her across the stallion's withers, sidesaddle style, and cradle her in his arms.

But she had other ideas. She slid into place between his thighs, riding astride, and all reason fled. Her soft backside fit into the cradle of his thighs, and she was all heaven and tempting woman.

Her silken hair brushed the sensitive skin against his throat. Her warmth touched him from thigh to chin, and desire cannoned through his entire being.

Instantly hard, he fought to control his body's raging demands. Marie stiffened, and he knew she'd felt his desire for her.

Shame engulfed him. She was a maiden. To react to her like this showed her great disrespect. What on earth would he say to explain? That his steely will melted like ice in the sun when she was near?

"It's a lovely evening, isn't it?" she said, glancing over her shoulder at him. A mysterious smile touched her lips.

Night Hawk strangled on a groan and sent Shadow streaking across the darkening meadows. The horse's gait rocked Marie intimately against him, mimicking an even greater act. Need hammered through him as his hands curved around Marie's hips, settling at her slim waist.

She didn't protest; she pressed boldly against him.

They were like a tree and the wind, moving together, one caressing the other, in a rhythm as old as time. Every rolling step Shadow took brought them closer as dusk gave way to night. Stars glittered on the eastern edge of the world where darkness gathered and lit their way.

He didn't dare breathe for fear of shattering the moment. Of waking up to find this was only a dream. That he would awaken to find her fading like mist from his arms when he wanted to hold her forever.

Too soon, the fort loomed shadowy and ominous in the clearing ahead. The settlement was quiet, and they were alone as he guided Shadow down the lane toward the closed gates.

With regret, he slid from the stallion's back. His feet touched the earth, ending the dream.

Even in the darkness, he could see her face, the hint of a smile as she leaned into his hands. He caught her arms and cherished the feel of her one last time as he lifted her safely to the ground.

"I'd like to come in the morning and check on our hawk."

"I'll send Meka to meet you."

"You could meet me." She lifted her chin, breathless with her own brazenness.

His knuckles brushed her cheek. "I will."

She craved a deeper, bolder touch. Her entire being felt aflame, and she longed for the feel of his arms again. For the hard wonder of his chest against her back and the powerful thighs cradling hers. For the thrust of that part of him that now strained at his trousers.

She'd done that. It seemed impossible that this noble and exceptional man wanted her.

"Your father will be angry."

"Probably."

Night Hawk's gaze dropped to her lips. Even in the dark, she could see his pupils dilate.

She wanted his kiss more than anything. And no polite demure kiss, either. She wanted one intimate and tender, deep and passionate. The kind lovers shared.

As if he read her thoughts, Night Hawk bent closer. *Yes.* She tilted her chin to meet his kiss. Her lips tingled with anticipation and a bright joy gathered deep in her heart.

His mouth hovered above her own and lingered. All Marie could hear was the pulse of her heart and the moan in her throat when, instead, he leaned his forehead to hers.

"I'll stay until you're safely within the gates." His breath mingled with hers and the intimacy lashed through her.

Tomorrow, she vowed. She would kiss him tomorrow. The beautiful light of this love she felt for him blazed bright enough to blind her. She would not be ashamed of her feelings or of the honest passion that thrummed through her veins.

"Good night, Marie." He spoke and his words rumbled through her. He stepped away, and her skin burned with his heat.

She watched while he hopped onto his stallion's back. It took all her self-control to turn and knock at the closed gates. In the seconds it took for the soldier to call out, Night Hawk stood guard, a part of the night, mysterious and magnificent and—she hoped—her one true love.

Then the gate swung open. She returned to her world. Leaving Night Hawk to return to his.

Chapter Eight

Night Hawk watched as dawn came in gentle awakenings. Of light. Of life. Of color. The light frost on the grasses shimmered like diamonds as the new sun peered above the horizon with an eye-stinging brilliance.

He'd been up all night tending the hawk but his thoughts kept drifting to Marie. He was torn apart over how he'd treated her. He'd been weak last night. Weak and needy and playing with fire.

Nothing good could come from wanting to make love to the colonel's daughter. He could be honest with himself—he hadn't only wanted to kiss her last night. He'd wanted to lay her down in the shelter of the trees and love her as he'd done in his dreams.

Was he that weak? Lacked that much self-control? Angry with himself, angry at this life he'd chosen and his unbearable loneliness, he took off for the stables.

Fury fueled his harsh step as he threw open the door and returned to the main aisle. Horses nickered their greetings, and the cow in the end stall mooed a melancholy good morning.

New light filtered through the cracks between the logs and illuminated the makeshift nest along the back wall. The hawk lay motionless in a basin filled with soft hay. The creature remained balled up, head hidden beneath its healthy wing, stiff and cold.

Sadness battered Night Hawk as he rubbed one finger along the bird's wing. The hawk shivered once, barely alive.

Marie would be here soon. She wanted to check on the bird. And later, they would talk together. And he would have to fight to keep from kissing her again.

How was he going to resist her after last night? How was he going to restrain his desire for her when it was already out of control?

Was it too early to meet Night Hawk? Marie swept down the staircase, anticipation like a drug in her veins. The house echoed around her as she hurried through the dining room and into the parlor. Henry's footsteps tapped on the ceiling overhead.

Good. He wasn't down yet. She wasn't avoiding him, but she certainly wasn't up to explaining. He hadn't been home when she'd returned last night—he was probably at his office—but Marie had no doubt he'd been unhappy she'd gone off on her own to go berry picking.

Henry would simply have to get used to it.

Tying her cloak's sash, she faced the morning. The sun sparkled on the frosty ground, and the grass crunched beneath her boots.

The guards at the gates tipped their hats to her in a respectful hello. As soon as she stepped beyond the stout fort walls, she lifted her skirts and hurried across the frozen puddles in the road toward the awaiting forest.

Night Hawk stepped from the shadows just as he'd promised. He stood tall and regal like a knight of old. Her very own knight.

Her very own love.

"I can't believe he's alive." Marie bent close and the wisps that had escaped from her elegant knot brushed his jaw. "You saved him."

So much respect filled those words. Night Hawk felt shamed. His need for her raged, and there was no use denying it. Still, though he wanted her, he wouldn't give in to his feelings.

He cleared his throat and vowed to ignore the tantalizing brush of her dark locks against his sensitized skin. "I only tended his wound. He owes his life to the lady who found him."

"No, you knew how to tend him."

Night Hawk lifted the strip of cloth from the basin. Fat water droplets trailed down the muslin and dripped onto the hawk's beak. The creature tilted his head enough to catch the drops, too weak to do more than swallow.

"This is a good sign." He held the cloth patiently. *Concentrate on the bird and not on the woman,* he advised himself.

But she sidled closer, seemingly fascinated by his care of the bird. "Can I try it?"

Her shoulder brushed his arm.

He gritted his teeth. "Just move slowly."

Their fingers touched. Longing pummeled him. She took the muslin from him and reached across his chest to dunk the strip in the basin. Water splashed as she worked, but Night Hawk could hardly hear it through the roaring of the pulse in his ears.

The outside curve of her breast was like hot silk against his arm. Beneath those layers of wool and cotton, he knew her skin would be creamy silk. Her breasts would be firm and rosy tipped.

His throat constricted and he moved away.

"Look, he won't drink from me. You'd better do it."

A prudent man would walk away from this closeness. Night Hawk could think of a thousand reasons to head out the door and put as much distance as possible between them. And only one reason to stay.

Hating his own weakness, he took the cloth from her fingers. She remained at his side, smelling of meadow flowers and summer. The hawk tipped toward the water droplets rolling off the muslin strip.

"He's a blue hawk," he heard himself say as if from a great distance. "See the dark blue feathers on his wings?"

"He's nearly the color of the sky on his stomach."

"He's smaller than most of the hawks in these parts." He dowsed the strip, and the bird cried in protest. "I guess he's feeling well enough to complain."

Marie's hand splayed across his shirt, closing the scant distance between them. "You stayed up with him last night. I can see the exhaustion on your face."

"I wanted him to live."

"You are the most amazing man." She breathed the

words, as if she were looking at a night sky full of stars for the first time.

And he was deeply embarrassed by his ignoble thoughts. "You don't know me, Marie. The kind of man I am."

"I know what I see." She leaned closer. "I know what I feel."

Every instinct within him shouted for escape. If he wanted to save his heart and his dignity, he would leave now.

Her fingers curled into his cotton shirt. She rose on tiptoe and her mouth softened. Her lush pink lips parted.

He claimed her with a hard kiss. There was no holding back. No politeness. Only the raging raw-edged passion that drove him. She met him willingly, her tentative kiss changing from untried to ardent. Her lips were heated silk, her tongue damp satin.

Her firm breasts pressed against his chest, and he was rock hard against the soft curve of her stomach. Layers of cotton and wool separated them, but he could fix that. A few tugs at the buttons marching down her bodice and they could be skin to skin, man to woman, lover to lover.

A groan was torn from his throat. Agony filled him, greater than any pain he'd known before. She moved against him, an inexperienced maiden who didn't realize the consequences of this kiss. Or what he wanted from her.

He twisted away, breathing hard. "I shouldn't have done that. You deserve my respect, not this."

"You are the man I want." Her steps whispered

after him. Her hand splayed against his jaw, possessive and loving.

She kissed him this time, a tender brush of her lips to his. Her sweetness tormented him more than her fire. Every fiber of his being shouted for completion.

"You don't want me, Marie." He broke the kiss and, because he was powerless to move away, rubbed the pad of his thumb across her lush lips. "I'm wrong for you. Ask your father. He'll agree with me."

"I don't need to ask Papa anything. I'm old enough to know my heart." She laved the curve of his thumb with the tip of her tongue. "I want you. Only you."

"It can never be." He'd fight any foe, right all wrongs, fight for the rest of his life to make it different. If he could. "You deserve more than I could ever give you."

"You have more to give me than any army major." She leaned her cheek against his chest. "The only question is, do you want me?"

"Yes." He choked on the word. The one that dishonored him, destroyed his integrity. The one that would make her think they had a future together.

"Then we have everything we need." She smiled up at him, and he swore he could see forever in her eyes.

Their forever—hers and his bound together as man and wife.

If only it could be.

"I hurried back as soon as I could. I thought of nothing else all day," Marie confessed as she watched

Night Hawk offer the small chunk of smoked trout to the wounded hawk.

"Lucky bird."

"I wasn't only thinking of him." The memory of their kiss flared between them.

Desire engulfed her, hotter than any flame. *He wanted her, too.* The realization encouraged her, made her want and wish. It took every bit of her self-control not to lean across the makeshift nest and brush her lips across his.

"He's eating a little, but not much." Night Hawk set aside the remaining piece of trout. "Maybe he'll feed on his own later."

"Does this mean he'll live for sure?"

"It's a good sign." Night Hawk sounded more encouraged, but he walked away, chin bowed, a man of strength and silences.

The injured bird settled down to sleep, cozy in his nest. Alive because of this man.

All day long, she'd thought of little else but his kiss. Of how right it felt in his arms. Her body melted every time she thought of Night Hawk's hands touching her.

How she wanted him to touch her.

She followed him into the yard, where sunshine and wind rustled the changing leaves of the trees. Oranges, golds and reds clung to their boughs, reluctant to fall. Only a few skidded along the ground in a rustling dance.

The season was changing. Time was passing. All her life she'd waited for the right man to love. The one she could make a real home with. The husband she would make children with.

He looked so alone as he stroked his hand down Kammeo's neck. How long had he been isolated from his clan and his culture? Keeping himself apart from the growing settlement?

She ached for him. Trembling with her boldness, she joined him at Kammeo's side. "I never thanked you for her. I would have paid you."

"That's the problem." His chiseled features turned to stone. "I could never accept money from you."

"Because I'm a woman."

"Because you're *the* woman." He turned, and she could see all he'd been struggling with shadowed in his dark eyes. All he wanted. All he feared.

"I want to learn to ride her." Marie pressed a kiss to his lips, a quick one, shy when she wanted to be brazen. "I want you to teach me."

His eyes turned black. Tendons strained in his neck. One bronzed hand curled around her nape, and a thrill washed through her. Their mouths met in a clash of desire and tenderness, each battling, each winning.

When he pulled away, they were both breathless.

He knelt before her and held one hand low. "I'll give you a foot up."

She set her shoe on the flat of his palm and curled her fingers through Kammeo's flaming mane. Suddenly she was airborne. Night Hawk's strength guided her to the mare's withers. She swung her leg over the horse's broad back and laughed when her skirts hiked up to expose her crinolines.

"Don't tell me you walked her all the way here." Night Hawk handed Marie the reins.

"I don't know how to ride. That's why I asked you

to teach me but you had better ideas after listening to my father.''

Night Hawk cupped the side of her face in his strong, tender hand. ''You should listen to your father.''

''This time he's wrong.'' She pressed a kiss to Night Hawk's palm, and her whole body burned. ''Are you going to teach me from the ground?''

''That was my plan.''

''I prefer a more active teaching method.'' He moaned when she kissed him again. ''I'll learn better that way.''

''I wouldn't want you to fail.''

''Exactly. I want to get this right.'' Marie wasn't certain that she was speaking about learning to ride.

Night Hawk mounted behind her and pulled her into the cradle of his thighs. Marie burned and hardly noticed when the young mare pranced, uncertain about the weight of two riders.

Night Hawk soothed Kammeo with low, gentle words.

''Trust.'' He spoke in Marie's ear, a fanning heat on her skin. ''It's what a rider and horse need most of all. The horse to trust you won't lead her into harm. And you to trust what she has to say.''

''You talk to horses, too?''

''Something like that.'' Night Hawk's hands settled at her waist, holding her against him. ''Knot the reins and lay them down.''

Her muscles tightened. Her entire body felt sizzling and expectant, as if waiting for something marvelous to happen. She couldn't seem to make her fingers obey the simplest command. She dropped one rein and had to lean forward to retrieve it.

When she leaned back, Night Hawk was there, his chest like stone, his thighs cradling hers, the hard ridge of his arousal seductive. She leaned into his hardness, into that rigid part of him.

His arms came around her, drawing her closer. Nothing but their clothes separated them. Not distance. Not differences. His chin brushed the top of her head.

"Tighten your knees just a little." His voice vibrated through her chest, as if she'd spoken the words. "Now lean forward."

Incredibly, Kammeo understood and began walking.

"She's bridle trained, so lay one hand on the knot of the reins." His words ruffled her hair and every breath he took seemed like her own.

"Like this?"

He answered by kissing her temple, where she knew he could feel the crazy beat of her heart. Feel how much she wanted him.

"Just a small pressure of the rein to her neck." His hand caught hers to show her. "And a slight squeeze of your knee." His thigh pressed hers.

Kammeo circled easily toward the sparkling lake and green-gold leaves.

"I can't believe it." How could life get any better? The mare felt alive and wondrous beneath her. And Night Hawk's intimate embrace made her melt with a strange need.

They rode down the trail where sunlight played on the water and the cool breeze teased the last of the meadow's wildflowers. With every breath Marie took, she felt more alive. More certain. Desire pulsed thick and heavy through her veins.

"I want her to go faster. Tell me how."

"More thigh pressure, and lean forward.

Kammeo broke into flight, taking them with her. Amazing. Marie could only hold on as she felt the horse fall to earth and then push off. The wind snapped the mare's mane against Marie's face, and she felt as if she were falling. But Night Hawk steadied her with his strong arms and legs. They moved together as one.

He was the one who slowed Kammeo to a walk. He was the one who stopped her. Marie wanted to go forever into the wind and meadow.

"I can't do this." He sounded strained as he dismounted. "Ride home, Marie."

Even from her perch on the mare's back, she could see his erection straining his trousers. She'd felt his arousal throughout their ride. Maybe it was wrong, but she lifted her right leg over the mare's withers and slid to the ground.

He caught her as if without thought. As if this moment between them was meant to be. He folded her close and their kiss was a perfect, tender caress.

"This isn't right." Torture twisted Night Hawk's face. "You don't know what you're asking."

"I know." She boldly met his gaze. "I want you. The only man I will ever love."

Her words were like a drug in his veins, destroying his steeled will. He could no longer resist her.

Their kiss deepened. Her arms curled around his neck, pressing her breasts intimately to his chest.

"Don't stop," she whispered as their breaths mingled. As her tongue swept across the tip of his.

Pleasure speared through him as he wound his fingers through her hair and her delicate knot tumbled down around his hand. The sweet scent of wildflowers and the sultry scent of woman filled him.

His knees went weak and he guided her to the earth. To the soft carpet of grass and fallen leaves. He was faintly aware of the cry of a gray jay and Kammeo wandering away to graze. The world seemed distant compared to the hammer of need within him and the touch of Marie's hand to his chest.

He cupped her jaw, kissing her lovingly. Her fingers tugged at his shirt. He eased her onto her back so it was easier to kiss her. Easier to look into her dark eyes and see her love for him burn.

Incredible that a woman like her would want him. But she did. Truly and deeply. The knowledge chased away every burden from his shoulders. Every darkness from his heart. The years of loneliness. The bitterness of grief. The loss of a way of life he still missed.

It had all happened for a reason, he realized as he drew her bottom lip into his mouth and gently sucked. All his losses, all the change had brought him his *kammeo,* his one true love.

Touching her was rapture. He treasured the feel of her pulse thrumming against his hand when he unbuttoned her collar. And the feel of her breast filling his palm. He couldn't believe she was tugging at her buttons until layers of fabric fell away to reveal the luxury of her bare breasts, creamy and rose tipped.

She smiled at him, a shy and bold invitation. Not only seductive but something greater.

He took his time, caressing her warm skin and kneading her firm breasts. She cried out when he finally drew her nipple into his mouth. She held him, pressing kisses to his brow as he suckled.

Time stood still. She caressed his chest, her fingers working magic on his skin as he caressed the lower curve of her stomach. Dipped lower to curve his fingers into her damp heat.

She moaned in pleasure as they kissed. Her arm curled around his back and drew him over her. The beauty of stretching out above her left him speechless. He gazed at her passion-flushed face and kiss-swollen mouth and knew this wasn't enough. He needed to be closer. He needed to be a part of her.

"Please." As if she were afraid he would stop, she pushed down the cotton undergarment that separated her from his sight.

He loosened his straining trousers. "You have to be sure."

"I love you, Night Hawk." She opened to him. "Please love me."

Marie felt as if they were made for each other before time began. Balancing his weight, he pressed her thighs apart with the strength of his. She gazed up at him and saw only him—the depth of his heart, the beauty of his love as his hard heat pressed against her.

She loved him so much. Freely like the wind that skidded over their heated skin. Wildly like the horizon that knew no end. The thrill of her body opening to him rushed like wine in her veins. He joined them in one slow thrust.

A sudden pain heightened and then faded, leaving her more vulnerable. Leaving her hurting in a frightening way.

"You're crying." He kissed the tears on her cheek. "I was too eager."

"No." She buried her face in the hollow of his shoulder and pressed against his throat. She could feel him breathe. She could feel him inside her, above her, and it was more incredible than she'd imagined.

They moved together and the beauty of it overwhelmed her. Pleasure gathered and built, twisting her tightly around him. He moved within her, and she rose against him. Every muscle tensed and she clung to his shoulders. Heat streaked down her limbs and vibrated in every muscle. Her entire body was tightening around him. Pleasure felt like pain and she couldn't endure any more. Relentless, Night Hawk rocked against her, stroking her deeply. Then she shattered into a thousand pieces.

He cried out, his body stiffened, and she held him as he came. She kissed his face and wrapped her ankles around his hips, feeling him pulse deep within her. She climaxed again, a sudden ripple of pleasure that left her clinging to him.

Night Hawk's kiss was infinitely gentle. He brushed the hair from her face with heartrending tenderness.

"Don't leave me." She kissed him, holding him to her with her arms and thighs, feeling his heavy shaft within her swell and stiffen again.

His kiss became a smile. He loved her slowly, as if

the day would never end. Thoroughly, as if night would never come.

From this moment on, whether together or separated, he would always be a part of her.

"It's nearly dusk." He kissed the crown of her head and breathed in her silken scent. "Time to get you back home before your father misses you."

"You had to mention him, didn't you?"

"He stands between us. You can't deny it." Sadness filled him. "I'm no army major."

"I told you that's not what I want." She kissed him passionately enough to make him wish he could lay her back down in the grass and love her all over again.

But she stood and smoothed her wrinkled skirts.

"I'll walk you." He climbed reluctantly to his feet and whistled for Kammeo.

At the far side of the meadow, the mare swung her head up, whinnied, then loped toward them.

The shadows from the sinking sun fell cool and long across the earth. He couldn't strong-arm the sun back up into the sky. He couldn't stop this treasured moment from slipping away.

Now there were consequences to face.

"I want to come visit you tomorrow." She allowed him to boost her onto the mare's back. "Right here. In this meadow. I want to make love to you again."

"You think that's wise?"

"Absolutely." Her smile chased away all the darkness from his heart. "I can't wait."

The world stood between them. She was too young to believe that, too optimistic to see that this choice they'd made had only one outcome. Even if he wished otherwise.

He mounted behind her and cradled her against him. She relaxed against his chest, sated and happy. They shared kisses as he guided the mare down the trail and toward the woods.

"I don't want you to speak to anyone about this," he told her when the trail narrowed and the fort lay just ahead. "Not even your father."

"I'm not ashamed of loving you."

He kissed her hard, loving her more. "I want you to think this over. We were impulsive in the meadow. I should have been in control. I should have made sure we didn't go too far."

"But I wanted—"

"I know." He silenced her with one last kiss. "But there are consequences. Your father is right. You have your reputation to consider. As his daughter. As a schoolteacher. And as a white woman."

"Night Hawk." Her hand caressed the side of his face, reassuring and devoted. "I'll do as you ask, but I already know what I want. My heart's desire is you."

"I love you, Marie." He wished otherwise. He wished he'd behaved more honorably. He had no right to take her virginity. No right to take what rightfully belonged to another man.

Yet part of him hoped. And wished.

"Good night, my *shaylee*." He slipped to the ground, hating this parting. Hating that by tomorrow, she might see him differently. Might look at him with regret.

"That means 'brightest star in the heavens,'" he told her.

When she left, she took his heart with her.

"You seemed distracted during supper." Henry hesitated in the hallway just outside Marie's room. "I thought you'd enjoy seeing Mrs. Webster again. Her husband is one of my best trackers."

"I have a lot on my mind, Papa." Marie closed her reading primer. "I have exams tomorrow. The first of the term."

"School seems to be going well. All the parents I've spoken to are pleased." He remained in the shadows, just outside the throw of lamplight. "You do me proud, daughter."

Proud was a start. "I'm glad, Papa." She pushed away from her desk. "I'm happy with the school. Coming here has been the best decision of my life."

"I'm glad you see things that way." A small smile broke through Henry's constant reserve, barely visible beneath his mustache. "I know it's been strained between us. I can't help but feel it's because I chose the career I did instead of staying in Ohio after your mother died and raising you."

If it was an apology, it was a start. "My only regret is that you didn't take me with you. I know—" she held up her hand before he could start his usual explanations "—the wilderness is dangerous. The frontier is no place for a child. You wanted me raised in my aunt's home."

"And you're the better for it." Henry looked sad. He looked defensive. He looked weary. "You are a real lady, Marie. The kind any well-bred gentleman would be proud to make his wife.''

''Does it always have to come down to marriage?'' She tried to control her anger, because it covered a greater fear and a deeper pain—the little girl inside her needed her father's love and feared she would never be good enough for it. ''I might want something different.''

''Spinsterhood?'' He raked one hand through his thinning hair. ''I want to sleep at night knowing my daughter is safely married. Before I die, I want to hold my grandson in my arms.''

''That will happen.'' Remembering Night Hawk's words, she kept their secret. ''But I need to choose for myself.''

''Now Marie, what does a girl your age know about making a good marriage?''

''Maybe more than you think.''

''I know what you want. Love. Isn't that what you're waiting for?'' He shook his head wearily. ''Love doesn't last. Marriage needs to be built on a more solid foundation.''

Sorrow filled her. ''What kind of love doesn't last? Romantic love? A father's love? All kinds of love?''

''You confuse the issue on purpose, Marie. I'm talking about duty. About united purpose. Working together to achieve goals.''

''That's how you run your fort, Papa, and you do a marvelous job. You have the respect of everyone I know. But there is more to life than duty and discipline.''

He stared at her as if he couldn't imagine what. ''At

times it's hard to believe that you're my daughter at all. You have too much of your mother in you.''

''How can you talk about her that way? I loved her. And I love you, although heaven knows it isn't easy.'' Anger shivered in her voice, and she hated that she couldn't control it. But her heart hurt too much over her mother's memory.

Duty, indeed. Bitterness filled her and she turned her back on Henry. Long painful minutes ticked by, measured by the small clock on her mantel. Then his step shuffled down the hall, slow and hesitant and almost dragging.

Was that how she was created? Not from a love so great, but from a sense of duty? A cold union without passion or beauty?

Tears burned. Not tears for herself, but for all her father would never know. What he'd missed. And how he'd failed her and her mother.

Wiping her eyes, she collapsed on the window seat. She grabbed the decorated pillow and hugged it tight. Through the crack in the curtains she could see a scattering of stars in a deep black sky.

Shaylee, Night Hawk had called her. The brightest star. She closed her eyes, treasuring the memory of making love with him. Of lying beneath him. Of the beauty of their tender union.

Their child would be conceived in love. As all children should be.

She longed for Night Hawk as she watched the sky. Waited while the disk of the moon traveled away from her window. Ached to hold him. Hungered for him.

Just as she would for the rest of her life.

Chapter Nine

"We cannot stay long," Spring Rain explained as she halted her pony. "Morning Star insisted on seeing your wounded hawk."

"Night Hawk!" Morning Star hopped from her pony and hit the ground running, twin braids flying behind her as she raced toward the stable. "Is he eating yet?"

"A little," Night Hawk called after her. "I left some smoked fish by his nest."

She was already out of hearing.

"Come, I have hot coffee." Night Hawk held out his hand, and Spring Rain, her sixth pregnancy beginning to show, accepted his help as she dismounted her pony. "I have sugar, too."

"You know my weakness." Spring Rain rubbed her back as she climbed the front steps. "Running Deer forbids such things. He clings to the past fiercely."

"We all do." Night Hawk took Spring Rain's elbow and led her to his most comfortable chair. "Put your feet up and rest. You look tired, sister."

"There is always so much to do. And Running Deer—"

Night Hawk didn't like the man who'd married his brother's wife, but it wasn't his place to say so. "What can I do?"

"You do too much for us." Spring Rain settled into the chair with a sigh. One that spoke of a deep weariness. "Great-Grandfather has sent a message from the western mountains where our clan has settled."

"What did our great-grandfather ask?"

"For us to join him. He's never seen my sons. He wishes Morning Star to be raised in the ways of our people." Spring Rain covered her small belly with both hands. "Running Deer is considering. If he decides, then we will leave now while the weather is fair."

Hundreds of emotions churned within him, and Night Hawk stalked away to the kitchen. He wished the solutions could be simple ones.

He filled a cup with steaming coffee and looked over his shoulder at his sister-in-law. The woman was too thin and dark circles haunted her eyes. Her smile was genuine as she accepted the cup he offered.

"Oh, you put in lots of sugar." Her eyes glittered with this small happiness. "If we move to the place of great mountains and rivers, I will miss your coffee. Unless you come with us."

"You know I won't leave this land." Night Hawk said it as gently as he could.

"I know." Sadness chased away the brief glitter in her eyes, and she sipped the brew deeply. "There is another matter we must speak of. The colonel's daughter.''

Shame filled him. Joy filled him. Images of loving Marie flashed through his mind. Of her eager touch. Her head thrown back in ecstasy. The trust in her gaze as he entered her.

Torn, he paced to the window. ''What do you know about me and Marie?''

''I saw you bringing her home last night. I saw you *kissing*.''

What if someone else had seen them? The meadow was a private one and he owned it, but that wasn't the only problem. He'd taken her virginity. He could have gotten her with child. What of her reputation? What about her father? There were great consequences he wanted to shelter Marie from.

He'd wrestled with little else all night long. He loved Marie with all his heart. All his soul. How could he ever be ashamed of that?

But he was a man of steel control. And he'd let his passion rule. He didn't need Spring Rain to tell him he had no right to love the colonel's daughter.

''Did you tell Running Deer?'' he asked carefully.

''No.'' Sorrow drew harsh lines in her pretty face as she shifted in the chair. ''I don't wish you harm, brother. Times have changed since Henry Lafayette came to the fort. Life has been better for all of us. He's a decent man. But how far can you trust him? He won't want an Indian for a son-in-law.''

''I can't argue that.''

''If you love her, you'll be the one hurt.'' Spring Rain stood, balancing her weight and the nearly full cup, and placed her hand on his shoulder. "Dissolve your relationship with Marie. She is a kind woman, but she doesn't understand."

"I keep hoping—" He did not finish his thoughts. Maybe it was too risky to put his greatest wish into words.

"You are lonely. Get yourself a wife, Night Hawk. Someone like us. There are other tribes nearby. Surely they have a pretty but dim-witted woman who would not mind being married to the likes of you."

Now she teased, and it hurt—her concern and her truth.

She padded toward the door. "I will not be long."

He knew where she was going—to his brother's grave. To the graveyard deep in the untouched forest at the far edge of his land. Where his family was buried.

Spring Rain was right. Loneliness had become a hunger inside him. But that wasn't the reason he'd been swept away by the gentle beauty of Marie's love.

More images assailed him. The honeyed taste of her skin. The moan she made low in her throat of surrender and hunger when he caressed her breasts. The way she brought laughter to his life. No woman had ever made him feel like this. No other woman ever could.

But the question remained, one that ate at his conscience. Did he have the right to wish? Was there a way he and Marie could be together as man and wife?

"Look! The hawk eats from my hand," Morning Star told him the instant he stepped inside the stable. "He's still very weak."

"The bullet went through his wing and into his

body." Night Hawk joined his niece at the table where the bird cocked his head to study the newcomer. "He still may not live."

"Oh, I want him to live. He likes me." Morning Star smiled.

In her face Night Hawk saw the faces of the children he wanted.

Children he wished for from the woman he loved.

"Night Hawk." Marie couldn't believe her eyes. The stylus tumbled from her fingers and plummeted off the desk. It really was him standing just inside the schoolhouse vestibule. "How did you know I was daydreaming about you?"

"Lucky guess."

Two little girls, the last of the students, scurried past him, chattering about their plans to visit the mercantile for penny candy.

Night Hawk closed the door after them.

How good he looked. From his dark hair tied back at his nape all the way to his leather moccasins, she loved everything about him. Everything.

Memories exploded through her, hot and forbidden.

"What are you doing in town?" She pushed back from her desk and retrieved her stylus from the floor where it had rolled. "I figured we might meet at the meadow."

"The meadow? And just what did you think we'd do there?"

"Oh, talk. Skip stones on the water." Three steps and she was in his arms. Cradled against his strong chest. "I dreamed about you all night. I wanted to be with you."

On a tortured groan, his mouth slanted over hers. *Yes.* She wanted this, too. Desire built with every tender-rough stroke of his tongue and every brush of his lips to hers. Claiming. Demanding. Heaven could not be better than this.

"All night I wanted you," he confessed against her lips. "Just you."

How incredible to hear him say those words. She wrapped her hand around his back, delighting in the hard luxury of him. "Take me home with you. I need to make love with you."

"No, Marie." He pulled away, and his face twisted as if in agony. "Not until we talk."

"There's no need." She let her fingertips dance along the back of his neck. "I don't have to think anything over, like you've asked me to. I'm absolutely certain about wanting you."

"Do you know what you're risking?"

"There's no risk. Not if you feel the same way."

"You know I do." Desire beat in his blood, and he was already hard. He wanted to love her. To lose himself in her over and over again until all these doubts vanished.

He could not relinquish the hard-won control he'd neglected yesterday. He pulled out the chair in front of her desk and held it, gesturing for her to sit. "We have to discuss what happens next, Marie. You are old enough to know there are consequences to what we shared."

"I know."

"It's not too late to change your mind." It killed him to say the words, but she deserved to hear them. "We can stop right now before this goes any further. Any man who truly loves you is going to understand one lapse of judgment. He'll forgive you."

"You're not listening to me, Night Hawk."

"I want you to consider carefully." Everything about him was tense—his face, his shoulders, his hands. "Your father will disapprove. I don't want you to be hurt. If you pledge your life to me, then it could bring you much heartache—"

He bowed his head as if he could not finish.

"Loving you could never bring me heartache." She pressed a kiss to the side of his face. "As long as you want me."

"No, *shaylee*. Making love with you was the greatest moment of my life." He knelt before her and took her hand.

A sense of rightness filled her. "Then we have no problems. And as for my father, Papa prides himself on his broad-mindedness. He's not a prejudiced man."

"Yes, but you are his daughter. The young woman he hopes will make an advantageous marriage to one of his majors."

"Then he will learn to accept you." Marie's chin lifted, as if ready to fight the world to defend their love.

How he loved her for it. "We must tell him. Now."

"This very moment?"

"Unless you hold secret hopes for Major Gerard."

"Very funny."

"This is important to me." Night Hawk stood, taking her hand in his. "You could be carrying my child, and I won't have either of you shamed."

She came into his arms as if she belonged there and intended to stay forever. "No one has ever cared the way you do."

"You are all that matters to me." He pressed a kiss to the crown of her head.

He wasn't surprised to hear Marie's confession. There was much to admire about Henry Lafayette, but he could be an overzealous man determined to run the fort and the settlement his way. He was even more rigid where his daughter was concerned.

That did not bode well for them.

"I want to speak with my father alone."

"I don't want you hurt. If I'm there with you, I can shoulder the blame. I am responsible for your welfare now."

"I'm responsible, too. This may be the last chance I have to make everything right between him and me." Her eyes filled with unshed tears. "He's going to be disappointed, I know. But maybe I can make him see the woman I've become. Maybe he'll surprise me and be the father I need."

"I can't stand by and let you take his anger."

She smiled, her unshed tears sparkling, her lovely face a mix of happiness and suffering. "Papa will not be himself with you there. He's so determined to be the colonel in charge."

"You will tell him?"

"I promise." Her words became a kiss, one that reassured him more completely than any vow.

It was anguish to release her. Anguish to step away still tasting her lips on his.

He would not hide. He would not lie. He would not compromise an innocent, spirited woman. Marie was a part of his soul. He could not defile his love for her by acting as if they'd done something shameful. That their affections should be kept hidden from sight.

"Marie, I was just thinking about you." Henry pushed away from his paper-piled desk in the large corner office. "Come, sit. Sergeant James will fetch some tea for us."

"I—" She wasn't in the mood for refreshment. Not when her stomach was coiled so tightly. "That would be fine, Papa."

"Good." He nodded to the man, who left the door ajar, presumably to fetch the desired drinks. "You look serious. You've come to resign your teaching position, haven't you?"

Resignation? Surprised, she slipped into the chair facing him. "No, Papa, but we do need to talk."

"I know." He held up his hand, in control. "How was school today?"

"Well enough—"

"Good, Marie. I knew you would do me proud with the school. I want to clarify something I said last night. Something I think might have caused you grief.

"I gave you the impression that I don't love you, my own daughter." Staring hard at his cigar, he pinched the end off and lit it, never lifting his gaze to hers.

Yet his words touched her. Words she'd never heard

before. Hope filled her, quiet and tentative. "Then you agree there is more to life than duty?"

"There is both for a father." He rubbed a hand over his face. "I may have given you the impression that I regretted that you were not a boy. A man wants for a son, I won't deny that, but a daughter is precious and needs to be taken care of accordingly."

Marie stared at the window, shaken. Was he saying that all the years they'd spent apart were his best effort to take care of her? "You did what you could for me, Papa, and I do appreciate it. I can take care of myself. You don't have to worry."

"Not until you're married to an ambitious major with a future ahead of him. Someone who can provide the world for my daughter." He exhaled cigar smoke with a contented smile. "And my grandsons. I will hold a grandchild in my arms before I die, won't I?"

You could be carrying my child. Night Hawk's words filled her with hope. Every time she loved him would bring a greater chance of conceiving their child. The thought of Night Hawk's baby brought joy to her heart.

She felt happier than she dared to believe. "One day, Papa. I'm sure of it."

Meka's bark rang across the meadows, announcing his and Marie's arrival. The injured bird startled. Night Hawk soothed the creature with his voice and touch.

"How's our hawk?"

"Improving. I just finished feeding him." Night Hawk wrapped the bundle of smoked fish and set it aside. "You're smiling. I can't believe it went well with your father."

"I didn't tell him. I tried, but some urgent business came up." Marie led the way toward his house, swinging her basket. "Something about missing livestock at one of the ranches."

"Did he think it was thieves or a wild animal?"

"He didn't say."

"What else did he say?" Night Hawk fought to keep from touching her. "You gave me your word that you would tell Henry about us."

"I know. It's just—" She pushed open his door and stepped into the kitchen. "He said some things that made me see him differently. I doubt that he and I will ever see eye-to-eye on some things, but maybe he understands a little. I think he's realized that I'm not going to marry Major Gerard or any other military man he pushes in front of me."

She set the basket on his table, looking as if she belonged here. "I think Papa has come to understand that he can't choose a husband for me. He'll accept you, Night Hawk. I know he will."

"He said that, did he?" Night Hawk didn't believe it for a second, but her excitement filled his house and made his heart whole. "He told you he'd welcome an Indian for a son-in-law? And a farmer, at that."

"He didn't say the words, but he respects you. I know he does." Marie reached inside her basket and withdrew a cloth-covered bundle. "Papa won't be home until late, and Mrs. Olstad had already started supper, so I packed a meal for us. I hope you like buttermilk biscuits and fried chicken."

"I would love anything as long as I'm with you." He laid his hand to her face, holding back his worries and fighting the growing need to lay her over that table and love her. Just love her. "I want us to wait. I want your father's permission."

"Wait to make love? I can't." Her eyes twinkled. "I've dreamed of nothing else all night and all day. I want to share supper with you at your table, and then I want you to take me to your bed, Night Hawk. Love me as if I were your wife."

Her words stirred tempting and forbidden images to life in his mind. Desire raged as he pulled her against him. She came willingly, molding like heaven against his thighs and chest. Her moan became a kiss.

"Please, Night Hawk." Her lips teased his as she spoke. "Make love to me now."

"We will wait." He was resolute even as his blood thickened.

Her fingers played over the fabric of his trousers, teasing his straining shaft. "I can't wait to feel you inside me. To feel my entire being enfolding you."

Longing, lust, love and forever warred within him. "You undo me, Marie."

"I haven't even started." She twisted away, but the devil flashed in her eyes as she finished setting out the meal. "Hungry?"

"Not for food." He laughed. He couldn't help it. The woman was trying to seduce him.

Just how long would his iron will last?

Marie moaned as he withdrew from her, separating their bodies, and she wanted to pull him back. "Now admit it. This is a better dessert than Mrs. Olstad's cranberry cake.''

"Fine. You win." He stretched out on his side and caressed her breasts with his hand. "You make me weak. I don't know what to do about that."

"You don't seem weak to me." She let her fingers creep down his abdomen. He felt warm like new gold and solid like a fortress wall. "You seem pretty hard. You're going to be uncomfortable sitting at the table like that. Maybe there's something I can do to alleviate your condition."

His breath became a hiss when she curled her hands around him. She loved this part of him that brought her so much pleasure. He was velvet steel and pulsed against her palm.

"You tempt me too much." He caught her by the wrists and kissed her knuckles tenderly. "I meant what I said. We should wait."

"We've been successful at waiting." She laughed when he pulled her on top and she straddled him. "You and I both know that love like this is too precious to waste. I don't want to miss a moment with you."

Her words touched him and he couldn't argue. Helpless to resist, he grasped her hips to guide her over his shaft. A smile touched her lips as her head tipped and her back arched, accepting him into her tight heat. Into the greatest intimacy.

You must tell him tonight. Night Hawk's request echoed like an overactive conscience in her mind as she padded through the dark parlor to the room Henry used as an office while he was at home. A swath of candlelight from the partly opened doorway guided her through the unfamiliar room.

And toward probable disaster. No, not disaster. She believed in Henry with all her heart. In his goodness. In the part of him she'd seen earlier when he'd said he loved her. *That* man would understand.

And then she could begin planning a wedding with Night Hawk!

Excitement skidded through her like a giant shooting star. She hadn't even thought that far, but with Henry's permission, she could become Night Hawk's bride.

A whole new world spread out before her in the eye of her imagination. Living with Night Hawk on his land. Keeping his house, cooking his meals and looking out through the many windows of his beautiful log cabin to watch him work with his horses. To think how wonderful it would be having the right to sleep in his bed and love him late into the night. To wake each morning in his arms, happy and at peace.

She could feel the change loving him had made in her body. She was more aware. More alive. She could still taste the tangy wildness of his kiss on her lips and feel the wetness of his seed within her. Children, there would be children one day. The thought of little boys with Night Hawk's smile and little girls with his dark eyes filled her with such joy.

"Marie." Henry's no-nonsense voice sliced through her reverie. "Is that you standing out there in the dark?"

"Yes, sir." She pushed open the door.

"Mrs. Olstad told me you were out berry picking this evening." Henry's face clouded.

She had not told the housekeeper that's what she was doing. Maybe the woman assumed. "Actually, I—"

"There's been trouble at the Meyers claim." He looked up from his newspaper, probably arrived on the last stage. "I don't want you straying from the settlement, you hear?"

"What kind of trouble?" Marie skirted the heat from the fire blazing in the stone hearth.

"It could be nothing. Every now and then a wild animal gets too close and decides to feast on a rancher's hen." He turned the page, newsprint rattling harshly as he frowned. "Sometimes it's more serious. We won't know if it's a problem until it happens again. Then we need to decide if it's a thief or a predator."

"I'll be careful." She took a shaky breath. Henry didn't look as approachable now as he had for that brief moment in his office. "There was something I tried to tell you earlier—"

"About your decision. I know." Papa actually tossed aside his paper, rose from his favorite chair and embraced her. "I'm so pleased with you, Marie. I've never been more proud of you."

Her mind reeled, her senses spinning. Before she could move past the shock of feeling her father's arms banding her and smelling the cigar smoke on his shirt, he stepped away, beaming from ear to ear like a brand-new, first-time papa.

Something wasn't right. What had happened since the last time she'd seen him?

"You've made me a very happy man." Papa simply glowed. His sadness had ebbed away and he looked younger, stronger, like a man with hope. "I've taken the liberty of inviting Ned to accompany us to the chapel services this Sunday. If you're going to make me a grandfather one day soon, then you'll have to start letting the major court you."

"Oh, Papa." Realization slammed into her with the force of a runaway horse. "I didn't mean that I wanted Ned. I've already chosen—"

"Ned Gerard is a wise choice. Family name, old money and he graduated fourth in his class at West Point. Imagine that." Henry's chest puffed up with happiness. "Now *that's* the kind of father my grandson needs."

"Papa!"

"I love you so very much, daughter mine." Unbelievably, he smiled again. A smile from the father she'd longed for all her life.

Had he really called her precious? How did she break his heart? She tried, she honestly tried to find the words. But they didn't come.

What did she do now?

Chapter Ten

"You didn't tell him?" Night Hawk's anger boomed like thunder across the lake. "You promised me."

Marie couldn't deny it. The cool wind buffeted her wide bonnet brim and the ribbons cut into her chin. She tugged at the knot to loosen it. It gave her something to do beside look at the disappointment on her lover's face.

Disappointment in her. She lifted the hat from her head and wedged it against the side of the canoe where the wind couldn't catch it. How did she explain?

Night Hawk rowed harder, turning the dugout around and taking them back toward shore. He didn't speak but the rigid set of his jaw said everything.

Beneath his silent anger lurked pain. She'd hurt him.

"Night Hawk." She laid her hand on his arm but he kept rowing with great force, sending them gliding across the smooth waters where mist rose beneath a late autumn sky. "It's not what you think. I'm not ashamed of loving you."

"You will not tell your father," he bit out between teeth tightly clenched. "I have asked you repeatedly, yet you refuse."

"I'm simply trying to find the right words. You understand, don't you? I'm not trying to hurt you."

"I've behaved dishonorably toward you." Agony twisted his stony features. "I cannot disgrace my family's name in such a way. I had a father, too."

Marie felt even more ashamed. In Night Hawk's culture, family must be very important. She hadn't thought about it, because he lived alone.

"I don't want to dishonor your family." She had to make him understand. "I want time, that's all."

"This is how it was for my people. A father chose a bride for his son." Night Hawk stopped rowing, and the canoe glided along the water. He laid the paddle across his powerful thighs and stared toward the hills far behind his house.

"Don't misunderstand." Whatever he'd been thinking drew sadness onto his face. "A son had a choice. He would tell his father, that is the girl I want. And if she were suitable his father would speak to the young woman's parents. Still, a father controlled who his child married when the time came."

"My father doesn't control me—"

"That is not my point." He slipped the paddle into the water once more, allowing the *slap-slap* of the tide against the boat to carry them. "My father would never have allowed me to marry you. Your father feels the same way. That is why you can't tell him the truth."

"No, that's not it."

"The truth, Marie."

She couldn't breathe past the sharp pain lashing through her. She felt as if a part of her was on the verge of shattering. Maybe it was the girl within her so hungry for her father's affection. Maybe it was the woman in her who felt she must choose. That she had to choose.

"Fine," she admitted, saying the awful truth she didn't want to admit. "He isn't going to want me to marry you. He thinks—" She saw Night Hawk's face sadden even more. "He thinks I've accepted his idea to let Major Gerard court me."

"Fine." Night Hawk's paddle groaned as he rowed so hard that tendons strained in his neck. "Is that what you want?"

"You know it's not. Night Hawk, slow down and listen. I talked with Ned —"

"Ned?" Jealousy blinded him and, with a roar, he jammed the paddle deep in the water, driving them forward.

"I told him right away how wrong my father was. To use both of us like that." Marie didn't look ashamed. She looked determined and caring. Like a woman doing her best to make things right. "I came here to teach at this settlement so that I could be with my father. I want to mend the heartache of our pasts. I've been given this chance to make things right with my father and I can't pass it by. Please understand."

"You cannot have a relationship with your father if it is based on a lie. If he believes something that is false and loves you for it."

"I won't lie. I just want to find a loving way to tell

him the truth. In a way he can accept and celebrate. Instead of feeling as if he's failed me as a father and I've failed him as a daughter.''

"I cannot bear this.'' Pain thundered in his chest. Desire pulsed through every inch of him. The way she was looking at him, as if she had everything to lose, hurt in a way that made him want to leap from the canoe and swim in the icy water until he grew too numb to feel.

"This isn't about my not wanting you.'' She came to him, rocking the dugout, and knelt between his thighs. He was hard when her hand found him through his trousers. "I'm already yours. You made me yours in the meadow not far from here. Remember?''

How could he forget? He craved her like the air he breathed. He gritted his teeth, determined not to give in to the pleasure flaming beneath her playful fingers. "My vow remains. I won't make love with you again until I have the right.''

"What do you mean?'' Her hand stilled. "You're still angry?''

He rowed the canoe onto the sloping shore and stowed the paddle on the floor behind him. "Out. Here, give me your hand.''

"I can manage.'' She didn't touch him as she grabbed her skirts and stepped onto the beach. "What about the fish we were going to catch?''

"I can't be alone with you.'' He snatched her bonnet from the floor and handed it to her.

"We're alone right now.''

"Yes, and you know what we both want.''

"There's nothing to be ashamed of, Night Hawk.

We've done nothing wrong." She took the hat from him, looking so vulnerable with her eyes wide and her face slightly pale. It was a silent plea he could not ignore. He stepped out of the dugout.

"Loving you is not wrong, *shaylee*." When he should be pushing her away, he drew her into his arms. He could not bear if she thought— "You cannot have things both ways. You either decide to claim me or you don't."

"But—"

"No. I will not let you change my mind. I cannot yield, Marie." He hauled the canoe up the shore out of the water's reach. "Take the time you need with your father. If you still love me, then come to me rightfully. Or not at all."

"You're making me choose between my father and you." She couldn't believe he didn't understand. "If I have to, I will choose you, Night Hawk. Are you afraid I won't?"

"I'm afraid of making you pregnant, and your father sending you back to Ohio before my son can be born here with my name." He looked dark with fury, hard with pain. "The clan of Hawk is one of honor. I cannot destroy who I am. Not even for you."

"I would never ask you to—"

"You already have."

How had this happened? Didn't Night Hawk want her? His words taunted her, slicing like a blade with every breath. "You're afraid that my love for you isn't strong enough in case my father opposes us."

A muscle jumped along his jaw. "*My* love is strong enough."

Without saying the words, he accused her. Their love was new, but if it were true then he should have no doubts. No doubts about her fidelity. About her devotion to him.

That made her question if he loved her at all. "How could you think I would leave you? After what we—" The lovemaking, his vows of love and her dreams all shattered into irrevocable pieces.

Had she been that wrong? she wondered wildly. Night Hawk strode toward her as if he were preparing another lecture on his honor. The pain of her heart breaking had her running toward town, Meka barking at her heels.

"Marie! Wait!" Night Hawk called after her.

The bonnet slipped from her fingers and rolled onto the leaf-covered grass. She kept going, not caring. Let Night Hawk call to her. Let him chase her. She had a good head start, and he didn't really want to catch her. He didn't believe that after pledging her life, her body and her heart that her love was as strong as his.

Maybe she was too young. She had no experience with men. With her aunt far away in Ohio, she had no one to trust. No one to ask for advice. What had Night Hawk said about her loss of virginity?

Any man who truly loves you is going to understand. He'll forgive you.

"Marie!" Night Hawk was dangerously close.

She ran harder. What would she say to the man who had no faith in her? Who made her question her faith in him?

She broke through the trees and onto the road. She

raced into the shadows of the fort and never looked back.

"I saw you with the colonel's daughter." Running Deer's accusation held immeasurable disdain. "What were you doing on the lake with her? Teaching her to fish?"

"None of your concern." Seeing Running Deer was the last kick in the bucket of a bad day. His argument with Marie left him weak and frustrated. As much as he loved her, as much as he would sacrifice to be with her, why had he ever thought there was a chance for them?

The pain inside him swelled like a festering wound, and he spun away from Running Deer, who was eyeing his latest batch of foals.

"Doing well for yourself. Farming land. Making white man's money." Running Deer wouldn't relent. "Do you think that you'll take her for a wife and fit in? Will you betray our people's ways completely?"

"I have betrayed no one." Night Hawk hated the vehemence in his own voice. He was upset over Marie and anger was no way to handle Running Deer. "Why have you come?"

"I've decided to travel to the western mountains. To this place our leader says is green and blessed." Running Deer stopped to covet a fine young mare in her stall.

"You would take your pregnant wife on a dangerous journey?" Night Hawk roared, unable to hold back his outrage. "Spring Rain does not look well."

"She is not your wife, though often I have thought you wanted her."

"She was my brother's wife and love of his life, and I swore on his deathbed I would care for her as a sister. You know this to be true." Thinking of his beloved brother, dead from wounds he received in the Great War when Night Hawk was but fourteen, was a great grief. "You will leave soon?"

"Within the next few weeks. I wish to leave immediately, but there is much to do." Running Deer ran his hand down the mare's neck as if calculating her worth. "White Hawk wants you to come with us. He said there is a place for you. I have no doubts he will groom you to replace him."

"He is a great leader, and you know my aspirations lie elsewhere." Night Hawk steeled his will. He would not fight with Running Deer. "I will not be leaving."

"Set your sights higher, have you? The pompous colonel will have no choice to accept an Indian for a son-in-law if his daughter is carrying your son."

"Marie has been good to your children and kind to Morning Star. You have no reason to malign her."

"If she takes you from your duties to the clan, then that is reason enough." Fierce, Running Deer fisted his hands. "I will send word to White Hawk that you have forsaken us all."

Night Hawk kept his temper until he was alone. His curse echoed in the rafters and startled swallows from their nests in the loft. The horses protested by neighing in their stalls. The wounded blue hawk squawked nervously in his nest.

Night Hawk whistled to Shadow, and leaped on the

stallion's back in midstride. They took off together, racing the wind through wild meadows and endless forest.

As fast as Shadow galloped, it wasn't enough to escape the anguish in Night Hawk's heart.

Henry wasn't home. Another emergency had come up at the Meyers's homestead, Mrs. Olstad explained as she polished the parlor furniture. More trouble with the bear.

Great. That made it difficult to have a private conversation with her father. Marie headed out the back door and took sanctuary in the private fenced yard.

The garden was fallow, the last of the pumpkins long since picked and stored. The remaining leaves tumbled from the maple. The bare limbs were stark against the graying sky. Dusk came early this time of year.

She sat on the wooden bench, huddling in her woolen cloak for warmth. But the air cooled and the sun sank below the horizon. Her breath clouded in the crisp air and fog collected on the ground, a strange mist that rose upward, shrouding all but the tallest of tree branches from her sight.

He loves me, I know he does. She had to believe that. To think anything else would hurt too much. Now that she was calmer, she thought over what had happened in the canoe. Night Hawk's words. The anguish on his face.

I am afraid of making you pregnant, he'd said. The clan of Hawk is one of honor.

He wasn't rejecting her, she realized. He was taking

care of her. Acting in a way he believed would be best for both of them.

He was right. She'd been reckless, a romantic daydreamer as always, so carried away by her powerful love she hadn't stopped to think. To consider Henry's opposition to a match like theirs. They shouldn't heedlessly make love until their future was assured.

What if she carried his child? She laid her hand over her stomach. How she wished with all her heart that she was. But she doubted she was that lucky. Wouldn't a baby solve everything?

No, it wouldn't erase the terrible torment she'd witnessed on Night Hawk's face. He'd spoken of honor while she tried to seduce him. All she could think about was being with him. Loving him. She was old enough to temper her desire with reason and couldn't.

Is that why he seemed to doubt the strength of her love?

Troubled, she sat until dusk became darkness and ice frosted the ground.

Tired of tossing and turning, Night Hawk crawled from his bed. He could not sleep without dreaming of Marie, passionate and sweet, ardent and tender. How he hungered for her. Memories of her in his bed tortured him.

For a short foolish time, he'd let his heart rule his head. She was so beautiful and as kind and tender as dawn. How could he resist loving her? Keep from wanting her here forever?

She wasn't certain. That's what it came down to.

The true crux of the issue. She couldn't displease her father even for love.

He wanted to hate her for it, but he could never hate her. He loved her from the depth of his being, and he always would. Whether she came to him or not.

She was young. He had to remember that. Even though he was only a year older, he'd known a world that had hardened and aged him. She'd been raised as the colonel's cherished daughter.

What real chance did he have to make her his?

None at all, he feared. He stared at the heavens for much of the night, watching the stars journey across the endless sky.

Black, barren boughs raked across the coal-black clouds. Marie's boots crackled on the frozen ground, accompanied by an armed soldier. The wind cut through her wool cloak like a sharpened blade, but the discomfort couldn't match the one inside her heart.

Many weeks had passed, and she hadn't seen Night Hawk. He hadn't come to her. She hadn't gone to him because the fort was on alert.

A cougar had nearly attacked a child at the Meyers's homestead. The father had frightened the wildcat with a panicked gunshot, but a farmer's musket was no match for the dangerous predator. The child had made it to the house in time, without injury, but the settlers' panic could be felt like the chill wind.

To search out Night Hawk would be foolhardy. And even if she did, what would she say to him? That her father was so busy hunting the cougar and seeing to the settlers' safety, she hadn't seen him. Or had the chance to tell him about her love for Night Hawk. Would Night Hawk understand?

Smoke already curled out of the schoolhouse's chimney. Marie pushed open the door to find Major Gerard kneeling in front of the hearth adding fuel to the fledgling fire. The two Holmberg children huddled close, still in their wraps, their little faces red with the cold.

"I'm early, I know." Ned set the wood in the flames and grabbed the metal poker. "A few men were sick this morning and we were one soldier short, so I decided to fill in. I'm heading back out to the Braun farm. Morning Star won't be returning to school. Something about the whole family moving farther west."

"The whole family?"

"That's what Running Deer said." Ned shrugged good-naturedly as he dug into the flames. More air made the fire roar brighter, radiating more heat for the students. "If you want to take over, I'll head out and bring in the Braun children. Guarding them is the best we can do until your father brings in that cougar."

"Are the men still out hunting? Papa didn't come home last night."

"He slept in the barracks for a few hours, and he's back out with the tracking party." Ned grabbed his musket from the corner and slung it over his shoulder. "At least he's too busy to try and marry the two of us off."

With a wink, the major strode out into the cold.

Hours later, when her students were quietly studying, she felt a tingle at the back of her neck. She looked up from her work. The curtain was pulled back to let in the precious warmth of the sun. Through the glass she saw a dark horse and rider trotting by on the lane. Night Hawk.

He looked so good. Powerful, dignified, he guided his stallion bareback through the busy street. Love for him welled within her like a too-full cup. She craved his touch. Needed his lovemaking. Ached to hold him one more time.

He halted Shadow in front of the mercantile and swung to the ground with an inbred grace. The shoppers and soldiers around him didn't acknowledge him with greetings. Like a stranger alone among friends, he opened the front door and stepped into the shop and out of her sight.

Her conscience smarted. For some reason she recalled Sergeant James's words the day she'd arrived. *Night Hawk doesn't seem to have much need for us. He's a real lone wolf type.*

No, she realized. He was protecting himself. He'd been hurt so much. Now his only remaining relatives were moving away. How did a man lose everything and still have the courage to start anew? Surely that's what he'd done in building his ranch. In laying claim to a new future and working toward it.

His strength amazed her. She felt small in comparison. A man as noble as Night Hawk deserved a woman who would stand by him. Whom he would never need to doubt.

Could she be that woman? Would he let her be? She watched until he reappeared, breezing down the mercantile steps with two bulging packs. He didn't look her way as he mounted Shadow.

As Night Hawk rode toward the shadowed woods, tiny crystalline snowflakes fell like promises from sky to earth.

"There is room for one more," Spring Rain said quietly in their native tongue as she handed him the deerskin pack holding the children's winter clothing. "I want you to come with us, brother. You will be happier among our own people. Happier living our old way."

"I cannot in good conscience leave." Night Hawk shouldered the pack, hesitating in the cabin's doorway. Cold wind buffeted him and yet the regret within him was colder still. "My family is buried in the wooded hills I tend and I cannot abandon them."

"But to preserve our heritage—"

"I have not abandoned it." Night Hawk thought of the horses raised from his father's herd. His father's stallion still sired half the annual foals. "I am content with my life."

"You are lonely. Without me and Morning Star you will be without family at all."

Night Hawk heard what Spring Rain didn't say as she retreated into the meager lodge. She'd become his only family through these long, difficult years, watching over him as an older sister did while he grew to manhood. He owed her a lot.

Enough to approach her now. "If you do not wish to leave, you and little Morning Star may stay with me. I will build you a house on the far knoll overlooking the lake. You will have morning sunshine through your windows.''

Her hands stilled. When she spoke, there were tears in her eyes. ''I would love nothing more, but there is Running Deer.''

''I am not afraid of Running Deer. I care about you, sister. Tell me what you wish and I will do it.''

Tears brimmed but did not fall. ''I cannot leave him. He married me when others wouldn't. When I was with Swift Hawk's child and had nothing to bring to a union. Come with us, please. That is my wish.''

''The one wish I cannot grant and well you know it.'' Night Hawk pressed a kiss to his sister's cheek. ''You should not be traveling.''

''I will be fine.''

''You can wait until the babe arrives and I will take you to these western mountains myself.''

The tears fell one at a time, a slow sadness that broke his heart.

''You are a good man, and I am proud to call you brother.'' She pressed her cheek to his chest and let him hold her. How frail she was. Yet her heart was strong and loyal.

''You help Running Deer with the wigwam.'' She stepped back, rubbing away her tears with the heel of her hands. ''Go, the travois will be nearly full. Tomorrow we will leave this land forever, and I must not cry.''

Night Hawk walked out into the yard where the mood was no better. Tiny mistlike snowflakes hung in the air, too fragile to fall. Morning Star bounded up to him, ready to help secure the last pack of the day on the travois.

"Running Deer says you might come with us." The girl's fingers nimbly finished the last knot before Night Hawk could reach it. "Is that true?"

"No. I intend to stay." He pulled a small package from his pocket and handed it to her. "To share with your brothers on the trip west."

Her eyes lit up when she peered inside the brown wrapping. "Peppermint! Uncle, you know it's my favorite."

"Yes, and this is the last time I'll be able to spoil you."

"Every time I eat peppermint I shall think of you." Morning Star dove into his arms and he held her, drinking in her child's sweetness, missing her already.

"I'll write you and tell you of the blue hawk's recovery."

Morning Star held on tightly. "I will miss so much."

"Yes, but think of the good things to come. Take care of your mother for me?" He smoothed back the dark wisps that had escaped from her braids. "The trip will be hard on her."

"I will make all the fires."

How could his heart stand one more loss?

"Soldiers." Running Deer appeared from the back woods and gestured toward the frozen road. "Two riders."

Morning Star darted into the narrow lane. "It's my teacher!" She took off at a full run, arms flung wide.

Marie? Why would she come here? Night Hawk

fisted his hands, trying to gain control. With the way he felt, he was going to look at Marie and do anything to have her back in his bed.

A sergeant from the fort trotted into sight, then stopped, keeping a watchful distance. Then Marie rounded the corner on Kammeo, bareback as he'd taught her, although she did use reins. He saw her all in an instant—her wind-reddened cheeks, her sweet oval face, the shadows beneath her eyes and her gentle pride.

Everything within him ached for her. How could it be? He wanted her so fiercely, this woman who was ashamed of him.

"Miss Lafayette!" Morning Star's delighted shriek carried clearly on the crisp winds. "Did you come to tell me goodbye?"

"I did." Marie's smile was genuine as she looked upon the child. "I heard from one of the fort's majors that you're leaving tomorrow. I have a gift for you, if it's all right with your stepfather."

Running Deer nodded in agreement.

Night Hawk watched as Marie held out three books, the same ones she'd lent Morning Star earlier. "When you returned these to me, you told me how much you liked reading the stories. I thought they should be yours."

"Oh, Miss Lafayette!" Overcome, Morning Star could say no more. She turned and ran to show her mother the treasured books.

Night Hawk closed the distance between him and Marie. Perched on her horse and with her skirt hem fluttering in the wind, she looked out of his reach.

When she saw him, her face lit with happiness.

"Morning Star will enjoy your gift of the books." He met her gaze and held it.

She paled. The kindness, like a light in her eyes, remained. "She's one of my best students. The top of her class."

"Spring Rain will like knowing that." It felt awkward talking like this with an audience when private words needed to be said. "If your sergeant will allow it, I will see you safely back to the fort."

"Sergeant Pierce?" She turned to address the silent soldier, who was already shaking his head.

"I'm under strict orders, ma'am."

Marie winced. Night Hawk did not need to ask by whose orders. Colonel Lafayette would make sure his daughter was protected from hungry cougars or unsuitable lovers.

"It's all right, Marie," he said when it wasn't.

"I've been wanting to talk with you," she said quietly.

"Have you spoken with Henry?"

He could read the answer in her eyes. She hadn't. He was afraid he knew why. And then, maybe he didn't. If his father were alive, wouldn't he try to find a way to keep a relationship with him? What would he do in Marie's place?

Her love for him shone in her eyes, brighter than a thousand suns and he couldn't mistake it. Just as he could not mistake the unhappiness drawing small lines into the soft skin around her eyes and mouth.

Lines made by him. He'd put the mark of sadness

on her face. It humbled him. Yet how could he risk his honor?

"As I told you," he said logically when his entire being called out for him to take her in his arms and never let go. "You come to me when you're ready. When you won't be ashamed."

"But I—" She glanced up and, even though he'd whispered, their intense conversation had gained more attention. "I could never be ashamed of you. Is that what you think?"

He could not answer. The sergeant called to her, for it was growing dark, making the return journey dangerous. The truth left him vulnerable, and he'd already lost too much of his heart.

"Bye, Miss Lafayette! Thank you!" Morning Star called out, racing down the road.

"Write me when you arrive safely. I want to hear all about your exciting trip west." Marie's caring was genuine, and it made it harder for Night Hawk to harden his heart. To insist she was a woman afraid to love a man like him.

Her gaze pinned his. In the space between one heartbeat and the next, he read the longing in her eyes as clearly as if she'd spoken of it.

Had he been wrong to withhold his heart?

Chapter Eleven

"Marie." The male voice seemed to come out of the night's darkness.

"Night Hawk." She'd thought only of him since she'd visited his niece. Equal parts of regret and longing filled her. Did she go to him? Did she run from him? She didn't know what to do.

"Did Morning Star's family leave safely?"

"As far as I know. My niece promised to send me a letter but it's only been a few weeks." He stepped close, so the candlelight glowing through the window tossed shadows over him.

He looked exhausted, as if he hadn't slept well during the past months. As if he, too, were tormented by dreams that came like touches in the night. Images of him so real and loving that she woke in her lonely bed wishing to return to the dream.

How did she begin? How did she reveal to him her deepest fears?

Before she could speak, he cleared his throat. "I've come to speak with your father."

"Papa?" Not her? She gripped the porch rail tightly.

"There was another cougar attack earlier tonight. A settler by the name of Meyers was attacked."

"Is he all right?"

"The fort doctor is on his way." Not speaking further, Night Hawk grew more serious. He could have been a stranger standing before her and not the man she'd made love to.

"I've come to join the hunt. Who in this fort knows where Henry is?"

"Major Gerard."

A muscle bunched along his jawline. She could feel his tension, feel his pride and how it would not bend. How he believed she was ashamed of their love. Of the beautiful lovemaking they'd shared. Of the true bright passion that lived in her heart. Could they still recapture it?

He turned away, a man of dignity and silence, before she could find the words to make him believe in her. This was not the time, but her heart ached to say the words.

Her body ached for his touch.

She watched him stride down the dark path briefly touched by fading starlight. Beside the musket slung over his shoulder was another weapon—a hand-carved bow.

A part of her feared she would never have the chance to say the words locked in her heart. Never have the opportunity to more deeply love this great man.

It all came down to him. Would he give her the chance?

Seeing Marie again stirred up too many emotions. Emotions that hindered him on a hunt. Night Hawk shook the snow from his cap and tried to purge her from his mind. But her image remained, standing on the porch washed with dwindling starlight.

A cold wind drove hard from the north as if to remind him of his mission. To catch the killer cougar who was threatening his neighbor's children.

Beside him, a handful of soldiers halted to nip at the whiskey in their flasks. Brought to keep them warm, or so they said. Night Hawk gave Shadow time to nibble at enough snow to quench the stallion's thirst while he listened to the men's conversations.

Some didn't trust the tracker. Others thought he was a genius. Others complained, wishing for a warm bed and a full night's sleep.

"There's no sense casting for a sign in this weather," Webster, the main tracker, boasted. "With this snow and it being nearly midnight, we won't get a sighting until morning."

"I'm not satisfied." Exhaustion marked the colonel's face. He hunched in the bitter cold. "We didn't keep trying to flush out that cat and look what it did. Attacked Meyers when he was bringing in his cows for milking. No, we can't stop."

"That kill we found a ways back means the cat won't be hunting for a few days."

"Not that cat." Night Hawk pushed through the

ring of soldiers surrounding the colonel. "What about the other?"

"Cougars don't share territory." Webster rounded on him, eyes narrowing. "There's only one cat. And we've been tracking him for three weeks."

"He isn't the cat you're looking for."

The soldiers silenced. Even the wind died, leaving the snow to whisper silently to the earth as Night Hawk steeled his spine, refusing to back down.

"Are you saying I can't do my job?"

"Your job is to hunt the right cougar. Kill the one you've been tracking and it won't stop the attacks on the settlers."

Negative comments from the soldiers rose, men who'd been working in the bitter cold and through long hard hours, so Night Hawk didn't take them to heart.

"A cat desperate enough to attack easy prey like children and fenced livestock doesn't kill a deer."

"What do you know?" Webster bit out. "*I've* been a tracker for the U.S. Army for fourteen years."

"I've been tracking and hunting since I was five years old. My grandfather was a great hunter and taught me." Night Hawk heard the soldiers' silence. Tension vibrated in the frigid air. "I know every animal who lives in these hills. What tracks they make. How they live, what they eat, when they rest. The cougar hunts at night and early morning, so why are you tracking it during the day while it sleeps?"

Webster's face reddened. "You don't belong here. Colonel, are you going to listen to his word over mine?"

The colonel rubbed his chin, considering.

He's going to listen to his trusted soldier, Night Hawk predicted. Even the visionary colonel who'd brought harmony and tolerance to this land would not trust an outsider. Or an Indian.

"Let's hear what Night Hawk has to say," Henry said thoughtfully. "We need to work together, soldier and civilian, white and Indian if we are to keep our settlement's children safe. Night Hawk, what more can you tell us?"

Many gazes turned on him, some assessing, some curious, some resentful. He was proud of his heritage, proud that he'd been raised to know the forest and its creatures.

He was grateful Henry respected his people's knowledge. He turned now to face the colonel, and maybe to impress Marie's father. It made him ashamed, but he was a man with weaknesses and fears like any other.

"Cougars are like spirits," he explained. "You may never see one in your entire life although you walk right past one. They decide when and if you see them. For example, Sergeant Samms stopped to take a sip out of his flask and didn't see the cougar on a bough not five feet above him."

"There was no cat," Webster insisted, contempt heavy in his voice.

"The cat had already feasted on his kill and he wasn't hungry. He allowed the sergeant to live. I had my arrow notched to make sure."

"You didn't tell us." The colonel looked greatly displeased.

"Why let you kill a creature behaving as it was made to do? It caused no harm, and it is not the cat you seek." Night Hawk met the colonel's gaze and felt the man's powerful pull.

The man who stood between him and the woman he loved.

"Can you find this killer?" Henry's gaze narrowed but there was respect there, visible even in the darkest shadows of the night.

"I will catch him before dawn breaks over the hills." Night Hawk knew the soldiers doubted him and he could see Webster's growing contempt. He laid his hand on his bow. "On my honor."

The blizzard hit full force, but the icy winds didn't touch him. He'd been trained for this as a boy and he'd completed his vision quest before his thirteenth birthday. A blizzard wouldn't stop him from bringing in the animal. Nor could these men.

Disgusted they would not help, he spun Shadow toward the trees. "Fine. Have your doubts."

"It can't be done, Colonel," Webster guffawed.

Night Hawk had heard insults before and kept riding. He had nothing to prove to the too-proud fort tracker who couldn't distinguish between a male and a female paw print. He did not need these men to bring in the killer. He would do it on his own with the skills his grandfather had taught him.

Skills to first serve his clan. And now to serve his new community.

"Night Hawk." The colonel's gelding labored to plow through the drifting snow. "I've relieved my soldiers for the night. Sent them back to the barracks for a warm meal and some sleep. There are a few of us who would like to join you.''

Night Hawk looked past the colonel to where three other mounted men sat proudly on horseback, as determined as he. ''Fine. But this is not a military mission, Henry. I will not take orders.''

''I won't issue them.'' Deep fatigue lined the colonel's face, but his spirit would not be bowed. ''This is Linwood, my junior tracker. He's eager to learn anything you want to show him tonight. Especially since our efforts have failed.''

''I would be glad to teach him what I can.'' Night Hawk nodded to the soft-faced lieutenant. Though he couldn't be more than eighteen, there was a man's respect in his gaze and he deserved the same. ''Linwood, stay with me. I hope you men are ready for a hard ride. We have a great distance to cover.''

''I should have come to you and asked for your help, Night Hawk,'' Henry said sincerely in front of the men.

It felt good to be counted. Good to make a difference.

Night Hawk sent Shadow deep into the heart of the forest.

Marie heard Night Hawk's voice, nothing but a low rumble through the thin stable walls. He was back safe! The worry she'd harbored all through the night faded like shadows at dawn.

Kammeo complained with a low nicker and butted her hand. Marie couldn't help it—she laughed and pulled the last peppermint piece from her pocket.

"Spoiled, that's what you are. Come on, let's go see Night Hawk."

Kammeo tossed her head as if in agreement. Or maybe she was demanding more peppermint. Either way, she came willingly out of the stall. Night Hawk's voice grew fainter and then Marie heard nothing at all.

She rounded the last corner and there, brushed by new snow and daylight, stood Henry just inside the stable's double doors, handing over his gelding to a stable boy. "Papa. Where's Night Hawk?"

"Said he had to hurry home and look after his livestock." Henry swept the snow-caked hat from his head and raked his hand through thinning gray locks. "Heard he came looking for me last night. Good thing, too. We caught that cat about an hour before dawn. The tough old tom tried to jump us, but Night Hawk stopped him with an arrow through the heart. Before the rest of us could even aim our muskets, the cougar was on the ground."

Pride filled her. Her Night Hawk had done that. "You mean the cougar could have killed you?"

"Night Hawk saved us. It was something watching him in the forest. He knew how to flush out that cat, and there's not an ounce of boastfulness in the man. It was a pleasure working with him."

Could she be hearing him right? "Papa, I can't believe it. You're actually praising a man who isn't a West Point graduate."

"Getting soft in my old age, that's all." Henry dusted the snow from his shoulders.

"Next, I'll have to convince you that a man like Night Hawk could make a fine husband." She couldn't believe she'd been so bold. Her heart skipped five beats. Maybe six.

The lines carved deep around Henry's eyes appeared deeper. "I don't think that's something to joke about."

"Maybe I'm not joking—"

"Marie Janelle! How you test me!" Henry exploded, his face flushing, his fists clenching. Knowing several lieutenants and stable boys were nearby, he leaned close and lowered his voice, but there was no mistaking the look of steely righteousness in his eyes. "If you even think of allowing a man like that to court you—"

"A man like what? An honorable man? A hardworking man—"

"A man who is not from our social standing."

Marie's stomach balled into a nauseated knot. "Papa, that's not fair. You're from a family without means. You know it's what is inside a person that counts. That's why your policies here have been so successful."

"Public policy is one thing. What concerns my daughter is another." Fury smoldered in his gaze. "I won't have you marrying beneath you, Marie. I've worked too hard."

"Papa, I—"

"Cross me on this, and I will send you back to Ohio on the next coach." Always the colonel, always in charge, he stalked down the aisle, his gait broken, slack-shouldered and uneven. "I mean it, Marie."

Her heart broke watching him walk away, clinging to the past. This was her father, the man who should be the epitome of unconditional love in her life. But when he looked at her, he saw duty. His to her. Hers to him.

Life was about more than duty. Love was more than duty. Or at least, that's what she wanted. What she believed.

Watching her father disappear around the corner, she had to wonder. What is love? Or was she clinging to a foolish ideal, a girlhood dream of romance that could never exist?

"I'll speak with him."

"Ned!" Marie jumped, startled. She'd been lost in her thoughts. "I hear the cougar is caught, so now Papa and the rest of the men can get some sleep."

"Looks to me like the colonel could use more than sleep." Sympathy warmed his gaze. "He has to know by now the two of us aren't going to visit the altar together."

"He won't see. He won't listen. He's so set on having everything his way."

"That's what makes him a good colonel. And maybe not so good a father. I know a little something about that. Let me speak with him. And don't worry."

As she led Kammeo out into the grounds, she was grateful for Ned Gerard's understanding. Maybe he could make Henry see reason.

What if he made good on his threat? Henry ran the fort. He had final authority over the school his soldiers built. He could send her back to Ohio and away from Night Hawk.

She hopped onto Kammeo's back and guided the mare down the snowy path through the grounds. She had to get away. If only she knew where to find the answers. If only she had someone she could trust.

Kammeo shot through the gates and kicked up snow as they headed down the lonely road. Cloaked in white, the black limbs of the trees reached over the lane like arms raised in joy, but she couldn't enjoy the beauty of the morning. The cold wind burned her face and forced tears from her eyes.

The mantle of snow transformed Night Hawk's property from magical to mystical. It looked as if heaven had touched earth at this exact spot.

"You shouldn't be here, Marie." Night Hawk stalked from the stable, his face a stony mask. There was no telling what he thought. She thought of him last night in the dark and how she'd desperately hoped—

Something squawked, a sharp intelligent cry. A hawk, blue feathers bright against the stark white world, hopped on Night Hawk's gloved left hand. One wing hung useless at its side as the creature cocked his head, looking at her.

"As you can see, he's doing better." He turned away, as if they were strangers. As if they hadn't shared tender intimacies.

"Wait." She slipped off Kammeo's back.

Night Hawk acted as if he hadn't heard her. Tall, proud, shoulders unbowed by hardship and heartache, he strode through the double doors and out of sight in the dark interior.

The hawk cried, and his low voice answered, soothing.

"I heard you brought down the cougar with a single

arrow." Marie dared to follow. "You saved the settlers from a terrible threat."

"Go home, Marie." He said the words kindly.

That only made them hurt more. It took all the strength she had to step closer when the fear in her heart screamed at her to run away. "The settlement's children might not be grateful to you. School was canceled last week because the cougar became so bold, and now vacation is over."

Was that a twinkle of amusement in Night Hawk's eyes?

"And think of poor Webster, shown up by a civilian. His pride may never recover."

Had Night Hawk's mouth twitched in the left corner, as if he fought against a smile?

Encouraged, she waited by the table, the bird's nest between them. "Papa actually paid you a compliment."

"Me?"

"Shocking, I know. He was impressed with your skills. And combined with the fact that you saved his life, he likes you."

"Not as a suitor for his daughter." He laid a small fillet of smoked meat in the nest and the hawk dove at it hungrily. "There is nothing new to say, Marie."

"Yes, there is." She reached out, but he moved back.

"You would give up too much being with me." He ran one gloved finger across the crown of the hawk's head, then headed for the door.

She took a steadying breath, not sure at all how she was going to do this. *Just tell him.* She didn't want to think about her failings. About the way she'd run from him in the meadow when he'd only been doing the right thing.

She wouldn't run. Not this time. ''I owe you an apology. I thought that you'd rejected me. That because I wouldn't tell my father, then that meant I didn't love you.''

A muscle pulsed along his jaw and he swung away from her into the wintry whiteness. ''You are ashamed.''

''I failed you.'' She couldn't lie. ''I've never felt this way about anyone, and it's frightening. You are my heart. It's scary to love someone this much.''

''No more. I cannot listen.'' The right thing to do was to walk away. To make sure nothing remained between him and the colonel's daughter. But the honesty of her words left him reeling.

Her touch to his shoulder set him on fire.

''I have to know something. Please, just tell me the truth.'' She paused, and only the quiet whisper of falling snow filled the charged silence between them. ''I've been struggling all my life to earn my father's love. I can't spend the rest of my life doing that for you.''

''Are you saying that's what I've done?''

''No. But I'm afraid you will.'' The sadness in her voice broke his heart. ''I'm afraid that's what happened between us.''

''Marie, that's not why I haven't wanted to be with you.''

''Then what could it be?''

The truth weighed heavy as a stone on his chest.

"You have a chance to marry a man who has more than a barely profitable farm and a herd of horses. I may not be the man you want to be with."

Pain clouded her eyes, but it was anger that drove her forward and made her hand fist. "You truly think I'm ashamed of you."

"I think you cannot tell your father because you know I'm right."

"You're just as bad as Papa is!" She grabbed his arm and pushed hard, knocking him back a few steps so she could march by. Snow flew from her heels and her breath rose in great billowing clouds.

"I can't believe this. After all we—" She grabbed Kammeo's mane and mounted with one swift leap. "You don't even know me. Or you'd know that I could never be ashamed of the most amazing man I've ever met. The one I wanted to marry. To father my children. To grow old with."

Night Hawk stared in amazement. He'd never seen a woman so furious.

"Too bad my one true love is a stupid jackass." Marie spun Kammeo around on her haunches and sent the mare flying across the snow-covered meadow.

What did he do now? Feeling as though he'd been struck by a summer tornado, he whistled to Shadow and leaped onto the tired stallion's back. They'd been without sleep through the long night, but the valiant horse managed to catch up with Kammeo on the road to the fort.

"Marie, I'm sorry." He called out the words so she could hear them above her galloping horse.

''Tell that to the next woman you make fall in love with you.''

Her words cut like a tomahawk. ''I want only you, *shaylee*.''

''Don't call me that. Not ever again.'' She pressed Kammeo harder.

The fort loomed in plain sight, guarded by soldiers. He hesitated, not wanting to damage Marie's reputation by having others witness an obvious lover's quarrel. Yet his heart broke watching her go, long wavy hair trailing in the winds, shrouded by the mystical beauty of winter.

Snow tumbled harder, and it was the coldest he'd ever felt.

He turned toward home, unable to chase her. To pull her from her horse and into his arms and hold her until she saw reason.

A sharp cry rang overhead, cutting through the thick mantle of falling snow and the forest's reverent silence. Night Hawk's spine tingled. He knew even before he gazed upward into the dizzying snow what he would see.

The dark majestic wings of a hawk soared overhead, circling patiently through the storm. Although the flakes buffeted it, the great bird glided with amazing ease as if it were more spirit than animal.

Not his spirit guide, but his father's. The knowledge left him trembling as the gray hawk circled again. What had he told Marie? *My father would never have allowed me to marry you.* Gray Hawk was a fair and a compassionate man but had he lived, he would have refused Marie as a daughter-in-law.

Was that why the hawk circled overhead, calling out to him? To tell him to find a woman who would not have to give up privilege, a comfortable life and her father in order to marry him?

The great bird made one final revolution. Instead of circling again, the magnificent hawk headed straight toward the fort and disappeared behind the tall watchtower.

Night Hawk shivered as the icy wind buffeted him. He waited and watched, but there was no sign of the bird. It was as if it had vanished into the clouds, a spirit guide after all.

Maybe Marie was his destiny. Maybe the hawk had come to tell him that a man should never turn away his *kammeo*. But he should be like a warrior of the honorable Hawk clan and fight.

What did he think she wanted? Another man? What other man? She had been turning down beaus and her father's top choices for the past five years. For what? To have a quick affair as an act of rebellion?

That's what *he* thought—that man who needed a swift smack upside the head with a stick. A *big* stick.

Marie's stomach churned as she stepped into a fresh pair of crinolines. Oh, she knew what his problem was. And he was trying to blame her for his shortcomings.

A thousand gentle memories threatened to break apart her tirade, but Marie was strong. She wouldn't let the images of him tending the wounded hawk or the tenderness of his lovemaking sway her from her path. She was angry, and she intended to stay that way. Come hell or high water.

"Marie Janelle, you're taking too darn long." Henry was clinging to his anger at her, too. "Our dinner guests are going to be here any minute."

"I don't think you want me to greet them in my undergarments."

His curse was drowned out by a loud knocking on the front door.

Henry didn't need to worry about firing her from the school and sending her away. Because she was never going to see *that man* again. The one who drove her completely insane. The one who made her more angry than she'd been in her entire life. *Ever.*

Her stomach twisted with a faint sickness, and she steadied herself against the bed. When she saw herself in the beveled mirror, she looked pale.

It just went to show how much *that man* had upset her. Between him and her father, she'd been half-ill all day. Not even an afternoon nap had helped.

Voices rumbled through the floorboards, merry and congenial. The last thing she felt like was having more people at the supper table, but Henry loved to entertain.

She selected a gown she knew her father despised, a gray damask that set off her dark hair and eyes, with touches of light blue. It was a spinster's dress, he'd told her the first time she'd worn it to supper.

Good. Being a spinster sounded just fine to her.

Finally ready, she headed down the stairs. Voices rose to a near crescendo, and it sounded as if more people were arriving. What was Henry doing? Throwing a full-fledged supper party to celebrate the cougar's capture?

It wasn't as if he'd invite Night Hawk to supper. At least there was one bright spot. She'd never have to see Night Hawk again. *Ever.*

Marie rounded the corner and descended the last steps. Mrs. Olstad rushed past, efficiently distributing steaming cups from the gleaming silver tray she carried. The din of too many voices, the competing scents of eggnog, whiskey, wood smoke and perfume assaulted her. She wanted to head back upstairs and hide in her quiet room.

The door breezed open, admitting more revelers, and the party silenced. The cold breeze enveloped her, and Marie turned to see a man dressed in a black jacket and trousers like any of the guests. Except there was something different about him—something proud and noble.

Night Hawk. Marie's knees buckled and she sat on the bottom step. The silence in the room grew thick and uncomfortable, then Henry wove through the crowd, hand outstretched.

"Night Hawk. Welcome. This is the hero of last night's expedition. The man who saved my life and countless others. This supper is in his honor."

Applause broke out, but Night Hawk appeared indifferent. He shook Henry's hand and accepted a cup of eggnog. Others crowded around him, asking him questions about the hunt. The colonel stood at the warrior's side, like two old army buddies.

Papa likes him. The anger within her shattered, leaving her trembling. What lay beneath the anger frightened her more.

What if Henry could learn to accept Night Hawk as

a son-in-law? Then nothing stood in the way of their love but her pride and his scarred heart.

The last thing she wanted to do was to spend the rest of her life trying to earn another man's love—not even Night Hawk's.

Chapter Twelve

She wouldn't look at him all through the meal. Night Hawk thought of nothing else as the officers and their wives spoke of the cougar, of the injured settlers now recovering, and the upcoming Christmas holiday.

She's still furious. It didn't show, but Night Hawk could tell by the way her soft mouth narrowed whenever he spoke to someone else. Regret filled him. He should have measured his words more carefully. Memories from his boyhood returned as he cut the steak on his plate and gave his opinion on the recurrent problem with wildlife. Like ghosts in this fine room, he could see the past as clearly as the present.

Father with his patient respect for Mother. Of his care for her. Of a tender regard that even a boy could notice and remember decades later. How Father said a man's words were something he could never take back. Once said, they could be forgiven. They could never be forgotten.

Shame filled him. He'd spoken out of hurt and jealousy. Looking at her beauty, feeling every piece of his soul cry out in joy at her presence had frightened him.

Made him realize that loving this woman rendered him more vulnerable than he'd ever been.

When the meal was over, he saw his opportunity. The men gathered in the parlor for brandy, and Marie headed through the kitchen while the housekeeper poured coffee for the women.

The back door closed just as he stepped into the kitchen. Was she still so angry that she'd rather face the bitter night air than him?

She froze, as if by not moving he wouldn't spot her there by the garden bench beneath the reaching boughs of the old sugar maple. The man in him heated at the sight of her softly rounded shape. Too well, he knew how she would feel lying beneath him. The warrior in him saw all that was at risk.

"I see you, Marie." He took bold steps toward her. "You can't hide from me here like you could among all those people."

"I'm not hiding. I just needed some fresh air." She seemed as cold as the night when she faced him. "Some of Papa's supper guests make me uncomfortable."

"Like me?"

"Yes." She looked him straight in the eye with a woman's fury, but her lower lip trembled.

"*Shaylee.*" He ached to hold her.

"I told you not to call me that." Not angry, but hurting.

"But you are the only star in my heavens. My life is dark without your love." He cupped the side of her face with his hand. "How good it is to touch you again. I want nothing more than to hold you forever."

"And what about what I want?" Her lower lip trembled again, and her eyes were big and filled with pain. "Maybe I don't want to live always waiting for you to doubt me."

"You take this too far, Marie. All I worry about is that you are ashamed of me."

"You would think that of me?" She pushed past him, breaking away, and his hand burned where they'd touched. A great fire flamed within him and he stalked after her, hunter and quarry. She reached to open the back door, but he pulled her against him. He trapped her between the log wall and his chest and left her no way to escape.

"You drive me crazy, woman." He kissed her hard and deep. How good it was to taste her again. To feel the lush texture of her lips caressing his. Their breaths mingled, their tongues met and plunged and danced. He scraped his teeth along the sensitive curve of her bottom lip and delighted in her moan of pleasure.

"I don't want you to kiss me," she told him sincerely, and caught his lip between hers and sucked. Her hands circled his back and held him to her, hip to hip, his shaft trapped between them.

"I don't want you to kiss me." His fingers fluttered over the peaks of her breasts, and he groaned aloud when her hand closed over his erection. Her touch through the layers of clothes was nearly enough to undo him.

Whatever it took, he would win her heart, body and soul. He wouldn't stop until there was no doubt, no fear and no opposition between them.

She was his missing half, and he would never be whole without her.

"Night Hawk, I'd love you to come take a look at one of the fort's horses for me." As the evening came to an end, Henry pulled Night Hawk aside at the door. "It's late, and if you'd rather come back in the morning, I'd understand. But the truth is I've got a mare ready to foal and I don't trust the man in charge."

"Then you should fire him. For that you do not need my help."

"True, but I'd still like you to take a look at the mare. I just received word from one of my stable boys that it's her time." Henry waved goodbye to the Websters and then tugged Night Hawk deeper into the parlor. "The lad you recommended I hire, Winter Thunder, is a good worker. I know he's been the one to ask when a horse requires special care."

"Winter Thunder is the son of my friend, a Winnebago. You fired him last week."

"My captain of horses did, I'm afraid." Henry led the way through the kitchen.

The moment Night Hawk strode through the threshold, a plate clattered to the floor and shattered. Marie stared at him across the length of the cozy room, eyes wide and a dish towel dangling from one hand. She wasn't looking at the shattered china at her feet but at him.

He wanted her. With every breath he took and every beat of his heart. How on earth was he going to make her his? She wore a dress more expensive than every penny he'd spent on the building of his house. Her shoes cost more than a fine saddle.

Wealth and privilege surrounded her, and it wasn't limited to the parlor where only guests could see and be impressed. No, it was here in the kitchen where crystal glittered in the lamplight and polished silver sparkled on the shelves.

"Let me help you." He spotted the broom in the corner and grabbed it.

Marie's hand curled around the handle. "You're a guest."

"I'm no guest." He said it low, so the snoopy-looking housekeeper couldn't hear, and he watched Marie's eyes dilate.

So, she was remembering their kiss. *Good.* This close to her, he could see the long graceful curl of each individual eyelash. He wanted to lean close and kiss her there, then claim her mouth with his.

That's all he had to do to brand Marie as his. Let Henry Lafayette toss him out of the house or make war on his land. The driving, pressing pulse within him was more than lust, and his love for Marie would not be short-lived.

But she yanked the broom from his grip, surprisingly strong for a lady gently raised, and gave him a look that said it all—*Leave or I'll hit you with this.*

Maybe his kiss hadn't worked enough magic, but the next one would.

Marie pushed open the stable door just enough to slip inside, anticipating the peaceful darkness. Emotions jumbled inside her, and all of them were painful. Night Hawk's kiss still tingled on her lips.

What should she do? She never wanted to see him again; she *had* to see him again. The need to feel the weight of his hard male body over hers drove her mad as she hurried down the dark aisle. It took her a full minute to realize the barn wasn't as dark as usual or as quiet.

She wasn't alone.

The candy in her pocket chinked together in counterrhythm to her gait. Kammeo leaned over the top rail of her stall and nickered a welcome. Marie dug out the peppermint absently. The mare crunched contentedly as the voices in the back of the stable swelled angrily.

One voice drew her—Night Hawk's. Then her father's brawling baritone ended in silence. Marie was too far away to make out more than a mumble. Were Henry and Night Hawk arguing?

Had Night Hawk told her father the truth? What if Papa sent her away? Fear bolted through her as she tore down the dark aisle.

She heard a loud sound like wood striking wood and a different man's curse.

"Damn it, Colonel, I know what I'm doing," the third voice spat. "I don't need no Indian in my stable telling me what to do."

"This man has the skill to save the mare."

Marie peered around the corner. Henry stood with his back to her, proud and commanding. Night Hawk knelt in the shadows of the large foaling stall, where a mare thrashed with terror.

"Colonel," Night Hawk said quietly. "I need this man out of the stall. He's frightening her."

"She's just being stubborn, that's all. Making a big fuss out of nothing." The stable master, a stick-thin captain with a hard face, snapped a riding crop at the mare's flank.

Night Hawk caught the strap before it could strike. The slap against his palm reverberated in the rafters, but no pain registered on his granite face. "Out. Before I take you out myself."

"Get out of here, Hooper," Henry barked.

The lesser officer grumbled but released the riding crop and climbed through the wooden rails. "No-good horse if you asks me. Won't be alive by morning anyhow."

Night Hawk tossed the riding crop down, letting the man's viciousness roll off him. He was quiet, his touch and voice a comfort the panicked mare understood. The horse made one final turn around the pen, then stopped before the man who commanded her. Her skin snapped, wave after wave of nervous ripples. She sidestepped, and Marie saw the splash of blood along her flanks where she'd been struck.

The mare was in labor. How could anyone strike her? The poor animal looked to Night Hawk for reassurance. She sidestepped again, fighting to stand, flicking her tail and whinnying.

Night Hawk's confidence, as quiet as the wintry night, changed the atmosphere in the entire stable. Tension melted away and the mare calmed. She lowered her head and leaned against his chest, trusting.

"She's fighting to stay up." Henry sounded worried. "She's a damn fine saddle horse and I'd hate to have anything happen to her."

"She's young and this is her first foal. She's frightened." Night Hawk laid his hands on her heaving sides. "You should have had someone come for me earlier, Henry. We'll do our best and pray that she is strong enough."

Brushed by lantern light and half-hidden by shadow, Night Hawk walked the mare and soothed her until finally she collapsed onto the fresh bed of straw he'd made for her. She fought, her legs thrashing dangerously. Night Hawk's touch was like enchantment, and the mare allowed him to hobble her.

Marie remained crouched in the aisle against the wall as the hours passed. As the mare's sharp neighs rang through the growing silence. It was as if the entire night held its breath waiting for birth or death.

Marie had never seen anything like Night Hawk's patience. He stroked the mare's flank in endless comfort. As the hours passed, the tenderness in his voice never wavered. The mare's pain increased as she thrashed and kicked her hobbled legs. Bright blood gleamed in the flickering light.

As the mare released a shuddering breath and the first gray light of dawn spilled through the slatted boards, Night Hawk pulled a foal's wet pair of hooves and nose into view.

He tore the sack, his voice changing as he greeted the new life. The mare didn't move, and Marie wept. Seconds ticked by as Night Hawk brought the foal into the world with the strength in his powerful arms. It was his kindness that made the foal collapse trustingly on Night Hawk's knee. The mare stirred and gently nuzzled her new baby.

"You saved them both." Henry spoke from the shadows.

"No. She's a fighter." Night Hawk stroked his hands over the foal's beautiful head.

Never had she seen anything as amazing as this one man.

The winter sun fought the thin layer of clouds that occasionally shifted fine snow onto the land. No wind blew, and the earth felt still, as if asleep. The great silence of the forest spoke to him and reminded him that there was a cycle to life. Birth and death, winter and spring, and there was awe in both.

He felt good. Exhausted, but good. When he'd left the stable, the dam and foal were both healthy and feeding. The colonel had complimented him again and invited him to his fine house for supper.

Marie had been absent and, while that troubled him, he had enjoyed talking with the colonel. Feeling the man's renewed respect for him felt like a victory.

He'd known the man was a fine colonel and his far-thinking policies had brought harmony to this land. But sitting at a man's table and being treated like an equal was a different thing entirely. He harbored a new, deeper respect for the colonel.

He spotted the tracks leaving the main road onto the forest path. Only one person he knew rode his shortcut along the lakeshore.

Marie. Hope beat within him as he followed Kammeo's hoofprints through the ancient forest to the clearing where weak sun shimmered on the snow like stars fallen to earth. It hurt his eyes to look into the brightness, but he was rewarded by the sight of a flaming red mare racing back and forth along the shore.

A swirl of gray and blue caught his gaze. Marie ran and slid on the thick ice. Her scarf fringe and her wavy dark brown hair danced behind her as she twirled. Her merry laughter trilled as sweet as a goldfinch's song and warmed him like nothing else could on this frigid morning.

"Night Hawk!" She spun breathlessly, her cheeks rosy from the cold. "I didn't hear you."

"Shadow and I tiptoed through the snow." He almost laughed when she did. Why did simply looking at this woman fill him with joy? "A lot of women would be afraid of falling through the ice."

"The stable boy told me he and a friend had been out ice fishing, so I figured it was safe." Her feet flew out from under her and she crashed to the ice, spinning on her backside. She laughed again. "I was waiting for you. Come, help me up."

"No." He dismounted. "I see that sparkle in your eye. You want to pull me down with you."

"Never." She laughed when he stepped onto the ice. She held out her hands, and the moment they touched, longing speared through him. How sweet she felt. How passionate.

She came into his arms as if they'd never parted. Many obstacles stood between them, but he no longer cared. He'd found his heaven, and he was never going to let her go. Their kiss was magic, like winter wind and passion. He drew her hard against him and drank of her. She opened to him, heated velvet and desire, and he couldn't get enough.

He broke away breathlessly, wanting to love her with every tenderness he knew.

She smiled at him, teasing lighting her up. She dashed off, slipping and sliding on the dazzling ice. "Bet you can't catch me."

"Beware. Warriors of the Hawk clan are swift of foot." He took off after her, his winter moccasins gripping the ice. The specially tanned buckskin gave him an advantage over her fancy boots and he outpaced her easily.

"Hey, that's not fair! Your legs are longer." Laughing, she grabbed his arm and they went down together, spinning freely. He cushioned her fall with his body, pulling her between his thighs as they whirled to a stop.

He pulled her across his chest. How good it felt to be with her! Kissing her tenderly, he held back the pounding drive to love her intimately. To make her his once again.

"I saw you in the stable last night." He brushed dark locks from her face. "You could have come closer. It must have been cold there in the draft near the door."

"Papa would have sent me back to the house." Her chin lifted, pure fight and determination and all woman. "He doesn't believe the young lady he's raised me to be should see the real side of life."

"Maybe he feared frightening you."

"It was beautiful. The struggle of birth." She leaned her cheek against his chest and hugged him tight. "It made me think about a lot of things. About how fragile life is. How easily lost. And the beauty that can be made from love."

"I doubt the stallion had love on his mind, *shaylee*." He kissed her brow, knowing full well what she meant but could not say. The truth was too intimate, and he let himself think of what it would be to make a child with her. To watch her grow round with their baby. What a gift that would be, one they gave to each other.

"I have to get back," she apologized, holding on to him more tightly. "Papa has a thousand things for us to do for the Winter Ball. I told him I didn't know a fort on the frontier could have a ball. I thought those were reserved for fancy mansions farther east, but he scowled at me. He doesn't always have the best sense of humor."

"No, but he is a fine man. And he wants to display his beautiful daughter in front of the best in the countryside." He kissed her once, twice. "I do not blame him."

"Will you come?"

Her face filled with longing. How could he say no? "You would dance with me in front of everyone?"

"All night long." She took his hand and allowed him to help her to her feet. She wobbled a little.

He pulled her to his chest. "Are you all right?"

"Just dizzy." She rubbed her brow. "I guess I twirled too much."

"Then I should see you home."

"Whose home? Mine or yours?"

"Which do you want it to be?"

"Yours, Night Hawk." She didn't know what the future held for them, but one thing was certain. No man could drive her to such heights of joy and to such depths of confusion as this warrior who stood before her.

It didn't matter what happened next, whether he could believe in her love or not. If their love ended with the winter or lasted forever. All that mattered was this moment and this man.

His grip on her elbow held her steady as she stepped onto solid ground.

"You look far too pale, *shaylee*." His kiss grazed her temple. "I will take you to my bed another time. Now you need to rest alone in yours."

"I'm fine."

"You're not." He lifted her onto Kammeo's back. "Should I ride behind you?"

"Yes." Not because she was so dizzy, but because she wanted him against her.

Heaven couldn't feel this good, she decided, as he settled behind her. The glory of his hard chest, the luxury of his steely arms, the cradling strength of his thighs thrilled her.

She only felt dizzier as he kissed her hair. Don't think about the future, she told herself. Sunlight glimmered like a thousand diamonds in the meadow and lit up the snow-heavy trees in the forest.

But the brightness felt dark next to the brilliance of love in her heart.

"Are you still feeling sickly, Marie?" Henry hesitated in the parlor, dressed in his best black suit. "You look as pale as a sheet.''

"I'm starting to feel better," she lied as she slipped into her warmest winter coat.

She'd been fighting on and off a light case of the grippe since final examinations, when all her students were either sniffling or queasy. "I'm not used to these bitter winds, I guess."

"Then you should try staying out of them and off that half-wild horse of yours," Henry scolded, but his heart wasn't in it, not tonight. "Is my beautiful escort to tonight's ball ready?"

"Oh, Papa." She grabbed her fur muff from the coat tree. "Don't try to charm me. It's not going to work."

"But I think you are beautiful." He was looking like a proud father again, and she couldn't despise him for it.

"Compliment me all you want," she warned, not fooled and delighted at the same time. "I'm not dancing with Major Gerard, so stop your scheming."

"I'm just eager to be a grandpapa, that's all." He opened the door for her. "You can't blame a man for that."

"I can."

The biting wind knifed through her clothes and she was shivering by the time she made it to the bottom step. Ice sheened the path and she was grateful when Henry offered his arm. Her party shoes weren't made for winter walking.

The enormous log building that usually served as the soldiers' dining quarters lit up the night. Boughs of holly and fir encircled the posts at the front, and candles flickered against the dark snow to light the path to the door.

Inside the hall smelled like hot cider and eggnog, evergreen and cigars, and a handful of soldiers sang carols to accompanying string and brass players, not quite in tune.

"Colonel!" Ned met them with two fresh cups of eggnog. "Marie, why don't you come with me? I'd wager half my month's paycheck that your father is going to push us together anyway."

"I hate to encourage him, Ned."

"Go on, Marie. You two kids have some fun." Henry gave a little wink. "The band's starting a new song just right for dancing."

Marie earned a warning look from Henry, and she laughed. She let the major lead her away. "You're only making matters worse, Ned. Look at him grinning from ear to ear."

"He'll figure it out soon enough." Ned led her to a table where his jacket hung over the back of one chair, and pulled out a second chair for her. "I tried to argue with him, but he issued an order. I have to look after you tonight."

"But you're not on duty."

"You know the colonel." Ned didn't seem upset about it as he helped her settle into her chair. "I decided not to argue because I could use some help."

"With what? Name it."

"With her." Ned gestured subtly to the left through the crowd.

Marie saw a young woman seated with the Meyers

family. One of her students, little Gretta Meyers was talking earnestly to the pretty blond stranger. "I don't know who she is, but I bet you do."

A rogue's smile changed Ned's good looks to something breathtaking. "Her name is Claudia Heintzelman, and she's Claus Meyers's sister."

"Married sister?"

"Widowed sister come to live with him." Ned nodded once, as if he were sure, gazing at the fragile woman, that he'd found his heart. "I can't go up there and introduce myself. She'll reject me."

Realization dawned. "You want me to talk her into dancing with you."

"It's a start." Longing showed on his face.

Marie knew what that felt like. "Fine. Come with me and I'll see what I can do."

"I'd owe you my future happiness." He stood, holding out his arm.

Night Hawk felt many curious gazes as he entered the hall. The melody and harmony of the music warred with the sharp din of conversations. Everyone had turned out in their best, from uniformed officers to modestly dressed farmers and their wives.

He was late. His gaze found her immediately amid the sea of people. She wore a shimmering red gown that sparkled almost as much as she did. Laughter touched her face as she whirled in the arms of an army officer he didn't know. Jewels glimmered at the base of her slender throat, but her beauty shone more precious than those rare gems. Her beauty came from within and nothing he'd seen in his life could compare.

He was at her side before he realized it, taking her hand from the young sergeant's and pulling her into his arms. She came to him like spring on the wind, quietly, radiantly, and snuggled against him.

They moved together to the white man's music, a rise and fall of slow concordant notes. Not the joyful rhythm of his people's music, but this had its advantages. Holding Marie so tightly in public, smelling the wildflowers in her hair and feeling her breasts against his chest made him proud.

He wanted to shout the truth of their love loud enough for the entire world to know, for it to ring in the air and the wind and across the hills. But she clung to him tightly as if to say, *Never let go.*

He wouldn't. Life came with few certainties, and he'd come here tonight to let her know. Time was slipping away each day. Time that belonged to them.

Chapter Thirteen

Night Hawk woke to the new day long before dawn came. The memory of holding Marie in his arms lingered. How proud he'd been dancing with her last night. Others had cut in wanting to hold her, and he'd always taken her back. She was his heart, and he would fight for her always.

As Night Hawk forked hay into the rows of stalls, he missed his father more than ever. He needed his advice and guidance. How do I prepare for a wife, he would ask his father if he were here.

Build her a lodge. He could almost hear the answer on the wind. Build her a lodge in the way of our people.

Maybe it would be a fine log house, the best he could make, but it would be in the old tradition. Meant not to show wealth but to provide a home for his wife and later his children. A place for happiness and love.

Yes, that is where he would start. Determined, he grabbed his best ax and headed into the forest.

Marie woke late feeling exhausted. She'd danced into the early hours of morning in Night Hawk's arms, and part of her was still soaring. The other part of her couldn't get out of bed.

The floor creaked in the hallway. She heard Henry's heavy gait on the stairs.

Henry wasn't one to tolerate sleeping in. Marie dragged herself out of bed and grabbed her housecoat. Getting dressed felt like too much effort. Maybe she'd feel better after a cup of coffee and toast.

The floor tilted under her feet, and she held the banister tight all the way down the stairs.

"Marie, you look pale. I know you arrived home terribly late last night." Henry sounded disapproving. "I ought to speak to Ned, but I'm sure you two had a good time—"

"Papa, I don't want to talk about Ned." Her stomach clamped hard. She wasn't feeling well. Not at all. She raced through the kitchen and out the door.

"Marie? Are you all right?" The privy door rattled as Henry pounded on it.

What was Henry doing? Standing there listening to her wretch? Head pounding, she leaned her forehead against her crossed arms in misery. "Go back inside. It's cold out here. You'll freeze to death waiting for me."

"I'm going to make Ned pay for letting my daughter stay out so late. You've caught the grippe that's going around, haven't you?" Papa sounded furious. "Let me in, Marie."

"I locked the door. That means I don't want you here."

"You've been in there for half an hour." Anger boomed as he banged on the wood panels, and the entire structure shook.

Another wave of nausea ripped through her abdomen. Her body shook uncontrollably.

She vomited again and then endured the dry heaves racking her body over and over. Finally, weak and exhausted, she collapsed against the wall.

"I'm getting the doctor, Marie." He sounded in anguish now.

"I'm coming out." Somehow, she made her legs obey her. She unlatched the door and tumbled into her father's strong arms.

"There now," he said awkwardly, doing his best. "We'll get you lying down. You'll feel better soon."

If only the ground would stop moving. She managed to stumble into the house. She had to grab the banister while her father held her steady. She'd never been so grateful to see her bed. She lay down on the cool sheets and the room stopped spinning.

"There, now. I'll have Mrs. Olstad send for the doctor." Henry drew a chair to her bedside. "Maybe I'll let Ned know you're ill. He could bring you a gift, a token of his affection."

Marie couldn't believe it. "Ned's not going to marry me."

"Why the hell not? Isn't my daughter fine enough for him?"

If she wasn't feeling ill, she would have laughed. "He's in love with someone else, I think. Or he's going to be."

"Why did you have to frighten him off, Marie?"

Henry pulled the covers to her chin. "I really liked Ned. I wanted him to be the one."

"There will be one. I promise."

"I'll hold you to that."

A warm feeling filled her, a sweet feeling of being protected. It was a feeling she'd never known before. Tears of gratitude burned in her eyes.

Night Hawk heard the clink of a heavily shod horse against the icy ground. He reined the team of work-horses toward the house, checking to make sure the chains held. The heavy logs they dragged gouged great tracks in the new snow. Meka dashed out of the forest, barking, and sat politely when ordered.

"It's not Marie," he told the dog, who appeared disappointed. "It's her father."

Henry broke through the woods mounted on his powerful gelding. Today he wore heavy layers of wool and waved a gloved hand at the debarked logs piled high near the side of the small cabin. "Looks like you're building on."

"Thought I might think of marrying someday. A wife might appreciate more than a three-room house."

"Good thinking." Henry nodded in approval. "That's why I insist on roomy houses for my married officers. Not that everyone accepts my philosophy, but if you keep the wife feeling content with her surroundings, then there's little reason for discord."

Night Hawk felt a wave of sadness for the colonel. For all his career success, he had very little personal happiness. "Keeping a wife happy is important."

"You're sensible, Night Hawk. But take my Marie

for instance. She's used to genteel living. After her mother died, she lived with her aunt, who was a real lady. Marie is used to a comfortable life, and what does she want? Instead of wanting a husband who can better her life, she spends half her time riding that horse you sold her.''

"She's young, Henry. There's nothing wrong with riding a horse.''

"Astride! I'm lucky no one has complained about it.'' Troubled, as if it mattered how Marie's reputation would reflect on him, Henry scowled.

Night Hawk wasn't fooled. He sensed Henry's great love for his daughter, one he hid carefully behind bluster and formality. What good was a love that never saw the light of day? "Let her have her fun, Henry. She will settle down soon enough.''

"She danced with Ned half the night at the ball, so there's hope. And you for the other half. I'm indebted to you again. You kept groping soldiers from taking a spin with her.''

"Groping?'' Night Hawk strangled on the irony. *He'd* been the one doing everything he could to keep his hands from roaming over Marie's delectable curves. Curves he knew well by memory.

"I remember what it's like to be a young man. I run a good fort and my soldiers are disciplined, but the toughest self-control can be destroyed by a pretty woman's smile.''

"You're worried because you want a better life for Marie.''

"That's right. A father's burden. When you finish

your house and find a woman, you'll know what I mean soon enough.''

The truth was urgent on his tongue, and Night Hawk almost told Henry. Almost asked for his daughter's hand right there on this humble land with only the most modest life to offer Marie.

He held back. There was too much at stake.

Henry leaned against the top rail of the corral measuring the unbroken filly trotting around the ring. ''I wanted to thank you for helping save the mare the night of my supper party. I'm impressed with your horse skill.''

''My father taught me what he knew. Horses are an important part of my people's culture.''

''Captain Hooper has been reprimanded and demoted, as you know. Captain McGee is young and doesn't know enough about training yet.'' Henry tossed him a sidelong glance. ''What we need is new stock. Well-trained animals instead of the cheap green horses Hooper insisted he could break. Are you interested?''

''To train horses for the fort?''

''I would pay good money.''

''Many of these horses come from my people's herds.'' It seemed wrong, yet a part of him knew that he wanted to make a living one day solely off his herd. ''It wouldn't be right to sell them to the army.''

''I see seven Arabian mares in that corral right there. How many do you have in the stables? Six dozen is my guess. Those are saddle horses to any man, army or Sauk. And money is money, Night Hawk. Good cash.''

"I'll consider it."

"Fine." Pleased, Henry offered his hand and they shook. "I have to head back. Marie's down with a bad case of the grippe, so I don't want to stay away too long."

"Marie is ill?" Alarmed, he tried not to show it.

"Oh, she'll be right as rain in a few days, no doubt. She has to be. The winter term starts soon." Henry snatched the gelding's reins and mounted, settling heavily into the saddle. "Give my offer some thought."

All Night Hawk could think about was Marie. He waved goodbye to the colonel and seethed inside with a hard, biting frustration. He loved the woman. He wanted her in his bed so he could take care of her. How long would it be before he had that right?

Marie's head pounded as she lay flat on the bed. The smallest movement made her stomach twist with violent nausea.

"You're not feverish." Mrs. Olstad set the cup of honeyed tea on the nightstand. "I still want you to drink every drop."

Marie's stomach somersaulted and she moaned.

"I'll leave the basin right here on the floor if you need to be sick." Mrs. Olstad left the room.

She'd never been this wretchedly sick. The steam from the fragrant tea wafted her way, and her stomach clenched. *Just don't move. Go to sleep. This has to get better.*

A sound startled her. The room wasn't spinning yet, but she didn't dare move too quickly. She inched her heavy head on the pillow so that she could see the rest of the room.

A shadow fell across her window. Before her tired eyes could focus, the shadow disappeared. Was someone at her window?

She levered herself up on one elbow. Her stomach complained and her head pounded, the dizziness and nausea were overwhelming as she inched toward the sparkling panes of glass. Something was on her sill. A tiny bird?

She crept the few feet to the window, but the small creature didn't move. No, it wasn't a bird. It was a carving. She eked open the window just far enough. Her fingers closed around cool, textured wood. Trembling, she studied the object she held in her hand. An exquisitely carved hawk the size of a hummingbird.

Every day that she was sick in bed for the next three weeks, Night Hawk left a carving on her windowsill. All were creatures of the forest and each was small, intricate and stunning. The polished wood gleamed with beauty and the handmade detail astounded her.

It was those carvings she thought of now as her stomach threatened rebellion in the middle of the doctor's examination.

"A case of the grippe shouldn't last this long," he said quietly as he rolled down his sleeves. "Maybe it's best if I ask you a few questions. Just in case we've got something else to deal with."

"I've never been sick like this before." Marie struggled to sit up, but her stomach turned. She leaned into her pillows and closed her eyes.

"Does it come and go? Or are you constantly nauseous?" His question was kind.

"It used to be constant, but the last week it comes and goes." She hated lying here. She'd missed the first week of the winter term, and without her the children had no teacher. "Is there something I can take to calm my stomach? I'm getting better, if I can just get past this nausea."

"I'll see what I can do. I have one more question." He cleared his throat, lowering his voice. The door was open, and Henry was out in the hallway. "How many monthlies have you missed?"

Marie blushed. Aunt Gertrude had told her it was something a married woman paid close attention to, so she knew when she was pregnant—

I can't be. Marie covered her face with her hands. Wouldn't she have known? How many had she missed? She'd been so upset arguing with Henry and Night Hawk she hadn't paid attention.

"How many, Marie?" the doctor insisted.

"At least two, maybe three. I'm not always regular." Ice-cold fear crept through every inch of her. *It's the grippe. It has to be. Now isn't the best time—*

"You're pregnant, Marie." The doctor stood and pulled the bedside chair back to its place at her desk, careful not to look at her. "Should I tell your father?"

"Papa? *No!* I'll tell him. I want to be the one to tell him." Marie gripped the edges of the comforter, holding on for dear life. Her head was spinning, her stomach twisting and she couldn't feel anything at all. It seemed as if she were as frozen as the icicles outside her window.

"Fine." The doctor shook his head as if in pity, grabbed his bag and hesitated at the door. "Try sipping a little ginger water. I'm told raspberry tea helps, too. And nibble on some dry bread. It will help with the nausea."

The pity on his face remained, and then he left her alone.

Henry was in the hall. Marie's heart stopped pounding. The doctor would keep his word, wouldn't he? She heard low voices, but she couldn't tell what the men were discussing.

A baby. Could it be true? It seemed unbelievable. Except for the sickness, she didn't feel any different. But she would soon, wouldn't she? The thought of Night Hawk's child growing within her filled her with a strange shivery excitement, one that was both fear *and* joy.

She remembered how Night Hawk had gazed at her with unquestionable love in his eyes the last time they'd made love. Sweetness shifted through her and she hugged herself tight. She was carrying Night Hawk's child!

A rapping sound startled her. She realized Henry was standing in the threshold gazing at her oddly. He no longer looked concerned over her health. He looked weary. More tired than she'd ever seen him. Deep lines gouged his face, drawing his mouth into a sad frown. His eyes drooped, lifeless and cold.

What had the doctor told him? Marie felt her joy ebb with each step Henry took. *He knows.* Terror stripped away all rational thought. "Papa, I need to be alone right now."

"Leaving you alone is what got you into this mess. You're pregnant, aren't you?" He said the word with such distaste that it sounded ugly. Dirty. Bitter.

Hadn't the doctor promised? "Papa, I'm not feeling well enough to fight about this."

"And just whose fault is that?" Anger crept up his neck in a bright red flush and he fisted his hands. "Tell me who did this to you. *Tell me.*"

She met his fierce gaze. Gone was the caring, compassionate father she'd briefly known. This man had a hard, cold heart.

"Tell me, Marie." He grabbed her by the arm and shook her.

She cried out at the burning pain in her arm. "Papa, you're hurting me."

As if shocked with himself, he released her. But the fury didn't ease from his rigid stance or his steely gaze.

"Ned Gerard didn't do this to you. He knows I'd make him pay for this. Pregnant." He spit the word. "How could you do this to me? What were you thinking? That you had to prove me wrong?"

"I didn't fall in love with a man just to spite you." She rubbed her arm where he'd hurt her. How could she make her father understand? "I'm in love, and he's a good person. I want his child more than anything."

Henry's face turned purple and he breathed hard, spinning away to the window. He hauled open the glass and let the icy air wash over him. Snow tumbled through the opening to speckle the floor.

Marie shivered, but it wasn't from the cold wind.

What was he going to do now? Night Hawk by rights should be the first to know. She wished she had climbed out the window and raced Kammeo all the way to the lake. She could be in her lover's arms telling him her news. Imagine the joy that would light his handsome face. She knew exactly how tenderly he would make love to her in his big soft bed in his snug little cabin.

Somehow, she had to go to him. She couldn't stand Henry's fury. He hadn't welcomed the news of this beautiful new life. He'd seen it as an act of rebellion! Worse, he worried how it would reflect on his reputation.

Willing the room to stop spinning, she pushed back the covers and swung her feet over the edge of the mattress.

"Where do you think you're going?" He turned around, and Marie gasped.

She didn't recognize him. The tall, square-shouldered colonel she knew as her father was now stooped. He looked beaten, as if he'd aged ten years.

"Don't you see? I was doing my best for you." He raked at his receding hair, and long shocks slumped forward over his brow, hanging limply in front of his eyes. "I could have given you comfort and class. A husband who was somebody, who would always have taken care of you."

"Maybe I don't want a husband who works all the time and cares only about his next promotion and how he looks to others. Maybe I want to marry a farmer and live in a log cabin surrounded by ancient forests. It's what I want."

"Is that what you think, foolish girl? That life is about getting what you want?" He shook his fist at her. "Fine. There's the door. Go to the man who loves you so much, and see if he wants you now."

"I know he will, Papa. You don't have to worry. Your reputation won't be harmed. No one will know—"

"He won't marry you, you know." Henry sneered, shaking his head as if he thought her the world's greatest fool. "How many times did you lie with him? And he didn't propose once, did he?"

No, her heart answered.

"Did he?" Henry said those words with such relish, as if he knew exactly how to hurt her. She wanted to lash out at him and make him stop. She wanted to shout the words that would defend Night Hawk.

But the truth was, he'd never mentioned marriage. He'd never taken her hand, bent down on one knee and asked her to be his wife.

But he would. She believed it with all her heart. Night Hawk loved her. And this child they'd made was a gift made from that love.

She refused to believe anything else.

"I thought you wanted a grandchild, Papa." She stood on wobbly knees, clinging to her dreams. "Didn't I promise you that one day I would marry? Think of how wonderful this is going to be."

"With a bastard child?"

She tried to forgive him his anger. He was hurt. He was losing his dreams. "No, Papa. I'll marry and the baby will be legitimate and no one will know. You will be a proud grandfather and I'll be happily married to the man I love.''

"You really believe that, don't you?" Henry pulled the chair from the desk and collapsed into it. He leaned his head in his hands like a broken man. "A bastard grandchild. A shamed daughter. How much worse could this be?''

He looked as if he'd lost everything. All the hopes he'd pinned his future on.

This was her father, and while she despised some of the things he'd said, he was still her papa. Still the man she wanted to love her unconditionally. Please understand, she silently pleaded as she padded across the room. Fighting nausea. Battling dizziness.

"You've ruined everything, Marie.''

She knelt beside him and laid her hand on his.

He jerked away from her as if her touch were poison. "You'll pack this morning, or I'll do it for you.''

"But everything is going to be fine. You'll see—''

"Now.'' He was the colonel again, hard as steel. "Every book, every dress, every scrap that will remind me of you. I want it packed and ready. I'm hauling you back to Ohio, true to my word.''

"You wouldn't! Papa, you said yourself that he was a good man. I heard you.'' He didn't have the right to send her away. "Night Hawk—''

"Night Hawk!'' he boomed with more fury than a raging twister. His face flushed. A vein throbbed in his temple. He shot out of the chair like a bullet. "You were intimate with Night Hawk?''

Alarm raced through her. "Papa, sit down or you're going to have a stroke—''

"Night Hawk? I can't believe it." More veins stood out in his neck. "You slept with *him?*"

"*Papa!*" She didn't like the way he said that. "Night Hawk is a decent, honorable man—"

"How could you do such a thing?" Henry looked at her as if she were dirty. As if she were the worst, immoral woman he'd ever known. "And with an Indian, Marie."

"But you're always saying—"

"That's policy. It makes sense for a community and a fort. Don't you see?" He shook his fists, and the cords in his neck strained like a man at the edge of control. "Public policy is one thing. Who sleeps with my daughter is another. How could you lower yourself like that?"

Confusion swirled around her. She took a wobbly step. "Papa, don't talk about him like that. Night Hawk is the man I love."

"He won't marry you, Marie. Mark my words." Henry slammed one fist against the wall, rattling the paintings in their frames. "Those people aren't like us. They don't always marry in church. If you're lucky, maybe he'll allow you to live with him. Be his squaw or some such nonsense. Is that what you want?"

"I can't listen to you." *This* was her father? The man she'd adored her entire life? She'd worked to earn his love. She'd agonized over not being good enough. She even came here to teach English at his fort, just to make him proud of her.

And this man was so ugly beneath the uniform? He was no great colonel. He wasn't even a decent man.

Disgusted, she grabbed the bedpost for support. Hurt, disappointment and shock all melded together, forever ruining the joy she'd felt.

"This is not the end of the world, Papa." She held her chin firm and willed her stomach not to flutter. "You'll see."

"Walk out that door and you won't be welcome back. In this house or in my settlement." He sounded as cold as a northern glacier, once again the colonel. *"Ever."*

"You don't mean that." He couldn't. Somewhere deep inside, she'd always believed he loved her. Or had the capacity to love her. "You're hurt, and I understand—"

"Hurt?" he raged. "I'm disgusted. Go to him or not, I don't care. If you stay with him as his woman, or I haul you back to Ohio, you're out of my sight either way."

His mouth twisted as if in distaste. Then he turned his back on her and simply walked away.

The room spun too fast and she dropped to her knees.

Had she heard him right? Had he just disowned her? He never wanted to see her again?

He's hurt. He's angry. That's all. She tried to make excuses, tried to cling to a little girl's illusion. But the woman in her knew that Henry didn't love her. He would never love her. Nothing in the world would ever touch his heart.

His cold, cruel, uncaring heart.

He was wrong about Night Hawk. Dead wrong. She believed that with the depth of her being.

Then why was she crying, a little voice inside her asked. Why hadn't Night Hawk proposed to her before this? He'd had plenty of opportunity.

What if Henry was right?

She'd dropped to her knees twice on the way to the stable, waiting for the dizziness and nausea to subside. *I have to get to Night Hawk.* She repeated that thought over and over in her mind until the memory of his touch soothed her.

He had come to her at the dance. He'd twirled on the ice with her. His touch, his words, all told her of his love. He called her *shaylee,* his brightest star.

Papa's wrong. He loves me. I know he does.

Kammeo nickered a welcome. At the sight of the mare eager to greet her, Marie cried out. She needed a friend right now. She wrapped her arms around Kammeo's neck, and the mare pressed her nose to Marie's cheek as if in comfort. As if to say, of course everything will be all right. Night Hawk will want you. You'll see.

She had to believe it. Their love might be new, but it was true and it was strong. Every time they'd touched, it was like finding the perfect peace. The greatest happiness. They belonged together, and Night Hawk wasn't like Henry. Night Hawk wouldn't let her down.

He would welcome her in his arms and cradle her close. He would take her to his bed and love her until all the pain in her heart melted away. Until there was only the two of them, body to body, heart to heart, joined by their love. Their bright, precious love.

Holding that dream close, she found the strength to climb onto Kammeo's back. Still in the stall and without a bridle, Marie leaned forward and clutched the mare's fiery mane. "Take it easy on me, girl. Take me to Night Hawk."

The mare nickered, well remembering the man who'd raised her. The mare seemed to understand her, ambled slowly through the stall door and into the aisle.

The dizziness had been bad before, but mounted on a moving horse made it ten times worse. The mare's rocking gait was like being awash at sea—up and down, up and down. Marie groaned and buried her face in the mare's neck.

Think of Night Hawk. She pictured the joy that would soften his dear face when she told him their news. She imagined how he would cradle her in his arms. The thought of his strong, unyielding chest felt like an anchor in her topsy-turvy world.

"Marie!" Night Hawk's voice. Night Hawk's moccasins whispering across the straw-strewn floor. It was his familiar touch that hauled her off the mare's back. "What's wrong? You look ready to fall down."

"It's really you. What are you doing here?"

"McGee asked me to show him how I shoe." Night Hawk frowned as he studied her, then he hauled her against his chest. "You still look very ill. What are you doing out of bed?"

"I had to see you." Her voice cracked with emotion, and she closed her eyes, afraid the tears balled in her throat would dissolve into endless pain. "Alone. I have to—"

"Shh." A man's comfort. A man's love. "Come. I'll find us a private place."

Marie felt the last of her energy leave her. She clutched his shirt with both hands. The buckskin was velvet soft beneath her fingertips, warmed by Night Hawk's heat. She leaned into his strength, not noticing what he said to the new captain. Only that his voice vibrated straight through her, as if they were one.

He loves me. I know he does. Her heart felt near to breaking, that's how much love she had for him. For this man she could rely on when everything in her life had shattered into unrecognizable pieces. She'd lost her home, her father, her family and probably her job. But she had this man. This wonderful, amazing man.

"Hold on, *shaylee.*" He scooped her into his arms with ease and cradled her against his chest like a child. "There is no color at all to your skin. I should take you back to your bed."

"*No.* Not to Papa." She burrowed against the strong column of Night Hawk's neck. He was her anchor now, her home and her life. "Please, Night Hawk."

"As you wish." His lips grazed her brow with tenderness.

Her heart soared. His love was all she wanted. The only haven she'd ever known, and she needed him now more than she'd ever needed anyone.

She clung to him as he lifted her onto Kammeo's back, then mounted behind her. He drew her onto his lap, cradling her once again. Her mighty warrior who would never hurt her.

He guided Kammeo out the back door and down

the short path by the small gate. He unlocked it, never letting her go. She felt every ripple of his muscles as he moved. She loved the bunch and pull of power beneath her touch and the reliable beat of his heart at her ear.

Then they were alone, behind the gate, with the winter forest crisp and new around them. Snow struck like tiny bits of heaven, sweet and light. This was where she wanted to spend the rest of her life. In Night Hawk's arms. On these beautiful lands.

"Tell me what troubles you, *shaylee*." He produced a blanket she hadn't noticed and drew it around her. A soft Indian blanket woven with intricate care.

She ran her finger across the dark hawk in the pattern. Night Hawk's family, she realized. He came from the Hawk clan. If she married him, she would become a Hawk, too. She hadn't realized it before but somehow seeing the bird's image made her stop. Made something real that hadn't been before.

We are different, he and I. Different cultures, pasts and expectations. Something Henry said troubled her now. *Those people aren't like us. They don't marry. If you're lucky, maybe he'll allow you to live with him.*

Night Hawk had never mentioned marriage.

"Tell me, Precious One." His love enveloped her like velvet, rich and warm. A good man. An honorable man by anyone's standards. "Something is wrong. There are tears gathering in your eyes."

She wanted him to be a dream. A man she'd imagined all her life. An all-conquering hero who would right every wrong just for her. Who would stand up to her father, give her a home, a name, love her unconditionally and above all else. A fairy-tale love imagined by a girl who'd been lonely and unloved all her life.

Night Hawk was a man and no dream. His power pulsed beneath her fingertips with every beat of his heart. He had vulnerabilities like any man. He was flesh and blood, muscle and bone and no fantasy. As great as he was, he was a man.

A man who had never spoken of marriage.

Tell him, her heart urged. He would be happy.

But he would not marry you, her mind argued and she remembered Henry's warning.

"You seem so unhappy, Marie. Is it your father? Has he done something to hurt you?" Always stalwart, always true. Night Hawk held her as if she were the most precious woman on earth to him.

How could she tell him? What if he rejected her? What if he'd stopped dreaming of a life with her?

What if the dream had only been hers all along?

"Yes," she mumbled into Night Hawk's shirt. "Papa has upset me greatly."

"He is a hard man, but he loves you."

"That's what I always believed." She felt like the biggest fool, clinging to her lover when she couldn't find a way to tell him the truth. He deserved to know.

Then she remembered how father had made her feel. Dirty. Shameful. Night Hawk would never treat her that way. Would he?

Tears burned behind her eyes but they wouldn't fall. Telling him had been so easy when she imagined it. But now, she had doubts. Again, how very much reality and fantasy differed.

It's time to grow up, Marie. She realized it, a great truth from her heart. It was time to accept the consequences of her actions. To stand on her own feet without leaning on anyone.

"Yes, it's my father," she said slowly. She released her hold on Night Hawk's shirt, her fingers stiff from gripping him too tightly. She'd been hanging on for dear life. The world spun crazily, but she met Night Hawk's gaze and the spinning slowed. "He knows about us."

"I was afraid of something like this." Tenderness, such tenderness. He brushed stray tendrils from her brow as if she were a child to be cared for.

When she was a woman responsible for her unborn baby's life. "Papa took the news hard."

"He disapproves. I had hoped—" Night Hawk's face twisted as if in pain and he stared into the forest. He breathed in deeply, his wide chest lifting. She couldn't interpret the shadows in his eyes and could only guess.

"I am not the man he wants for a son-in-law." A muscle snapped in his rock-hard jaw. He held himself so stiffly he looked as if he were entirely made of stone.

Just as he had on the day she'd met him.

"Henry cares for his reputation most of all, you know that." Marie steeled her spine. She was an adult now, grown-up, able to gather up the pieces of her sorrow with dignity.

"Let me guess. He no longer wishes you to see me."

"No, he said I had to make a choice." She waited,

wondering what he would do. She would not cling to him like a needy girl.

"I see." His throat worked as if he held much back. Tender words? Or relief, she wondered.

Did he want a wife? Or a bed partner? Even a man as noble as Night Hawk could break his word. Or decide when it came down to it that he didn't want her. If Henry could admit to being prejudiced, then who knew what lurked dark and unseen in a man's heart?

Only time would tell for sure.

"What is your choice, Marie?" He said the words harshly, as if he were angry with her. "What do you want?"

You, her soul cried out. "I don't know," she managed, knowing it was the wise answer. "I can't decide these things alone because they concern you. Because what I do will affect you."

He looked so hard, like a man who had lived and prospered in this harsh wilderness. A man who was part of the land, part of the wild. And yet she still loved him.

She always would.

The sky opened, and the snow fell in sharp, mean strikes. The air grew colder. The flakes drove at a harsh angle. She waited while Night Hawk gazed at the far horizon, as if an answer would be painted there by the wind.

Would he reject her? What would she do if her father was right? Was the love they shared too new and fragile? Or had it been only a dream?

"I would sacrifice anything to make you mine." His

confession surprised her. "Anything but your happiness."

Say the words, she silently begged. She needed him to need her. She wanted him to reach out for her. To offer her the marriage she desperately wanted.

"I can wait for your decision." He pressed a kiss to her brow. Tenderly he leaned his forehead against hers so they were eye-to-eye, face-to-face. She could see all the shadows in his heart.

He's not going to propose. The realization weighed her down, so heavy that it took all her strength not to weep. The truth was, all along she'd been the one talking of marriage and wishing and dreaming.

A girl not yet a woman with lessons to be learned. Marie ran her fingers down Night Hawk's cheek. His bronzed skin was as warm as gold. The ridge of his high cheekbone and the cut of his face would be forever etched in her memory.

"You need to go, Night Hawk." She hated saying the words, but she would spend no more time waiting. No more time wishing. All their silences spoke louder than any words. "The captain is waiting for you."

"You are important to me." He kissed her gently and deeply, the kiss of a loving man. Not a hurtful one. "Can you tell me, is there a chance you will want me now?"

"Yes." She lifted her chin, fighting to stay in control. Once, she would have flung herself in his arms and let him lead her to his bed. Now she did not have that innocence of spirit. "There is a chance, if you want it."

"That is all I ask." He kissed her like a fantasy man with the right blend of gentleness and heat.

He left her trembling, he left her wanting. He left her ashamed.

What did she do now? She had no place to go. No one to cling to. Only her own two feet to stand on.

As the storm worsened and the snow turned to ice all around, she knew she could not linger much longer.

She would have to make her choice.

Chapter Fourteen

"Whoa! That's enough, boys," Night Hawk called down to his team of draft horses. The geldings halted in unison, keeping the ropes taut over the pulleys. The twenty-foot log they were lifting swung dangerously in the air, buffeted by the heavy wind.

Night Hawk rubbed his hands inside his jacket pockets to dry them, then reached through the driving ice. A gust slammed into the log and drove it straight toward him.

He ducked, slipping on his icy perch. The log swung over his head, slammed into one of the new main supports for the house and shook the entire structure.

Night Hawk caught the log and slowed its swing enough to nudge it into place. You're a fool, he told himself. What was he trying to do? Get himself killed?

Frustration roared through him with more force than the wind, and nothing would relieve it. Not working with his horses. Not walking the fences. And especially not sitting alone in his cabin. He could still feel the weight of Marie in his arms. The sweet woman scent of her clung to his shirt and tormented him.

There is a chance, if you want it. Her promise drove him now. She'd been different, distant. As if she were a stranger he'd never met before and not the woman who owned his heart.

Time was running out. He could sense it like the storm to come. The sky was leaden, and black at the horizon. Ice drove in heavy pellets, falling like snow, but when those warmer clouds arrived, there would be hell to pay.

Was that what his relationship with Marie was to be? Something that worsened until there was no chance for them?

Determined, he pulled the mallet from his belt and a wooden peg from his pocket. If Henry knew they were lovers, then what would he do? The colonel hadn't shown up with a loaded musket, but Night Hawk wasn't fooled.

Henry Lafayette wasn't going to accept him. Not as a husband for his daughter. If only he'd started work on the house sooner, the dwelling would be finished now, gleaming and new. A home that would tell Marie and her father that he was equal to any white man. That he was prepared to love her for the rest of her life.

The wind gusted. Night Hawk wrapped his legs around the unsecured log and placed the mallet over the peg. He drove the wooden nail deep into the belly of the log. Every pound of the mallet released frustration, but it did nothing to ease his fears.

Why had Marie been so distant? What had she been

telling him with her set chin and unshed tears? How furiously had Henry objected?

Yet her words bolstered him when the black clouds came. When the earth turned too slippery for the horses to work the ropes. He rubbed the geldings down and fed them warmed oats, but then he returned to his work.

There is a chance, if you want it, she'd promised.

Hope strengthened him and he faced the wind and ice. For her.

Marie heard the chink of ice skidding across the fort's stable roof. The hopeless sound of winter at its worst. The angry wind slapped loose wallboards and let in shards of ice. The temperature dropped until she was shivering.

She snuggled deeper in the extra pile of clean hay she'd forked into Kammeo's stall. She hated how the faint, pleasing winter scent of Night Hawk somehow lingered on her clothes, or maybe it was her imagination again. Yearning for him so much, needing him to stand tall and claim her. To charge through that door on his big black stallion, take her in his arms, give her a wedding ring and take her home. To his cozy little cabin in the woods.

That's what she wanted. To be his wife. To give this baby she carried his name.

The baby. She should have told him. Regret gathered in her chest until she couldn't breathe. All she would have had to do was say the words. But then what would he have done?

Married her out of obligation? Or worse, not married her at all like Papa had said. Those horrible, hateful words he'd spoken remained like a black cloud in her mind.

What was she going to do now? She could not beg Night Hawk to take care of her. She had too much pride for that. After all she'd been through, after the lessons she'd learned, she would never again lean on a man. He could be the noblest human being she'd ever met, and she still wouldn't lean on him.

A child depended on her now, and in four or five months she would be holding their baby in her arms. A helpless infant who needed her to make the right decisions now.

Where did she go? Back home? To face Henry's fury? That would mean accepting his threat to return her to Ohio.

Maybe that's for the best. She covered her stomach with her hand. If she returned to Ohio, no one here would know of her mistake. No one in the settlement knew she'd been with Night Hawk. In Ohio, she would have her aunt's help and guidance.

But what about Night Hawk? He'd said so little. He'd seemed so distant. Maybe he hadn't said the words she needed to hear, but he loved her. She knew that.

Is there a chance you will want me now? Night Hawk had asked. But didn't he understand that the next step could only be his?

The wind grew in fury and what sounded like a branch scraped over the roof. She was grateful for this warm place to think. Exhaustion settled over her, thick and heavy, but she wouldn't sleep or dream. She had too much on her mind and many problems to solve.

A branch thick with ice flew through the air and slammed into the half-built wall beneath him. Swiping the miserable sleet from his face, Night Hawk knew he had to head indoors. The next branch that came his way in these high-force winds could knock him ten feet to the ground.

He climbed down carefully, slipping and sliding all the way. Ice bit into him like nails, and the wind drove it deep into the layers of his clothes. His skin burned with cold. His bones ached with it.

The wind brought the scent of thunder, and Night Hawk's neck prickled. That wasn't good news. He could smell it in the air—the precipitation and the fury. The storm would get meaner and stay that way.

He had no choice. He had to go in. It was the last thing he wanted to do. To stop now when he was so determined. He felt as if his chance with Marie was slipping away.

After sliding up the back steps, he stumbled into the kitchen. Darkness surrounded him. The storm had bled all but the faintest light from the afternoon. The house seemed alive with the sounds of the howling wind and driving ice against the log walls.

The rooms echoed with every move he made. The rustle of his frozen clothes. The tinkle of ice hitting the floor like shards of glass. The thud of his boots as he kicked them off. The fall of his step on the un- heated boards.

This is how his life would be if Marie turned away

from him. He'd felt her sorrow today over her father's reaction. She'd been hurt, but she had stopped clinging to him. Maybe she no longer needed him. Or wanted to need him.

It was as if someone had reached through his ribs and yanked out his heart. Had he already lost her?

Restless, he set the fires and lit them. Soon the warmth drove the chill from his little house. Settling heavily onto the stone hearth, he held out his hands to heat them. Every inch of him ached from the cold.

The wind gusted against the house. Again. Then again. Big loud bursts that drove the ice so hard they sounded like steel through the thick shingles.

A storm like this could cause much damage. Night Hawk limped across the front room to look out at his stables. They were only shadowed humps in the growing darkness that came as the storm met dusk, but those structures were better built than his house. The horses would be safe in their stalls.

A bark rang outside, and Night Hawk let him in. "Meka! You look like a snowbound bear."

The huge dog smelled of the forest where he often ran, and brought in with him a shower of ice. His fur and paws thick with the sleet that had frozen to him, he clunked across the floor to the hearth. He dropped with a sigh on the heated stones.

How strong the wind was. Through the windows, Night Hawk could plainly see both large and small branches tumbling end over end along the frozen ground. A strange feeling settled over him, like the brush of a feather down his spine, and he had the sudden urge to run outside.

That made no sense. The winds and flying debris were dangerous. Troubled, he rubbed his hand over the nape of his neck, where the tingling was strongest. The sensation remained.

A hawk's cry pierced the howling wind. Was it the injured bird? It couldn't be. The creature was still unable to use its wing. Yet when Night Hawk heard the sound again, it came from the sky and not the barn.

The prickling at his nape began to burn.

"Meka!" he ordered. "Come!" He threw open the door.

The wind exploded with the sound of thunder. Lightning forked from the sky and struck a tree in the orchard. Fire mushroomed, engulfing the tree.

Hurry, a whispered force seemed to be saying, and he lunged off the steps. A tree sailed over his head and he rolled, hitting the frozen ground. Pain shot through him, rattling his spine and jarring his bones. When he sat up, he saw the giant fir, branches crippled by the ice, volleying like an enormous spear directly toward the skeleton structure of his new house.

The fir hit like a cannon's fire and the mighty logs exploded. The supports cracked into pieces and an avalanche of broken wood crashed over his cabin.

Night Hawk stared in disbelief at the ruins of his home. And his dreams.

Marie waited until the storm stopped before she crawled out of the warm hay. She'd had plenty of time to think. Determined, she pushed the stable door open and met the bitter cold head-on.

A half moon hung in the black sky, ringed by

blacker clouds. Silvered light filtered down to shine on the thick layer of ice. Like frozen water, the sparkling ice clung to branches and fence posts, walls and earth.

Broken limbs and fractured trees littered the dangerously slick path home. Slipping, sometimes falling, Marie skated around parts of roofs and what remained of a shed, a porch post and someone's outhouse door.

The bitter temperature sliced through her clothes, and by the time she skidded to a stop at her father's back door, she was trembling so hard she couldn't turn the knob.

The door swung open and a shadow stepped away from the threshold. Slow steps scraped on wood and then a chair grated hard against the floor.

She stepped into the cold room. No candles burned in the crystal holders on the table. No fire snapped in the hearth. She saw Henry's silhouette in front of the window, shoulders stooped, chin bowed.

"He didn't want you, did he?"

"I didn't tell him." Marie worked the ice off her cloak's sash with her fingernails.

"Too scared, huh? You were afraid I was right." There was no victory in Henry's accusation.

"Maybe." She wouldn't lie. The sash came loose, ice crackled to the floor, and she shrugged out of the heavy, partly frozen cloak. Finding the peg by feel, she kept her back to the colonel. Thank heavens for the dark, because she didn't want to look at him.

A knock rattled the back door. Startled, she jumped toward the knob. Her pulse rattled through her as she reached for the handle. It was Night Hawk. It had to be. He'd come for her.

Henry jerked the door open, blocking her view of the doorway.

"Colonel." Ned Gerard's baritone stripped Marie of her last hope. "We've got some serious damage—"

Fort business. She turned away, fighting bitterness. Always with Henry it was work first. Men looked to him for leadership, but there was no end to it. No end to being the colonel.

When what she needed was her father. A little girl's dream was shattered forever. Her illusions were dropping like flies in the first frost. Her feet dragged on the stairs as she climbed them.

There would be time in the morning to speak with Henry and settle the differences between them. She was not going to let him send her home like a shamed child. She had a job to finish and she had Night Hawk to deal with. Regardless of how painful it might be, she would tell her lover about their baby. If he rejected her, then she'd go home quietly. But if his love was as true as she hoped, then nothing could ever make her leave.

She wanted more than anything to be Night Hawk's bride.

There was nothing she could do now. She gave in to her exhaustion and slept.

The dawn's light shone gently on the ice-covered devastation. Diamonds glittered on the broken logs and the crushed cabin. The peaceful morning came quietly and beautifully. Night Hawk shivered in the frigid mists from the lake.

Two days had passed and still it was too dangerous

to move the logs. Thick ice covered every inch of the wreckage. Of the home he'd wanted to build for Marie.

It was just an ice storm, he told himself. They happened sometimes. Nature could have sharp teeth, and the morning was serene as if nothing had happened.

Had he and Meka been in the cabin when the logs came down on the roof, he would have been gravely injured. Maybe even killed. The loss of his hard work and his cabin ought to seem small by comparison. But it didn't.

He'd lost Marie's home, the only thing he had to offer her. His hands were empty. What if his future was empty, too?

"Night Hawk." Josh Ingalls rode over the hill, dressed warmly. "I came to see if you had any damage from the storm."

"Some." Night Hawk tucked away his sorrows and his worries for later. He faced his friend who'd always been someone he could count on. "How about you?"

"Lost a few trees, and a branch knocked out a window. Nothing I couldn't fix. Nothing like this." Josh gazed at the devastation, shaking his head as if he couldn't believe it. "The wind and ice are a bad combination. Heard there was damage like this at the fort. The wind took the roof off the new schoolhouse."

The schoolhouse? That made him think of Marie. He'd left her in the forest when the snow had been turning to ice. Surely she'd headed in before the worst of the storm hit. He fought the sudden and intense urge to whistle for Shadow and race all the way to the fort to make sure.

She might not be yours anymore, he reminded himself. He had to accept that truth no matter how much it hurt. "Was anyone injured in the storm?"

"Not that I know of." Josh dismounted. "That was a strong wind to take down those logs. I didn't know you were building an addition. You could have asked. I would have helped you."

He could see the toll the loss of his wife had left on Josh. It wasn't right to ask his friend for help when he was grieving. Besides, building the house had been something he had to do alone with his own two hands. It had represented his future with Marie.

Josh had no idea what was at stake, and it was best that way. Night Hawk gestured toward the stable where he'd fashioned a living space out of two box stalls in the back. "I dug the cookstove out of the wreckage, and I've got a hot fire. Come in and warm up. I'll boil some coffee."

"I'll have some of my ranch hands come help with this." Josh followed him, his gait slower these days. "We can get that mess cleaned up. A lot of the logs look in good shape."

"Some I can use when I rebuild." Night Hawk hadn't thought about the future until that moment. But he would rebuild. A single ice storm could not destroy the future he wanted so desperately. Hadn't the hawk spirit guided him to the fort? Hadn't he heard a hawk calling to him just before the cabin was demolished?

Night Hawk would continue to fight. Marie was his soul's desire, his one and only. The other half of his heart that made him complete. The right to claim her as his was worth any amount of work. Making her happy was worth any sacrifice.

Marie struggled against her afternoon dizziness as she stepped through the fort gates. At least the doctor's advice about ginger water had calmed her stomach enough so that she could return to work.

Classes would begin tomorrow in the fort's chapel, thanks to the chaplain's generous offer. She'd gone toe-to-toe with her father and found a compromise of sorts. Since the ice storm's destruction meant he needed to stay to oversee the repairs, Marie had talked him into letting her remain at the fort for a while.

Not because Henry liked the idea. He didn't even want to look at her. But because she would look irresponsible walking off at the start of a new school term. A month would give Marie the time she needed, and by then Henry would have hired a teacher to replace her.

A strange feeling shivered down her spine, leaving her tingling. It was the same way she felt whenever she was with Night Hawk—as if she were more alive. When she looked up, she saw him tethering two huge draft horses to the hitching post near the mercantile's front steps.

His back was to her as he looped the thick leather straps around the sturdy post. Long icicles hung from the wood, and he knelt to break them off in thick handfuls so the shards wouldn't damage the reins.

He looked so good. Even from behind. His back was strong and wide. He straightened from his work, and he saw her. The air snapped between them. Her hopes fell as she watched him react. His shoulders tensed. His eyes narrowed. He looked away as if he were trying to figure out how to avoid her.

Why did she have to pick this exact moment to go shopping? She couldn't stand the way he was looking at her, as if she were a mistake he'd made, as if he regretted the love he made her feel. He might love her, but so much pain was between them. She would not run to him and cling. She would wait until he was ready to claim her.

"Marie." He called out in a quiet, intimate way.

Maybe it was his voice, or seeing him again, but hearing him say her name as if they were still close, as if they were lovers tore her determination into shreds.

She wanted to run into his arms right here in the middle of the settlement. She didn't care if it was proper to show public affection or not. She wanted the entire world to know this man was the love of her life and that he'd given her his child. He was the only man she wanted to call husband.

But he did not open his arms wide to greet her. He held out one hand, as if to help her like any man would along the path.

He was being a gentleman, no more. She took a slow breath, accepting his help. Afraid she wanted more than he would give.

"I'm glad to see you looking better." He leaned close, his free hand cupping her elbow to give her more support on the ice. "I hear school starts tomorrow. Does that mean you'll be staying?"

His actions and his words seemed casual, but was

that a hitch in his voice? Had she imagined it or did his question tremble, as if her answer mattered to him?

"Yes," she said carefully. "I'll be staying for a while, although my father and I are not getting along."

"I see." The tension drained from his shoulders, and when he smiled, she dared to hope again. "Then it is not your father keeping us apart."

She waited while a sleigh slid past on the street. Every bit of her became perfectly still. Night Hawk seemed aloof, but exhaustion bruised the skin beneath his eyes and he looked raw, somehow hungry, the way she felt at the thought of losing him.

The tension remained tight in his shoulders, and his gaze did not waver but held her carefully, as if waiting expectantly.

"Is that what you still think? That I'm ashamed of you?" Remembering Henry's horrible words, Marie blanched. "That couldn't be possible. There isn't anything about you that I'm not proud of. The man you are. The way you work with horses. Your home and your land."

"Why do you say that?" His gaze narrowed, as if measuring her carefully. "You're used to a comfortable lifestyle, Marie. You are a gently bred lady who has always had a housekeeper."

"That doesn't mean I don't know how to cook and clean. And I take care of Kammeo's stall by myself."

His eyebrow shot up skeptically.

"It's true. Ask any of the stable boys." She felt the knot of pain and worry inside her loosen. "Is that what you think? That I want a pampered lifestyle?"

"It crossed my mind." The left corner of his mouth

twitched as if he were fighting not to grin. "It occurred to me a few times."

"I'm not like my father." She was angry, she was confused, she was in love with this man and she didn't know what to do. "Have you thought all this time that I'm a spoiled colonel's daughter? Is that why you—"

"No." He took her hand in his, and even through the layers of his leather gloves and her wool mittens she could feel his heat. It dazzled her.

"You told me that your father asked you to choose. But if you choose to be mine, I want you to come to me with no regrets." Night Hawk grew very still. "That is, if I am lucky enough that you would want me."

"I would have no regrets if you asked me."

He nodded once, as if he finally understood.

She wanted him to propose to her, to say the beautiful words that would make her his fiancée. Then she could tell him about their baby. But they were not alone, and this was not the place to tell him, where a passerby could overhear.

Although they were in the middle of the square with only the horses to shield them from view, Night Hawk leaned his forehead to hers. His skin was warm, and gazing into his dark eyes intimately made her see what he'd been afraid to risk. His heart was full of love for her, a silent and honorable love.

Just like the man.

Josh and his men had gone home at dark, but Night Hawk continued to work. An icy wind blew tiny snowflakes over him and kept trying to douse the lantern, but nothing was going to stop him. Not now that he knew for sure.

A while, she'd said. That's how long he had. Maybe he should have asked exactly how long that was—a couple weeks? A month? Two? Either way, he intended to work on their house every waking moment.

It had to be ready for her. He wanted it to be perfect for their life together.

He tied the rope around a thick log and whistled to the draft horses to start pulling.

It was too cold for them to meet, and she'd promised her father, as a condition of her staying for a while, that there would be no more unchaperoned visits to Night Hawk's home.

But she thought of him constantly. She dreamed of him at night when she lay alone in her bed. Watched for him in the settlement or at the stables, hoping for a chance meeting. Her morning sickness lingered, even when her waist began to expand a little more as the weeks passed.

Time was running out. Henry had gruffly spoken to her one evening to say that a teacher had been hired. He'd purchased tickets on the stage for her return to Ohio. Then he'd left before she could argue, treating her as an unwelcome visitor in his home.

It will all work out, she assured herself. It had to. Night Hawk wanted her, she was certain of it. They just needed time together to work out the details. A spring wedding, maybe. Joy filled her at the thought. She laid her hand on her stomach, carefully concealed by a pretty overskirt and apron.

Before she told him about their child, she wanted to hear the words first of how he loved her and wanted her for his wife. She knew for sure now that he would, and she could hardly wait for him to come to her. What a surprise she had for him!

The injured hawk cried in protest as Meka ambled into the stable. The bird and dog disliked each other, and their antics at least filled his lonely evenings.

"Don't let him get to you," Night Hawk advised the bird as he tossed a chunk of smoked venison in the air. "You'll be flying by the end of the month."

The hawk hopped into the air to catch the meat and nodded his head, as if he understood.

Night Hawk stepped around Meka and opened the cookstove door. Heat stretched the skin on Night Hawk's face as he loaded wood on the fire. Soon the flames were crackling merrily, and he hoped it was enough to drive away the ice in his bones. It was nearly midnight.

Every muscle in his back, legs and arms burned from exhaustion, but he'd finished clearing away the last of the rubble. There was no more devastation, and he could start over again.

For Marie. How he ached to see her. Soon she would be his wife. Sleep at his side. Fill his life with her joyful presence. *I would have no regrets if you asked me,* she'd told him and with all his being, he believed her. Finally.

Tomorrow he would start to rebuild. Maybe not the grand house of his dreams, but a large and roomy home. Satisfaction lifted him. Maybe it was because it was a part of his heritage, or maybe it felt satisfying to be simply providing a home for Marie, but he felt good about himself as a man and a Sauk. He would build a lodge for his wife, as his father had done for his mother.

Then he and Marie would fill the rooms with their love. And the children made from that love.

Children. That was an image that pleased him. The thought of Marie cradling his son in her arms filled him with a fierce, protective love.

What a happy life they would have.

The dream came on quiet wings and a stormy sky. Black clouds stretched from north to south and lightning slashed the horizon. The western horizon where the future lay.

The nearly silent beat of a hawk in flight circled overhead. Night Hawk's moccasins were stuck to the ice—to the thick glistening sheen of ice from the storm—and he could not move. Not west toward the future. Not east toward the past.

He could only tip his head back in wonder and watch as the giant hawk glided over the ruins of his lodge destroyed by the wind. A white man's lodge he'd built for the woman he loved.

The giant hawk, dark as midnight, glided over the ruins and saw all things. All that the dwelling meant. What it represented. And what would be.

Night Hawk watched, feeling the power of the bird and the wisdom of its spirit. As if in slow motion, the great hawk plucked a white feather from its own wing with its beak, then dove straight toward Night Hawk.

No, this cannot be. Even in dream, he fought the truth the spirit hawk brought him. He didn't want to take the offering, he would not touch the feather. He steeled himself against the mesmerizing pull of the majestic hawk, but as the creature neared, Night Hawk could see the sorrow in his eyes. The sorrow from a great sacrifice.

The hawk had come to him. There was no one else to accept the offering. Night Hawk held out his hand and the magnificent creature laid the perfect white feather on his palm. The hawk cried once and rose into the sky again, ready to continue its journey.

Ice fell in torrents, chilling him to the bone, freezing him where he stood. On the land where his father was buried. On the land where he'd dreamed of spending his life with Marie.

Thunder clapped, the hawk disappeared at the horizon's edge. Night Hawk snapped awake, his hand still clutched as if holding a feather.

Sweat dripped off his brow. His pulse drummed in his ear. He sat up, breathing so hard that the sound filled the darkness.

He did not have to ask what the dream meant. Or look at his empty hand where he'd dreamed of receiving the feather. A dream where a hawk sacrifices a part of his body can mean only one thing.

Night Hawk buried his face in his hands. In a place beyond tears, where pain was greatest, he tried to find the strength to do what he must. To do as his spirit guide told him—to sacrifice his love for Marie.

A white woman didn't belong with him. It was what his own father would have said.

But would his father have asked him to give up the one woman made for him?

No, it cannot be. He wouldn't believe it. Everything that was Hawk within him rebelled. He tossed off the blankets made long ago by his mother and sister-in-law and stormed across the aisle to the tack room. He pulled on white man's woolen socks and white man's leather boots. He tugged a white man's sweater over his head and grabbed a store-bought wool coat.

He would build his house. He would have his wife and his family. Nothing, not even the great Colonel Lafayette could stop him.

He'd given up everything else of his people and his past. Why couldn't he deny the dream and pretend it meant nothing?

And if he did, he would turn his back on his beliefs.

His ax. He needed his ax. Frantically he searched through the dark, but couldn't find it where he'd left it by the door. Cursing, he grabbed a lantern and struck a match. The single flame tossed shadows across the ax that had fallen on its side into the corner. Next to his mother's blanket bearing a majestic black hawk.

He nearly dropped the lantern. No! He would not listen to the dream. It was only a dream. If he gave up Marie, he would live without a heart. If he let her go, then he also lost their unborn children. Children whose faces he could almost see in his dreams.

The light flickered over the blanket, caressing his mother's fine skill. So long ago she had patterned the great hawk into that stormy sky.

He could not turn his back on his family's memory

any more than he could give up his future. What should he do?

He didn't know. There was no one he trusted enough to turn to.

Maybe he should just go outside, follow his feelings and start building the house for his wife.

But the light caressed the blanket in a way that seemed to make the hawk alive. Night Hawk couldn't turn his back and walk away.

He went forward instead. Through the door that led to the meadows. Through the meadows that led to the woods. Snow battered him. Frigid winds drove arrows of cold straight to his bones. He didn't stop until he came to his father's grave.

There he sat in the darkness, where the forest felt sacred, and asked for wisdom. For the strength to give up the love of his life.

Chapter Fifteen

He felt dead inside, as frozen as the ice at his feet. The pathway to her house had never seemed so long. Never before had he dreaded doing any task so much. How could he do this? How could he say the words that would tear Marie away from him forever?

All he had to do was knock on the door and tell her it was over between them. Simple as that.

Except what he felt for her wasn't simple. Giving her up so she would have a better life made jealousy stampede through him. The thought of another man taking her into his arms, kissing her, making love to her—

Red rage burst in front of his eyes. Blood pounded through his temples, and if he could, he would have pushed down the door and done anything to claim Marie as his. Anything.

But that would be the ultimate act of selfishness.

Torn, Night Hawk struggled with the need to step forward and the wish to turn back. But what would that accomplish?

The hawk in his dream had only told him what

Night Hawk had known from the start. He knew if he took Marie as his wife now, she would never find happiness with him.

So that is how he pictured her, happy with a white man her father approved of. That is how he found the strength to climb the steps and knock on the door.

The housekeeper answered. The surprise on her face at the sight of him quickly turned to disdain. "The colonel told me not to allow you in if he isn't here."

She must know about their affair, too. He splayed his hand on the door to keep her from slamming it in his face. "Is Marie here?"

"You are not allowed—"

"Thank you." He strong-armed the door open and stepped inside. "If you do not want me in her room, then I suggest you send her down."

"The colonel will hear about this!" Outrage drew the woman's narrow face into numerous prunelike wrinkles. She whirled around and marched up the stairs making enough noise to stampede a herd of buffalo.

Night Hawk was not afraid. He'd already lost everything of value. Let Henry do his worst.

Her shoes tapped on the stairs as she descended, and the sound was music. She swept into sight in a flowing gray gown that shimmered when the light touched it. Her beauty to him was the greatest in the world.

"Night Hawk. You came." She greeted him with a smile, running into his arms as if she'd been waiting forever for him. Her arms wrapped around his neck and held him tight.

My kammeo. He breathed in the sweetness of her

skin and rubbed his jaw against her satin-soft hair. For all the lonely nights yet to come, he memorized the feel of her. Her fragile frame and soft woman's curves, her buoyant energy and the way she lifted her chin to look at him.

Beauty. She was his beauty.

"I can't believe you came for me," she breathed, her face alight with a great inner happiness. "Even though I hoped you would. I told Mrs. Olstad to leave us, although she's probably sent word to Henry. But he's out tending to some property line dispute. We have time to talk. To say what needs to be said."

She leaned from his embrace so quickly he was too dazzled to speak. Everything about her seemed different, and yet she appeared the same. "Come to the kitchen. I'll put on some coffee. You must have had a very cold ride."

"No," he said quietly, breaking a little inside. "I cannot have coffee with you."

"Oh? Are you in a hurry? I told you, Henry can't be here for a while—"

"It's not Henry." He hated interrupting her. He hated the way her inner light faded a bit. What had she said to him? *I can't believe you came for me.* Sorrow battered him, but he could not back down. For her sake. She deserved a better life than he could give her.

"Then what's wrong? If you're uncomfortable talking here, we can ride out into the forest, even if it's cold. Or back to your place."

"No, I do not want you out in the cold."

What was wrong with him? Marie wondered. He

looked so stiff and formal, as if he were a stranger visiting for the first time. Shadows made his eyes appear darker and she wondered what had happened.

Something is wrong and he came to me. She reached out and held him tight. His arms came woodenly around her, and he did not kiss her hair or lean into her comfort.

She gazed up at him, at the implacable set of his jaw and the sorrow that drew harsh lines around his mouth. Something was tearing him apart, and she ached for him. If Henry had spoken to him and put that anguish on Night Hawk's face, he was in serious trouble.

"Come." She took his big hand in hers. "If you're not in the mood for coffee, we can sit here in front of the fire. You're as cold as ice."

"Yes, we should talk." He sounded odd and distant, yet when he looked at her, his eyes were not hard or cold but shone with great tenderness.

He sat on the footstool in front of her, which was lower to the ground, so they were eye-to-eye.

He's going to propose to me. Excitement zinged through her when he took her hand in his. It was there in his dark eyes and in the gentle affection of his touch. He loved her. And now he would honor her by asking her to be his wife.

Giddiness bubbled through her. She couldn't wait to tell him about the baby.

"Marie." He said her name as if he cherished it. He lifted her hand and pressed it against his jaw and cheek, an endearing gesture that made the whole world tilt.

She took a breath, certain she was about to faint. She'd waited for this moment all her life. The moment when someone loved her truly and without end.

"I came to say goodbye."

"What?" No, that didn't make any sense. He wanted to marry her, right? He'd practically promised to ask her the last time they'd spoken—

"I don't think we should be together," he said quietly. "I've thought it over, and I want to end this love between us."

"End it?" What was going on? She wasn't hearing him right. He wasn't making any sense. Didn't he want to marry her?

"It was good, Marie. Very good." He kissed her hand gently but without passion. "I do not think we will suit."

"No, you can't be saying this. You can't mean this." She jerked away from him. He reached out to stop her, but she darted around him. No, something was wrong. This didn't make any sense. "We love each other, Night Hawk. That's all it takes for a future together."

"I disagree, *shaylee*." He was behind her.

She could feel her skin crackle with his nearness. He was going to touch her, to comfort her in a polite passionless way and she sidestepped him before he could do it.

"Marie, listen to me. This makes sense."

"I don't care about sense." Everything within her screamed this couldn't be true. One minute they were talking of forever and now—

"I am like the bird who catches a star. They both

live in the sky, but the star is greater and she burns with her own light. When she flies, she touches the heavens, but when the bird flies, he does little more than skim the treetops.''

"Henry threatened you, didn't he? He broke his promise to me like he always does, took his musket and probably half his battalion to convince you not to marry me."

"That's not what happened—"

"Don't lie to me. I can tell that you're lying."

His head shot up, and he was all warrior, all fight. "I'm telling you the truth, Marie. I no longer wish to see you."

"That can't be true—"

"Why not?" Now fury hardened his face. "Because I love you? Love has no part in this, Marie. None at all."

"Of course it does. I love you and if you—" She hesitated, his words finally penetrating her hard shell of denial. Over and over she heard his words. *Love has no part in this.*

Shaken, she reached blindly for the nearby chair and sank into its cushion. "Y-you're saying you no longer love me."

He did not answer. Towering over her, his face granite hard and resolute, the faintest apology shone in his eyes where once love had been.

She felt her hand cover her stomach protectively. Pain like a lightning bolt seared her. No, it couldn't be true. She wouldn't believe it. She'd known Night Hawk's love. Henry had done this. He'd threatened Night Hawk so he would back down. That's what he'd done. If Henry had started yelling about his ugly prejudices, then it was little wonder Night Hawk stood before her now, as cold as stone, as if no love burned inside him.

"I want you to know," she began quietly, "that I do not share my father's opinions. I see you as a man, Night Hawk, the best I've ever known. Henry shouldn't have threatened you and said cruel things to you—"

"I am a Sauk warrior." He sounded merciless, like a man she did not know. "No one threatens me."

"I see." She started to tremble. If she looked at him, she could see the truth holding him up, proud and noble. He'd come to tell her he didn't want her, that's why he was here. Henry had to be behind this. He had to be.

She wouldn't believe anything else. Her soul cried out for him to admit he was lying. To take her into his arms and hold her for the rest of their lives.

"This is goodbye, *shaylee*." He stalked away like a predator who controls the forest, strong and proud and without fear. Without softness.

She couldn't say the words. She would not tell him goodbye.

The door closed, taking her dreams with her.

Run after him, her heart cried out. She wanted to grab hold of him and never let go. It didn't matter what Henry said, or anyone else for that matter. She had a child on the way. And she hadn't even told him—

A chill shivered over her. What if he knew? What if Henry had told him?

She wrapped her arms around her middle, where her thickening waist felt strange but welcome. So very welcome. No, Night Hawk would not walk away from his child. And that only made her angry. Maybe it was the hurt and fear melding together. Maybe it was seeing every one of her dreams shatter. She felt broken, as if the pieces could never be made whole.

The back door slammed hard enough to rattle the windowpanes in the parlor. Henry's vengeful step struck the floor in a sharp staccato that grew louder. He burst into the parlor, red faced and as furious as a charging bear. "Where is he?"

"He's gone, Papa." She lifted her chin, facing him, ready to fight for what she believed in. "He came here and ended our relationship, just like you forced him to do. You broke your word to me again. You threatened him."

"Is that what he told you? I didn't go anywhere near him. If I had, I would have taken my musket and used it. That's what I would have done. There would have been no threat. I hate what that man did to you."

"No, you did this to me." Marie stood, lightheaded, trembling with something beyond rage. It held her up, gave her power as she marched toward her father. "You wanted to break us up for good, and you have."

"Where is that worthless excuse for a man?" Henry jerked open the door and gazed into the fog that hung like a shroud. "He's gone, damn it. My musket is loaded and ready. He's to stay away from you, Marie."

"I told you, you're not to run my life anymore. Just

like you told me that I'm no longer your daughter."
She pushed past him, angrier then she'd ever been in
her life. "If I can't make things right with Night
Hawk, then when I leave, I am out of your life forever.
That includes your grandchild."

"You are out of my life either way, young lady."

His threats didn't hurt her. Not anymore. She was
on her own now. Another week of teaching. That's all
the time she had to fix this with Night Hawk. And to
tell him about their child.

"I didn't talk to Night Hawk," Henry called as she
climbed the stairs, his words echoing all around her in
the narrow well. "He walked out on you all by himself. What I can't believe is that he was man enough
to tell you face-to-face. I was right. Do you see that
now?"

She didn't answer. There was nothing left to say,
and she had better things to do than argue with a man
who only cared about being right.

The room was spinning a little, and she sat down
on the window seat. Through the boughs of the maple
and the thick fog, she could barely see the path below.
A man with long black hair and a gray wool jacket
was kneeling on the snow. His head down, his shoulders uneven, the brave warrior she'd fallen in love
with looked as if he were hurting.

The fog swirled, hiding him from her sight. As if
an unseen hand were telling her that Night Hawk
would never be hers.

The hawk attempted to flutter his wings, but the
injured one remained too weak to take flight. Night

Hawk tossed the bird a piece of jerky from his pocket, and the hawk caught it easily in his hooked beak.

The icy wind had sharp teeth, and the clouds racing across the northern sky told him a storm would strike before midnight. Dusk was swiftly arriving, and soon there would be no more daylight to continue his work.

It will be a house, but not one for Marie. The thought made his mouth bitter, and he tried to drive her from his mind. But thoughts of her lingered like summer in an autumn wind, and he knew he would never forget her. He could use every bit of his strength and exercise all his steely will and still he would be weak and remember. He would always remember.

He set the last log in place. The walls of his new house were slowly climbing. Not an elaborate structure, but larger than the original.

He heard a hawk's call in the sky but it was hidden by the lingering veils of fog that rose from the lake like ghosts coming out for the night. For one brief moment, he hoped it was a majestic gray hawk, but an ordinary brown hawk swooped from the clouds and lighted on a maple's bare limb.

The meager hope died within him. Saying goodbye to Marie had been the hardest task of his life, for it was cutting off an important part of him.

Even as he hoped there could be another dream to show him a different way, he knew he was being foolish by wanting something that could never be. To fight against the old ways would be to disrespect his father's and his father's father's beliefs.

He could not turn his back on the Sauk warrior beneath the store-bought clothes. Just as he could no longer run from the truth.

In giving up his future with her, he was giving her a better life. He would grieve, but in time she would not even remember him. She would only see the face of her rightful husband, a white military man her father could accept.

There was one task she had left, aside from teaching her last class tomorrow, and it would not be an easy one.

Marie halted Kammeo with the slight touch of her heels and debated which path to take. If she chose the regular road, she would arrive at Night Hawk's place as she'd first come, as a visitor and practically a stranger. If she chose the trail that bordered the lake, she would have to face her memories.

She squeezed her eyes shut, fighting hard not to take the lake path. She wanted to see the meadow where she'd made love to Night Hawk for the first time. That could even be where they had conceived their child. Memories made her chest warm with happiness.

But if she chose that path, then she would be clinging to what happened in the past. The thickening of her waist was still not too noticeable and her cloak hid it well, but she could feel the difference within her. No, she could not look back, only forward.

She chose the main road, and Kammeo seemed to sense what was to come because she held back, walking so slowly it seemed to take an hour to reach Night Hawk's land.

She didn't see him at first. There was no sun to

glitter on the shadowed ice and no wind to stir the trees. The snowbound fields held no grazing horses. Some of the beautiful animals drowsed in corrals next to the half-dozen stables. In the spot where the cabin used to be stood a structure half-built, golden logs a bright splash of color against the wintry world.

A dog's bark split the air, bouncing off the miles of snow, and she brightened. Meka! She would miss the dog that had been her companion to and from the fort all those months ago. He dashed toward her now, furry and big as a bear, his long tongue lolling.

"Meka!" A voice boomed like thunder across meadows, and the dog restrained himself.

Night Hawk strode into sight on the hill above. He wore heavy winter clothes and held a mallet in one hand. He stood proud and tall and with the wind snapping through his black hair. He looked valiant and dashing, a prince from one of her fairy-tale books.

"Night Hawk." She loved saying his name. She loved everything about him. Nothing could ever change that. "What happened to your cabin?"

He strode closer, lifting one wide shoulder in a casual shrug as if it were nothing. "Ice storm," he said simply, abrupt and curt.

He hadn't meant what he'd said in Henry's house, she knew he didn't, but it was hard to remember that now as he wore a frown that made him look intimidating and harsh.

This was Night Hawk, she reminded herself and took a steadying breath. "Where are you living?"

"In one of the stables. I made a room of two stalls, cleared away all the straw and added a stove." He spoke quickly and without inflection, as if he were speaking to someone he wished hadn't dropped by for a visit.

Her palms grew damp inside her mittens. "I'm leaving on the Friday afternoon stage."

"Is that so?" He looked at the horse, then at the road and at the forest. At everything but her. "I thought we already said our goodbyes."

"I only want the truth this time." He was so distant. How did she make him look at her? "This is the last time we have to sort this out. I told you when we spoke last that I don't share my father's prejudices. Whatever he said to you was uncalled-for, and he is not the man I thought he was. The man I wished he would be."

"Stop." He held up his gloved hand, the frown on his face twisting into anger. "I thought I made it clear. I have not spoken to your father since before the ice storm."

"But he's so angry with you—"

"Marie, this is very difficult for me and I'm only going to say it one more time." His face twisted and he stared hard at the horizon as if looking for something. Then he focused on her with single-minded intensity. "Goodbye."

His gaze was like an accusation, and it made her feel small and shamed. She saw that he was telling the truth, for his stare was uncompromising. If Henry hadn't spoken to him, then that meant—

She was ashamed of herself for coming here when she'd vowed to let him be the one to decide their future. That she would not try to influence him like an immature girl.

Pain washed through her like a mighty wave, drowning all her hopes. Leaving her without the will to fight him anymore.

He meant what he said. He didn't want her. She took a slow breath, trying to stay calm. She wouldn't cry in front of him. With deliberate control, she dismounted. When her boots touched the hard ground, it jarred her.

"I've come to return the mare." She lifted her chin, facing him, trying to hide the humiliation she felt inside. "Kammeo was a fine gift, but I can't take her back to Ohio with me."

"I should pay you for her." How noble he sounded.

She wanted to hate him for it. "No. She was freely given, and I don't want to profit from her. I will always be grateful she was my first horse. I will miss her."

Night Hawk stood waiting, as still as stone.

So, is this the way love ended? Marie wondered. With uncomfortable silences and awkward farewells? Love burned within her, rare and honest, and it was all she could do to turn her back and walk away.

She didn't want to say goodbye. She never wanted to say another thing to him.

As if he felt the same way, Night Hawk didn't follow her. Kammeo's neigh shattered the silence, seeming to call her back.

Don't look, Marie told herself. There was nothing else to do but keep walking.

Meka fell in stride beside her, a silent companion

back to the fort. His presence reminded her of better days when a new love shone more brightly than the autumn sun.

Or maybe she only thought so. Like Henry had said, maybe she'd been a foolish girl who'd only fancied herself in love.

She laid her hand over her stomach. Now she would pay the consequences.

Go to her, his heart called to him. How beautiful she'd looked on Kammeo, spirited and bright. Everything within him shouted with the need to claim her as his. To fold her in his arms and never let her go.

All evening he thought of her, saw the exact moment when she realized he didn't want her. Tears had filled her eyes but hadn't fallen. Her chin had shot up with pride, but the wobble to her bottom lip had shown her pain.

He tossed and turned all night, dreaming of her in his arms. Dreaming of kissing away the heartbreak on her face. They made sweet passionate love, and when he woke he cried out for the dream.

But she was gone forever.

"Are you ready, Marie?" Henry tapped on her door. "The sergeant has taken your trunks to the stage. It leaves in ten minutes."

"Yes. I'm just checking to make sure I have everything." Marie felt hollow inside, and maybe that was for the best. Dissolving into tears now wouldn't serve any purpose.

"I'll be downstairs, then." Henry marched away, his gait military and precise.

There was nothing for her at Fort Tye. Not a husband. Not a home. Not a job. Leaving was for the best.

She took her reticule from the bed and left the room. She descended the stairs and found her cloak by the door. As she slipped into it, she realized this place had never been a home. Even with all its finery, it was nothing without love. Henry would never understand that, but she did.

She would never marry a man who didn't love her, even if she was carrying his baby.

Henry walked beside her all the way to the stage. Several soldiers wished her luck. Mrs. Kelsey hurried out of the store to give her a goodbye hug and wish her a safe journey. Her aunt needed her was the story Henry had concocted to keep any tarnish off his reputation. No one knew the real reason she was leaving.

As she climbed aboard and waited while Henry settled on the seat beside her, she gazed out the small window. Business went on as usual. Farmers' wives were driving their family sleighs to the mercantile to trade eggs and butter for supplies. Farmers had come to see if an order had arrived on the stage. Horses and riders hurried by, and a cavalry unit trotted through the gates and disappeared from sight.

Then a movement in the sky drew her attention. It was a lone hawk soaring across the leaden clouds on wide, powerful wings. It circled once and then disappeared, as if it had meant to say goodbye.

Even though Night Hawk had shattered her heart, she couldn't stop hoping he'd come. Just a little bit.

The stage bounced forward and carried her away from the mercantile and the strong fort walls. It jounced on the road until there was nothing but forest on either side.

And only a future without Night Hawk ahead.

"New love burns the brightest, you know that now." Henry apparently thought he should dispense some fatherly wisdom.

Not that she thought of him in that way anymore. "I don't want to talk about this. I just want to head home."

But her heart would never forget the man whose bright, beautiful love had illuminated her world for a time.

She would be in darkness without him.

Chapter Sixteen

Night Hawk watched the bird wobble on his shaky descent. The injured hawk was almost recovered. Soon he would be able to return to the forest where he belonged.

Just like Marie was returning to Ohio. *Good.* Returning home was best for her. She belonged in a world where people hosted dinner parties in their finely furnished homes and drank coffee and brandy in the parlor. It wouldn't take long for her to find a wealthy white husband who would give her everything she deserved.

Everything Night Hawk would have to work a lifetime to give her.

Kammeo neighed, already lonely, pacing the corral as if looking for a way out. She'd been restless since Marie had left her. Even Meka sat on the knoll keeping a lookout should Marie return.

This is for the best. His loss was nothing when compared to the better life awaiting Marie. He'd never been to a large city, he'd never been far from this lake, but he knew Ohio would be the right place for her.

Thinking of her happy was the only thing that could ease the pain of his broken heart.

Henry had left her at Chicago, returning because he was needed at the fort. And probably because he knew there was no reason for her to return to Fort Tye. She wished there were.

She'd been gone for two weeks and so far the trip hadn't been easy. She watched the morning sun blare on the waters of Lake Michigan. Winter still gripped the land, but spring was fighting to take hold. Birds trilled as she waited to climb aboard the stage.

"Traveling all alone, ma'am?" the driver asked, eyeing her stomach, which was now harder to hide.

She blushed, grateful for the gloves on her hand, hiding the evidence that she was unmarried. "Yes. I am on my way home."

"Then your husband will be glad to see you. Here, let me help you up. The step's mighty high."

"Thank you." Marie knew the driver only meant to be kind. He couldn't know there was no husband. And the father of her baby didn't want to see her again.

Sorrow wrapped tight around her, and she settled on the seat. Across the aisle a married couple nodded at her, their two sons well mannered and quiet between them.

She tried not to think what Night Hawk's son might look like. Somehow, as she felt her body change, she knew she carried a boy. A baby she loved with all of her being, just as she still loved his father.

The door slammed, and the coach jerked into motion on the partly muddy and partly frozen road. Her stomach twisted, and she reached into her pocket for a cracker. Her morning sickness had never left her completely. The constant swaying of the stage didn't make her feel any better.

She nibbled at the edge of the cracker and watched the sunlight play on the water. She couldn't help remembering the lake she'd left behind, a place of endless wilderness and crystal-clear water where she longed to be.

If she closed her eyes, she could feel the heat of Night Hawk's touch on her skin. She could smell the winter and man scent of him.

A little more of her died with each passing mile.

"I'll take all four," Captain McGee nodded at the geldings trotting around the corral. He waded through the mud made by spring rains and melting snow, never taking his gaze from the horses. "They're the best-looking Arabians I've seen this side of St. Louis. You have a fine talent."

"It's a talent anyone can learn." Night Hawk joined the captain on higher—and firmer—ground. "You are making good progress in that direction."

"I still don't seem to have the knack, although I'm able to set a decent shoe." The young officer stuck out his hand. "I'll have the colonel sign the paperwork and you'll have your money by week's end."

"I appreciate it, Captain." Night Hawk sealed the deal with a handshake. "I'll bring the horses in on my next trip to the fort."

"Thanks." McGee mounted. Meka barked a fare-well and watched until the horse and rider had disappeared from sight.

"C'mon, boy, it feels like rain." Night Hawk whistled to his dog and headed toward the new house on the knoll. Only loneliness awaited him there, empty rooms that dreams had once filled. But he steeled his spine and opened the door.

Meka collapsed on the rug in the mudroom, and Night Hawk lit a fire in the new stove.

A hawk's faint cry penetrated the thick log walls. A bird sailed past the windows and landed on the front porch rail.

Night Hawk grabbed a handful of jerked venison and headed through the house. "So, you've been out testing those wings. Did you find any female hawks?"

The blue hawk cocked his head, squawking softly.

Even though he knew better than to make a pet out of a wild creature, Night Hawk rubbed his fingers over the bird's soft head. "Here. Catch."

He broke off a small chunk of jerky and tossed it into the air. The hawk dove after it, catching it neatly. While the bird thought it was a game, Night Hawk was helping him strengthen his wings to hunt. The bird was quick. Night Hawk would be surprised if the bird wasn't hunting on his own soon.

Then it would be another goodbye.

No, he wouldn't think of Marie. He stopped his mind before he even conjured her in memory. She'd been gone a long while.

She wasn't coming back.

* * *

"Of course you must stay." Aunt Gertrude lifted the cozy from the teapot and refilled both their cups. "I'll help you any way I can."

"I'm very grateful." Marie managed a shaky smile. "If you didn't take me, I wouldn't have anywhere else to go right now."

"And the father doesn't know about the baby?" Gently prying, Gertrude's gaze squinted, measuring. "Marie, you mean you didn't tell him?"

"I didn't have the chance."

"Oh, Marie." Gertrude pushed the sugar bowl closer. "He deserves to know about the baby."

"I know, but it was hard to find a way to tell him when he was explaining to me that he didn't want me anymore." Guilty enough, Marie stared out the window where the orchard was in full bloom. Bright new leaves and blossoms of light pink, dark pink, white and plum dappled color everywhere.

"Did he say those exact words?"

Marie nodded. "No. He said that we didn't suit."

"That's an odd thing to say. Men who don't want to marry usually turn tail and run, in my limited experience."

"He said we were like a bird and a star, but that didn't make any sense to me." Marie watched a pink crab apple petal feather by on the breeze. It looked as lost as she felt. "I don't want to bring shame to you, Aunt Gertrude. Papa and I have disowned each other over it, and what if our neighbors shun you—"

"Pish-posh! Let me deal with everyone. Why, you grew up here so we can hope our friends will understand. And if they don't, shame on anyone who thinks my Marie isn't a good girl. You were in love. There's no crime in that.'' The older woman's hand covered hers. ''You look unhappy. Is there anything I can do?''

''Not unless you can change the past.'' Another blossom sailed by on the wind, and she couldn't help remembering that Night Hawk had an orchard near his house. His trees would be blooming too, scattering color with the wind.

''It will be all right, Marie.'' Gertrude's hand squeezed gently. ''You can stay right here and raise your baby. Goodness knows I would welcome your child in my home.''

Overwhelmed, Marie could only nod her gratefulness. She had a place here with her beloved aunt, where she'd lived since she was very young. It was home.

But as beautiful as it was, it wasn't the home her soul longed for.

''Dear, are you sure you want to stay in the carriage?'' Gertrude asked while perched on the busy street corner. ''No one's going to comment on your pregnancy. Goodness, no one even mentions such a thing in polite company.''

Marie squinted against the sun in her eyes. ''You're not fooling me. You're trying to lift my spirits with a shopping trip.''

''Am I succeeding?''

''No.'' Marie pulled a book out of her reticule. ''I'll be happy reading right here. At least I'm away from the house.''

"You'll get too warm sitting here."

"Reginald will find some shade to park in." Marie motioned toward the driver, who'd been her aunt's hired man forever. "Go, run your errands. I will be fine."

"All right, but I won't be long." Gertrude pressed a kiss to Marie's cheek, then turned to the driver. "Reginald, take care of my girl and get her out of the sun."

Marie watched her aunt hurry down the boardwalk, arrowing through the crowd with single-minded focus. When Gertrude was coming, people moved right or left to get out of her way.

Love filled her heart for this woman who was the only mother Marie could remember. It came to her then with the buggy jerking as Reginald pulled out into traffic and the noise of the streets assaulted her ears, the truth she'd missed all along.

Gertrude was all that a mother should be. If Marie needed a parent's love, she didn't need to look any further. She'd spent her entire life trying to earn Henry's affection. When she'd had Gertrude's all along.

That lifted her spirits just a little. Reginald found a place in the shade by a park. The merry shouts of children playing distracted her from her book, and she gazed out the window.

Yearning filled her. The long stretch of green grass, the lush maples swaying gently in the wind. A finch trilled from a low branch as if rejoicing in the late spring day. Marie closed her eyes and saw, as clearly as if she were there, the endless forests and the gently rolling hills, the sparkling water and fragrant meadows.

She opened her eyes, and the images faded. The jangling of harnesses, wheels on the street, shouts of drivers back and forth, the bang of a delivery wagon, the slam of a door. It wasn't just the noise that unsettled her. The long row of shops that went on for as far as she could see. The traffic. The smell of someone's forgotten garbage. Unclean streets.

How could she raise Night Hawk's son here? He would never know the sound of wind through the trees in an ancient forest. Or see a hawk soar across the face of the sun. Or feel the power of a mustang beneath him as he raced through lakeside meadows.

A longing pierced her so sharp that she couldn't breathe. Hadn't she realized it before? Why the days had passed slowly here and felt as if without light? She missed Wisconsin. She loved everything about it. Somehow during her stay there it had become a part of her soul.

Just like Night Hawk had.

Thinking of him filled her with pain. She laid her hand on her round stomach. He would not want his son to be raised where there was no forest. Where the closest piece of nature was a small city park.

The carriage door swung open and Gertrude climbed inside. Her shopping bags were full and rustled and crackled as she set them down on the opposite seat.

"Here, dear, I have something for you. Henry had it forwarded here." She searched through one of her bags. "Now, where did it go? Oh, here it is."

Marie could only stare at the letter. What if it was from Night Hawk? Suddenly she was too afraid to take the folded parchment. She was afraid not to take it.

"It's not from him." Gertrude was kind as she pressed the letter into Marie's hand. "It's from someone named Morning Star. Is that an Indian name?"

"One of my former students." Pleased, Marie managed to unfold the piece of paper and turned it right side up. Morning Star's family had reached the western mountains. They crossed over peaks so tall they almost touched the sky, the girl wrote.

Reading the girl's letter brought warmth back to Marie's heart. She was glad to know that Morning Star had a new baby sister, and that her great-great-grandfather was proud of her reading and writing skills.

When Marie was finished reading, she held the letter for a long while and simply stared at the page. Not at the words written there, but in memory of all she'd left behind.

Her heart. Her soul. Her baby's father.

She missed Night Hawk. How she missed him. She could not allow herself to think about him for fear of starting to cry. And never being able to stop.

She missed his tenderness. His touch. His pride. His spirit. Everything she'd ever felt for him remained alive in her heart. A big bright beautiful love still burned.

Thinking back, she tried to remember all he'd said to her when he'd come to break her heart. And how she'd remained troubled over it all this time. Goodbye, *shaylee,* he'd said. Not goodbye and good riddance.

Not simply goodbye. But he'd added his private endearment for her. *Shaylee.* The brightest star in the heavens.

"I know, I can tell by the look on your face," Gertrude said as the buggy bounced along the cobblestone street. "But I won't have you traveling alone in your condition, and goodness knows with my lumbago I won't make it ten miles in a stagecoach. And yes, my dear Marie, I think you should go to him."

Marie felt the tears come, finally. Not from weakness or grief. But from gladness. Love was everywhere in her life. And it was good.

Chapter Seventeen

The miles passed, and Marie felt the baby within her strengthen and grow. Traveling was uncomfortable, but she would suffer anything for the chance to see Night Hawk again.

He'd said they wouldn't suit. He'd said goodbye. But he'd never given her a real reason why they couldn't be together. Maybe he was afraid. He'd lost most of his family. Maybe he'd been alone so long he didn't think he deserved to be loved.

And if she fought for their love and he still didn't want her, then so be it. She would return to her aunt's home certain she'd done the right thing.

But if Night Hawk saw she was pregnant and he wanted to try to make a marriage work, then she would stay. Love had blossomed between them once. Couldn't it bloom again?

"Do you need another pillow, Marie?" her cousin, John, asked as the stage bounced hard over ruts in the road.

Her stomach still felt sick and she shook her head.

"The wind's warm. Here, trade places with me. The

fresh air will do you good.'' John took her hand and helped her scoot against the window. ''How are you feeling?''

''I'll live. And don't look at me like that,'' she warned him. ''I'm not going to have the baby yet.''

''Good, that's the attitude.'' He was teasing her, trying to get her mind off her queasiness. ''I don't mind a trip through the wilderness, but I'm not about to deliver a baby.''

''Don't worry. You won't have to.'' She had another month. It seemed so far away. The baby kicked her hard and she winced. He had strong legs, that was for sure.

When she saw the sparkling waters of Lake Michigan, untouched and half-wild, she knew it wasn't far now.

''Boss, Haskins brought his filly by.'' Winter Thunder trotted through the sun-crisped meadow and hopped over the split-rail fence. ''I put her in the corral by the training stable.''

''Well-done.'' Night Hawk smiled at the boy, who was almost a young man.

Although Henry still refused to speak with Night Hawk, the fort's horse shortage had reached a crisis. Colonel McGee had made an offer to pay Night Hawk for training some of the fort's mounts and to buy Arabians as they needed. Soon, other settlers began doing business with him. He'd been so busy, he'd taken Winter Thunder on as an apprentice.

It had been a good decision. Night Hawk was well pleased with the lad's progress. He had a good hand with the horses, and it felt rewarding to teach someone younger the skills his father had taught him.

"I'll be back before noon." Night Hawk wheeled Shadow toward the road. "Fill the water troughs while I'm gone. And stay off Devil. He's got to learn some manners before you try riding him."

"All right." Winter Thunder rolled his eyes in the way of all boys his age.

Night Hawk chuckled. He couldn't help it. He had so much to be thankful for. His dream of a successful horse ranch was coming true. It wasn't a life with Marie, but it was something to be glad for. "I'll bring you back some peppermint."

"For me or the horses?"

"I'll bring enough for you, too." He pressed Shadow into a smooth lope and welcomed the warm wind against this face.

"Look!" Winter Thunder called out, pointing high in the sky where a lone bird soared across the face of the hot sun.

It couldn't be. Night Hawk drew Shadow to a stop and waited. Wonder filled him as the hawk circled once and then again. His call seemed like a greeting.

It was the hawk Marie had found injured. The bird Night Hawk hadn't seen since the day Marie left.

The hawk sailed on a gentle breeze and lighted on a nearby fence post. The regal creature cocked his head from side to side, and then called again.

"I don't have any food with me," he told the bird, who continued to beg. "Winter Thunder, ride up to the house and bring back some smoked trout."

The hawk preened, and a second bird glided out of the sky to perch on the rail at his side. A female.

"So, you found a mate, did you?" Night Hawk told himself it meant nothing. Nothing at all. He'd practically made a pet out of the hawk. It was no surprise the creature had returned here to nest.

But his people would say the hawk's arrival with a mate signaled something of great value was to return to him.

Coincidence, he told himself. It had to be.

Marie didn't mind the dust in the air that nearly choked her as John helped her from the stage. She didn't care that her back ached something fierce and her lower right leg smarted from a recent cramp. She was home!

Lush green trees crowded out the horizon and most of the sky. Finches and warblers darted overhead on the wind singing their cheerful songs. The settlement had grown some, and the schoolhouse had been repaired. The road was busier. People she didn't recognize drove by in wagons, calling pleasant hellos to one another.

"Where are we going to be staying, Marie?" John asked her, taking her arm to protect her from the crowd. "You shouldn't be in the heat like this. Let me take you over to the shade, and I'll take care of our baggage."

Marie's back muscles cramped again, and she didn't feel completely well. She probably needed to sit still and rest a bit. That was the sensible thing to do, but it was hard not to argue when she was so close. Only the length of the road heading north was between her and Night Hawk.

She'd come so far, surely she could wait another hour, she told herself as her cousin led her toward a new bench in the shade of the mercantile. Her awkward stomach felt enormous as she noticed several strangers looking at her.

"Marie?"

Night Hawk? Suddenly he was towering over her on the path, surprise marking the handsome face so familiar to her. She had to fight hard to keep from reaching out for him.

Her gaze lovingly worshiped him, from his black hair tied crisply at his nape to the blue cotton shirt he wore, and down to his polished boots. He looked the same—tall and muscular and trim. She knew how hard his chest would feel against her fingertips. She longed to touch him. To step into the circle of his arms and never let go.

Then it occurred to her why he was staring at her with his jaw slightly slack. Her very pregnant stomach was hard to miss. She laid her hand on the round of it and felt the life inside. Speech failed her. How could she find the words to tell him that this was his son? Their son. Not here in the path where anyone could see.

Surely he had to know. The surprise remained on his face, and finally he snapped to attention and offered John his hand.

"I am Night Hawk, an acquaintance of Marie's. She taught my niece for a time." How formal he sounded, as if he were making polite dinner conversation.

"Night Hawk?" John tossed a questioning look at Marie, then warmly accepted the man's hand. "Pleased to meet you. Marie has told me all about you. I hope, while I'm here, you could show me your ranch. I'm a horse trainer, too, and I'm always looking for business."

"Fine." Night Hawk nodded in agreement, then turned toward her.

She'd dreamed of this moment all the way from Ohio. Across every mile as her body grew rounder and the baby within grew into its own strong life force. A sharp kick to what felt like her kidney made her remember that this was no dream. The man she loved more than her own life was standing right here in front of her.

Just say the words, invite him over to the shade where it's quiet and tell him. But the look of heartbreak in his eyes made her forget every carefully rehearsed speech.

Sorrow darkened his eyes. A great grief shone there, deep and hopeless. He glanced at her stomach again, and she knew. He regretted what he'd said. He never would have sent her away if he knew. Because he loved her.

Now she knew what love was, and what it looked like. It was this man.

"I wish you well, Marie." Night Hawk's face twisted, his composure appearing to be shattered, and he simply walked away.

"He loves you," John whispered in her ear.

"I know." She was grateful for her cousin's steady hand on her elbow. She didn't feel so strong, suddenly.

But that didn't mean she would stop fighting for what she believed in.

She's married. She's happy. It's what I wanted. But that didn't wash away the agony in his heart. He'd thought saying goodbye to Marie had been the worst loss of his life, but this was worse. Seeing her pregnant and happy, with a decent-looking man—one with money—made it real. She was with someone else and would never again be his.

Except that judging by the girth of her stomach, the baby she carried wasn't one made *after* she'd left the settlement. He thought of the sun-swept meadow by the lake when the turning leaves had painted the forests amber, gold and orange. When he and Marie made love for the first time. It didn't take a genius to count the months to know that the child she carried was his and no other's.

"Boss! What's wrong?" Winter Thunder looked up from the well.

Only then did Night Hawk realize he'd been running Shadow hard. Foam flecked the stallion's black coat and the animal was breathing hard.

"Nothing, just got carried away. Here." He handed down the heavy packs. "Peppermint's inside." It's all he could manage before he pressed Shadow into an all-out gallop and they headed for the woods.

Leaves slapped against his face and arms. A limb struck his ankle when Shadow leaped over a fallen tree. The run was a hard one—the stallion racing half-wild through the forest. Wildlife scattered from their path. Night Hawk lost himself in the challenge of the ride. He wouldn't think about Marie. Or the baby she carried.

If he had to ride forever, so be it.

Then the forest opened into a small fragrant meadow. A pair of warblers took flight into the trees as Shadow skidded to a halt. This had been his mother's favorite meadow. Filled with wildflowers that made the air sweet. Shaded enough so that in midsummer she could sit all day with her work and gaze out on the lake where Father fished.

Remembering made him weak. It made him long for the family he'd lost. And the family he would never have. He slid off Shadow and gave the horse a pat on the flank. Understanding, the great stallion tossed his head, letting the wind catch his mane, and he was off, racing the wind on his own.

Anger, grief, regret. All three hit Night Hawk as hard as a twister chewing up everything in its path. He sank to his knees in the lush grass, breathed in the scent of early summer and gazed down at the lake below. Water glimmered cheerfully, birds glided by on joyful wings, trees rustled with the voice of gladness. He felt dark inside and lost.

All those times Marie had looked at him with loving eyes and a jubilant smile she must have known about the baby. Maybe she'd been trying to find a way to tell him. And what had he told her? *Goodbye.* When she'd been carrying his babe.

It was for the best. He clung to it, even though he felt dead inside. The last thing he would ever feel was this all-consuming grief that would never end.

For the loss of the woman and child he loved with all his soul.

He sat for a long while as the sun moved past its zenith. Shadow returned, walking peacefully, and rubbed his nose hard along Night Hawk's back.

"I don't have any peppermint," he said dully. "Go back to the ranch."

Shadow knocked him over.

"Hey!" He rubbed his hand down the stallion's neck. "What is your problem?"

Then Meka's bark echoed faintly in the valley below. A bark of joy and welcome, the one the dog always reserved for Marie. The dog bounded through the meadow and disappeared.

Night Hawk stumbled to his feet. His pulse pounded though his veins as he ran to the meadow's edge, where the hillside fell away and he could see most of the lakeshore. There, in the meadow that met the water, he saw a spot of gray. A woman. *Marie.*

With Meka at her side, she watched the placid lake lap the shore and felt a deep peace. Marie laid her hand on her stomach, wincing as her back tightened again. She was far too pregnant to have been sitting in a bouncing stage. This walk had helped stretch her tired muscles. After all, carrying a baby was a major undertaking.

Beneath her hand, she could feel the flutters of life as her child moved. Earlier, he'd been hiccuping when she and John had joined the Websters for dinner in their home.

Mrs. Webster had taken one look at them on her

doorstep, stared at Marie's obvious pregnancy and then rushed her right inside. Not another word was said about her supposedly shameful state, although Marie had the feeling Mrs. Webster understood. And could correctly guess who the father was.

She was supposed to be resting, but her muscles had ached and she'd wanted a walk. John had gone to speak with Henry. Marie didn't hold any hope the coldhearted man could change his ways. His love no longer mattered to her. She had Aunt Gertrude. She still had a chance with Night Hawk.

The image of heartbreak on his face told her everything. He wanted her. He loved her. Still.

Meka barked in welcome again, bounding away from Marie's side. There on the incline above her emerged a man as dark as the shadows. His stance spoke power. His black hair rippled in the wind.

When he stepped into the sunlight, joy splashed across her heart like the brightest dawn. Looking at him made her feel as if her life was just beginning. The sun shone only for them as he strode down the path. His gaze locked on hers and she felt a steel band wrap around her stomach and clamp tight. Everything within her cried out at his approach.

"Why are you here?" Night Hawk fought to keep the intense mix of emotions from his face and his voice. He saw her blanch, and he knew he'd failed. He cleared his throat and tried again. "I didn't think you would come to this place."

"I think of it as our place." She smiled shyly at him and lit up his whole world. The sun in the sky, the stars in the heavens could not be as beautiful as this one woman.

His love, like a banked flame, burst to life. Overwhelming and consuming, it made him feel weak. All he wanted was her. All he would ever want would be her.

She stepped close, bringing the sunshine with her, and laid a gentle hand on his arm. "There is something I have to tell you."

"I already know." He glanced at her swollen abdomen, ripe with his child. Sadness gripped him like sharp talons. What was he to do now? What was the right thing? He'd let her go to a greater happiness. Why had she returned? "Your husband looks to be a good man."

"My husband?" Confusion burrowed into her brow, and then vanished. "You mean John. He's my cousin on my mother's side. He graciously agreed to bring me back to you, since traveling alone would be a difficult journey for me."

She laid her other hand on her huge stomach, drawing his gaze there, where his child was nestled.

His child. The impact rocked him. "You aren't married?"

"No." Her words were quiet. "My father told me first love burns out quickly because it's so bright. But he was wrong. My first love for you burns so brightly it will never end."

Her words were like magic, like a dream often dreamed but forgotten come morning. He fought against it. And he couldn't. Everything within him cried out to claim her.

What about the hawk's feather? The dream of sacrifice? He could not have her.

But then a pair of hawks soared low over the glistening water of the lake, reminding him of something else. She'd returned. A woman of the greatest value. Is that why the hawk had returned with his mate, to tell Night Hawk he had the right to love Marie? That he had the right to finally make her his wife?

Far over the lake, the male hawk called out as if in answer.

Night Hawk's doubt vanished. Whatever journey his spirit hawk had wanted them to make was now complete, he was sure of it. Marie was truly his to cherish, his *kammeo,* his one and only love for all time.

"Night Hawk." Hearing his name on her lips drew his attention to her, to the woman he loved beyond all. But she wasn't smiling. She no longer looked happy. "I should have told you about the baby sooner. I should have given you more time. But I'm here now to ask you what I was too afraid to ask before."

Hurt darkened her eyes and it wounded him. He longed to touch her but didn't dare. He couldn't believe he could simply reach out and hold her. That this beautiful woman could be his.

"You loved me once." She searched his gaze. "Can you find a way to love me again?"

"My *shaylee.*" He pulled her into his arms and held her, simply held her. "My love grows greater for you every day. Apart or together, that will never change."

"Then you want me? And the baby?"

"More than my life." He kissed her and she tasted

like summer. Always summer. Her arms curled around his neck, and he pulled her more closely against him. Her stomach hit him in the abdomen, keeping them several inches apart, and she laughed.

So did he. He only laughed with this woman, who brought such joy to his soul.

"I want to marry you," he told her, brushing dark tendrils from her face, glad to have the right to touch her. "So much stands in our way. That hasn't changed."

"No, but I have." She looked different, too. Still his Marie, but there was more to her. Strength and maturity. Like when the sun reached its zenith and had more light and heat. "I want to live with you on this land and raise horses and our children. I have found my place in the world, and it is with you."

"Now I know I must be dreaming." He kissed her hard and tenderly. "I never thought I would hold you again. But to have a future with you, Marie, I would do anything for you. My house is plain but it is new—"

"Night Hawk." She laid her hand on his chest right above his heart. "I want you as you are, don't you understand? I love everything about you, and I love your ranch. I want only one thing, and that's all."

"What? Not a fancy parlor with fine furniture?" He teased, because happiness filled him. And because for the first time he believed her. She'd traveled all the way from Ohio uncomfortably pregnant with their child. What a difficult journey that must have been. He would never question her again. "What is this one thing I can do for you?"

"Marry me. Now." She laid her hand on her stomach and moaned. "Because I'm going to have our baby."

He froze. "Right now?"

"Y-yes." The moan continued.

"We need the doctor." He took her by the elbows and supported her. "I'll carry you back to the house—"

"No." She laughed and the pain eased from her face, replaced by a great joy. "I'm going to give this baby your name before he's born, and that's the way it's going to be. So go get your horse and take me to the chaplain. I want to be your wife."

"Then you shall be." He guided her to a soft patch of grass and knelt with her, helping her to rest. His bride. "I love you, Marie. Just in case I haven't told you."

Then he kissed her and ran for the horses.

"Maybe you should lie down in the back." Night Hawk gazed at her with great concern, as if she were ill instead of simply giving birth.

"I'm fine." To prove it, she sat straighter on the wagon's board seat. The pain was getting much worse, but it was a small price to pay. To think she would soon be holding their baby in her arms! "I wonder if he will look like his handsome father? Will he have your eyes?"

"I hope he has your smile." Night Hawk's arm gathered her protectively while he held the reins in one hand. "I still think you should lie down."

"I'm having a baby. I'm not sick." She didn't feel

well at all, but she felt too happy to complain. "There's the fort. In a few minutes we'll be man and wife."

"Do you want your father to attend?" Night Hawk kissed her brow. "I do not wish to bring up a painful subject, but we'll marry only this once. I don't want you to have regrets."

"My only regret is that my aunt can't be here. She's been a mother to me all these years." She would keep in touch with Aunt Gertrude. Maybe they could send a private coach for her later this summer, when the traveling would be easier.

The steel band tightening around her abdomen clamped again, stealing her breath. Pain knifed through her. She bit her lip to keep from crying out. She didn't want Night Hawk to know she was in this much pain.

Besides, it would all be over soon. Think of the baby, she told herself. Think of being able to see their son.

The pain didn't ease, but she did feel stronger.

"*Shaylee,* I hate that you hurt." Night Hawk's kiss was tender on her brow. "We should see the doctor first, then the chaplain."

"I'm told first babies take a long time. Don't worry." She smiled at him. "I intend to do this right. I want to have many more babies with you."

How proud he looked. How happy. "That would be fine, but let's see this child safely into the world first. You are what matters to me, Marie."

"I will be fine. And so will this baby." It had to be. She hadn't come all this way to lose her dreams.

The wagon circled the last corner. Mrs. Holmberg stepped out of the mercantile and stopped to stare at them, then waved brightly.

"I wonder if our secret wasn't as well kept as we thought," she told him.

"Many people noticed that I was dancing with you at Henry's ball." Night Hawk stiffened and drew his team to a stop in front of the fort's gates. The wagon bounced, then was still.

A guard stood in the open doors, his hand held out, signaling for them to climb down.

"Is there a problem?" Night Hawk asked.

"Seems so, sir." The private shifted uneasily.

Henry strode into sight in full uniform, his musket slung over one shoulder, polished so that it gleamed in the summer light. "I heard you came back, Marie. John is at the Websters' right now, packing your things. We have nothing to discuss."

"No, we don't." Marie felt pity for a man who would never know happiness. "I—"

"This is my battle, Marie." Night Hawk gently addressed her, then climbed from the wagon. "This is attracting attention, and I know you do not like this kind of notice, Henry. Let Marie inside, and you and I will settle this later."

"She is not welcome here." Henry growled, though, kept his voice low. "Take her back to your claim."

"I'm going to marry her, Henry. Your chaplain is the only man who can do it."

"Then travel to Fort Orchard." The man stood so straight he looked ready to snap.

"Fort Orchard is fifty miles away." Night Hawk did not see how a father could treat a child so. "Lower your pride for your daughter's sake. Let her in. I want to make the child she carries legitimate."

"I trusted you. I treated you like an equal." Humiliation flushed the colonel's face. "And then you slept with my daughter."

"I am your equal, Henry, and you know it." Night Hawk heard the wagon step creak behind him and he turned in time to catch Marie's arm as she climbed down. "Let us in, Henry."

"I won't," he boomed, but something changed on his face when he looked at Marie, so pale and vulnerable.

Marie clutched Night Hawk's sleeve. "We are going to have to argue about this later, because I've changed my mind. I need a doctor right now."

Night Hawk saw that she was too pale. She was trembling. When he looked down, blood puddled on the dusty earth at her feet.

"Stand aside, Henry." Night Hawk swept his woman in his arms and pushed through the gates.

No one stopped him as he headed straight for the doctor's home. He didn't bother to knock. He kicked the door open and stormed inside.

"Doctor!" he shouted, and a man came running.

The doctor looked from the pregnant woman to the blood staining his polished floor. "Up here. We'll put her in my bed."

Night Hawk took the stairs two at a time.

Chapter Eighteen

"This is all your fault," Henry Lafayette boomed in the doctor's small parlor.

Night Hawk's rage doubled. He'd been forced from Marie's side, and the fury of having to leave her and the image of blood on her skirts pushed him to the rawest edge of control. "Not another word, Henry, or I'll silence you myself."

"You did this to her." The colonel would not back down. "I could have kept her safe—"

"You told her she is no longer your daughter. That makes her welfare none of your concern." Night Hawk laid his hand on Henry's chest and pushed him out the door. "Don't come back unless you can be quiet. She can hear you through the ceiling. Now go."

He shut the door on the colonel's shocked face. Good. Let the man think about his role in this. If he could lower his pride enough.

Night Hawk fisted his hands and laid them quietly to the door. He would not harm Marie's father, no matter how much the man needed a lesson in humility. Then he saw the blood on his hands. Marie's blood.

Please, don't let her die. Don't let the baby die. He sank to his knees, unable to stand. What would he do if he lost Marie?

Pain had overtaken her, raking through her stomach like sharp cruel claws. She felt helpless against it. Unable to fight it. She could hear the doctor speaking to her as if from a great distance. The daylight had seeped from the room and now there was darkness and bright lamplight that hurt her eyes.

The midwife returned to the bedside, her voice kind. "The doctor needs you to push. Don't give up on us now."

"I c-can't." She felt as if she had no control. She tried to push, but pain tore at her from within at all angles, sharper than the finest blade.

A cool cloth stroked her forehead.

Marie could feel the blood draining from her. The contractions only heightened the pain but didn't push the baby. Her strength was fading as the night progressed.

The door opened. Let it be Night Hawk, she prayed. But it was a thin, gentle-looking man holding a Bible in his hand. The chaplain. Not here to perform her wedding.

Grief filled her, and she stared at the far wall. Another claw tore through her belly, but she didn't have the strength to scream. She wanted to see Night Hawk, but they wouldn't bring him back even when she'd begged. She wanted to at least tell him the name she'd chosen for their son.

But the light seemed so far away. And then there was nothing at all but the pain.

It is too silent. Night Hawk leaped off the sofa and raced to the foot of the stairs. This wasn't right. Marie's screams had died long ago, and not even the faint mumble of the doctor and the midwife speaking broke the stillness.

This is the way it feels when someone dies. He'd felt it before, that solemn hush as if the entire world had changed and would never be the same.

No. Grief rent through him greater than any pain. Any suffering. He fought to keep from racing up the stairs and charging into the room. The doctor had told him any distraction could mean death.

What if she was already dead? What then? Had something happened to their baby? Night Hawk forced himself to sit on the bottom stair and stay there. War raged within him. He couldn't sit helpless like this forever.

The front door flew open and Henry filled the threshold. Candlelight showed his panic. "I saw the chaplain come over here. What happened? Is there—"

"The chaplain is here?" Night Hawk flew to his feet.

"He came in the back way—"

Night Hawk raced up the stairs. He would not wait idly one instant longer. Fury and fear drove him down the hall and into the room.

Into the still, silent room. The doctor was covering Marie's motionless body with care. The chaplain was seated at the bedside, his head bowed. Night Hawk looked from one to the other and back to Marie, un-moving on the bed.

She was dead. And their baby—

"Night Hawk." The midwife turned with a small bundle in her arms. "Come and see your son. He's small, being born early as he was, but he's strong. Look at him."

Night Hawk staggered, leaning against the wall for support. "Marie—"

"Is still alive. Barely. All we can do is wait and see." Exhaustion shadowed her face, but she smiled. "I think she will recover. She's strong. Her love for you is what pulled her through. I don't think she could leave you."

Slowly the pain eased from his soul. "She looks so still."

"She needs her rest after what she's been through. Bringing a new life into this world is no easy task. Come." She gestured toward the bed. "Sit with her, and hold your son. Let her know how much you love her. That should help."

The chaplain offered his chair, and Night Hawk managed to stumble across the room.

She looked like an angel, his angel. He collapsed onto the chair and covered her hand. Her skin was cold. Her face was drained of color. The sheet over her chest barely moved with her breath.

"Your son." The midwife handed the bundle to him. "Hold your arms together like this. Keep his head supported. That's right."

The bundle weighed hardly anything at all, and it fit into his arms easily. The midwife pulled the blanket farther away from the small nose and mouth. Looking at his son for the first time, Night Hawk saw high cheekbones, a straight nose and a strong chin. So like his father's face.

Love filled his heart with such force that it washed away every hardship, every loss and every pain. The baby opened and closed his mouth, apparently asleep, but the movement grabbed hold of his heart with unbreakable force. Awe filled him.

This is what comes from love, he thought, a precious, amazing gift.

He loved Marie all the more simply watching her sleep.

Dawn came gently and Marie moaned. Night Hawk waited, hoping she had the strength to awaken. Her fingers curled around his, and he smiled. She was going to be all right.

"Night Hawk." She opened her eyes, looking around as if unsure where she was and what had happened. Then her eyes widened. "Where's my baby? What happened to my baby? Did he die—"

"He's fine." Night Hawk laid one hand against her face and made her look at him.

She relaxed when she saw his smile. "*He's* fine? We have a son?"

"Just like you said." He kissed her brow. There would be passion between them later, when she was recovered, but for now there was enough tenderness for a lifetime.

As if she felt it, too, tears filled her eyes. "Please, I have to see him. I have to know that he's all right."

"He's perfect. His grandfather is holding him."

"Papa?" She didn't believe that. "Now you're teasing me."

"I wouldn't tease the woman who just gave me a son." Night Hawk's touch was a heaven she never wanted to lose.

"Your father had a change of heart last night. He thought you died. He and I have talked, and we've reached a truce. He's a tough man, but he does love his little girl very much. Maybe he'll be better at showing it from now on."

"Your love matters to me the most." She pressed a kiss into the palm of his hand. "For you are my *shaylee,* the brightest star in my heaven."

Night Hawk held her tenderly. His touch chased away all the night's pain. It was a new dawn and a new beginning.

Footsteps tapped into the room. Marie didn't know what to feel when she saw her father, but when he handed Night Hawk the small blue bundle she saw that he no longer looked rigid or angry.

"A fine job you did, daughter." Henry smiled at her, a real smile. "I'll be downstairs waiting for the chance to hold my grandson again. A good boy he is."

Henry looked awkward, then headed for the door. She watched him in wonder. Somehow during the night, the colonel had found his heart.

"Look at our son." Night Hawk leaned close.

All it took was one look. Like a bolt of lightning striking her, she felt changed. Just like she had when she'd first seen Night Hawk. She was so in love with her baby boy, who was handsome like his father.

"Look at what love can do." Night Hawk kissed her on the mouth, a gentle caress that made her long for more.

They gazed at their new baby for a long while, simply gazed at him. Remarking over the shape of his mouth, his bright eyes and the strength in his tiny hands.

"I want to name him Blue Hawk." Marie waited, watching Night Hawk's reaction. She wasn't sure. Maybe it was his people's way for the father to name his son.

"Blue Hawk he shall be." Night Hawk nodded, pride radiating from him and she knew that she'd chosen well.

"Marry me, Marie." The man she loved said the words she'd been longing to hear. "The chaplain is downstairs, and I've already spoken to him. He's agreed to perform the ceremony."

"Now? Like this?" Marie laughed, unable to keep her happiness inside. "I'm wearing a nightgown. And it isn't mine."

"Yes, but the sheets are pretty." Night Hawk shrugged. "We can wait for the flowers and a special dress if you like. But I want to start our life together as husband and wife as soon as possible. I don't want to wait one more minute."

"Then yes, I'll marry you." Marie kissed him gently so he could feel each brush of her lips to his and know the depth of emotion that lay beneath.

It was so easy to see their future together. Living in

his log home, riding horses across the summer meadows and twirling on the winter ice. A lifetime of joy spread out before them. This beautiful day was only the beginning, for theirs was a true love, the greatest of all, and it would last for all time.

* * * * *

JILLIAN HART

grew up in rural Washington State, where she learned how to climb trees, build tree houses and ride ponies—a perfect childhood for a historical romance author. She left home, went to college and has lived in cities ever since. But the warm memories from her childhood still linger in her heart, memories she incorporates into her stories. When Jillian is not hard at work on her next novel, she enjoys reading, flower gardening, hiking with her husband and trying to train her wiggly cocker spaniel puppy to sit. And failing.

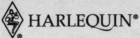

Harlequin truly does make any time special. . . . This year we are celebrating weddings in style!

A Walk Down the Aisle
WEDDING CELEBRATION

To help us celebrate, we want you to tell us how wearing the Harlequin wedding gown will make your wedding day special. As the grand prize, Harlequin will offer one lucky bride the chance to **"Walk Down the Aisle" in the Harlequin wedding gown!**

There's more...

For her honeymoon, she and her groom will spend five nights at the **Hyatt Regency Maui.** As part of this five-night honeymoon at the hotel renowned for its romantic attractions, the couple will enjoy a candlelit dinner for two in Swan Court, a sunset sail on the hotel's catamaran, and duet spa treatments.

Maui • Molokai • Lanai

To enter, please write, in, 250 words or less, how wearing the Harlequin wedding gown will make your wedding day special. The entry will be judged based on its emotionally compelling nature, its originality and creativity, and its sincerity. This contest is open to Canadian and U.S. residents only and to those who are 18 years of age and older. There is no purchase necessary to enter. Void where prohibited. See further contest rules attached. Please send your entry to:

Walk Down the Aisle Contest

In Canada
P.O. Box 637
Fort Erie, Ontario
L2A 5X3

In U.S.A.
P.O. Box 9076
3010 Walden Ave.
Buffalo, NY 14269-9076

You can also enter by visiting www.eHarlequin.com
Win the Harlequin wedding gown and the vacation of a lifetime!
The deadline for entries is October 1, 2001.

HARLEQUIN®
Makes any time special®

PHWDACONT1

HARLEQUIN WALK DOWN THE AISLE TO MAUI CONTEST 1197
OFFICIAL RULES
NO PURCHASE NECESSARY TO ENTER

1. To enter, follow directions published in the offer to which you are responding. Contest begins April 2, 2001, and ends on October 1, 2001. Method of entry may vary. Mailed entries must be postmarked by October 1, 2001, and received by October 8, 2001.

2. Contest entry may be, at times, presented via the Internet, but will be restricted solely to residents of certain geographic areas that are disclosed on the Web site. To enter via the Internet, if permissible, access the Harlequin Web site (www.eHarlequin.com) and follow the directions displayed online. Online entries must be received by 11:59 p.m. E.S.T. on October 1, 2001.

   In lieu of submitting an entry online, enter by mail by hand-printing (or typing) on an 8½" x 11" plain piece of paper, your name, address (including zip code), Contest number/name and in 250 words or fewer, why winning a Harlequin wedding dress would make your wedding day special. Mail via first-class mail to: Harlequin Walk Down the Aisle Contest 1197, (in the U.S.) P.O. Box 9076, 3010 Walden Avenue, Buffalo, NY 14269-9076, (in Canada) P.O. Box 637, Fort Erie, Ontario L2A 5X3, Canada.

   Limit one entry per person, household address and e-mail address. Online and/or mailed entries received from persons residing in geographic areas in which Internet entry is not permissible will be disqualified.

3. Contests will be judged by a panel of members of the Harlequin editorial, marketing and public relations staff based on the following criteria:

   - Originality and Creativity—50%
   - Emotionally Compelling—25%
   - Sincerity—25%

   In the event of a tie, duplicate prizes will be awarded. Decisions of the judges are final.

4. All entries become the property of Torstar Corp. and will not be returned. No responsibility is assumed for lost, late, illegible, incomplete, inaccurate, nondelivered or misdirected mail or misdirected e-mail, for technical, hardware or software failures of any kind, lost or unavailable network connections, or failed, incomplete, garbled or delayed computer transmission or any human error which may occur in the receipt or processing of the entries in this Contest.

5. Contest open only to residents of the U.S. (except Puerto Rico) and Canada, who are 18 years of age or older, and is void wherever prohibited by law; all applicable laws and regulations apply. Any litigation within the Province of Quebec respecting the conduct or organization of a publicity contest may be submitted to the Régie des alcools, des courses et des jeux for a ruling. Any litigation respecting the awarding of a prize may be submitted to the Régie des alcools, des courses et des jeux only for the purpose of helping the parties reach a settlement. Employees and immediate family members of Torstar Corp. and D. L. Blair, Inc., their affiliates, subsidiaries and all other agencies, entities and persons connected with the use, marketing or conduct of this Contest are not eligible to enter. Taxes on prizes are the sole responsibility of winners. Acceptance of any prize offered constitutes permission to use winner's name, photograph or other likeness for the purposes of advertising, trade and promotion on behalf of Torstar Corp., its affiliates and subsidiaries without further compensation to the winner, unless prohibited by law.

6. Winners will be determined no later than November 15, 2001, and will be notified by mail. Winners will be required to sign and return an Affidavit of Eligibility form within 15 days after winner notification. Noncompliance within that time period may result in disqualification and an alternative winner may be selected. Winners of trip must execute a Release of Liability prior to ticketing and must possess required travel documents (e.g. passport, photo ID) where applicable. Trip must be completed by November 2002. No substitution of prize permitted by winner. Torstar Corp. and D. L. Blair, Inc., their parents, affiliates, and subsidiaries are not responsible for errors in printing or electronic presentation of Contest, entries and/or game pieces. In the event of printing or other errors which may result in unintended prize values or duplication of prizes, all affected game pieces or entries shall be null and void. If for any reason the Internet portion of the Contest is not capable of running as planned, including infection by computer virus, bugs, tampering, unauthorized intervention, fraud, technical failures, or any other causes beyond the control of Torstar Corp. which corrupt or affect the administration, secrecy, fairness, integrity or proper conduct of the Contest, Torstar Corp. reserves the right, at its sole discretion, to disqualify any individual who tampers with the entry process and to cancel, terminate, modify or suspend the Contest or the Internet portion thereof. In the event of a dispute regarding an online entry, the entry will be deemed submitted by the authorized holder of the e-mail account submitted at the time of entry. Authorized account holder is defined as the natural person who is assigned to an e-mail address by an Internet access provider, online service provider or other organization that is responsible for arranging e-mail address for the domain associated with the submitted e-mail address. **Purchase or acceptance of a product offer does not improve your chances of winning.**

7. Prizes: (1) Grand Prize—A Harlequin wedding dress (approximate retail value: $3,500) and a 5-night/6-day honeymoon trip to Maui, HI, including round-trip air transportation provided by Maui Visitors Bureau from Los Angeles International Airport (winner is responsible for transportation to and from Los Angeles International Airport) and a Harlequin Romance Package, including hotel accomodations (double occupancy) at the Hyatt Regency Maui Resort and Spa, dinner for (2) two at Swan Court, a sunset sail on Kiele V and a spa treatment for the winner (approximate retail value: $4,000); (5) Five runner-up prizes of a $1000 gift certificate to selected retail outlets to be determined by Sponsor (retail value $1000 ea.). Prizes consist of only those items listed as part of the prize. Limit one prize per person. All prizes are valued in U.S. currency.

8. For a list of winners (available after December 17, 2001) send a self-addressed, stamped envelope to: Harlequin Walk Down the Aisle Contest 1197 Winners, P.O. Box 4200 Blair, NE 68009-4200 or you may access the www.eHarlequin.com Web site through January 15, 2002.

Contest sponsored by Torstar Corp., P.O. Box 9042, Buffalo, NY 14269-9042, U.S.A.

PHWDACONT2

Got a hankerin' for a down home romance?
Pick yourself up a Western from Harlequin Historical

ON SALE MAY 2001

CIMARRON ROSE
by **Nicole Foster**
(New Mexico, 1875)
An embittered hotel owner falls for the beautiful singer
he hires to revive his business.

THE NANNY
by **Judith Stacy**
Book 2 in the Return to Tyler historical miniseries
(Wisconsin, 1840)
A handsome widower finds true love when he hires a
tomboyish young woman to care for his passel of kids.

ON SALE JUNE 2001

THE MARSHAL
AND MRS. O'MALLEY
by **Julianne MacLean**
(Kansas, 1890s))
A widow wishes to avenge her husband's murder, but
soon loses her nerve—and then loses her heart
to Dodge City's new marshal.

Available at your favorite retail outlet.